Indivisible

— A NOVEL —

Indivisible

— A NOVEL —

Paul Martin Midden

PUBLISHED BY

Wittmann*Blair*

INDIVISIBLE

Originally published as
Indivisible? The Story of the Second American Civil War

ISBN-13: 978-0-9859223-5-1

Written by Paul Martin Midden
Published by Wittmann Blair
St. Louis, Missouri
wittmannblair@charter.net

The consolidation of the States into one vast republic,
sure to be aggressive abroad and despotic at home,
will be the certain precursor of ruin
which has overwhelmed all that preceded it.

—General Robert E. Lee
December 15, 1866

CONTENTS

I n the early years of the twenty-first century, the empire of the United States of America commanded a preeminent position among the nations of the world and a disproportionate share of the planet's resources. It stood mighty and alone, the sole super-power to which other nations deferred. While rapidly developing countries were bursting onto the horizon, none was as yet so eco-nomically vibrant and militarily powerful. None commanded the respect nor consumed the raw materials of the planet so voraciously. With an ambivalent eye, Americans beheld their good fortune and their great responsibility. There were those who believed the coun-try should rise to its natural stature and police and tame the world, using it, much as the Romans did, to luxuriate in their power and wealth. There were others, however, who saw continuing world domination as a path toward bankruptcy and moral and economic ruin. The histories of previous empires weighed heavily on the edu-cated classes.

Other fissures in policy began to make themselves felt: those who yearned for a return to what they believed to be a simpler time when faith and family governed the social lives of all citizens; these were pitted against those who saw the potential in human ability to solve problems and move forward. Some respected a governmental role in basic services, such as health care, while others thought the less government, the better. In short, there were those who looked to government for a solution, and there were those who saw government itself as the problem. This tension, of course, was not new in American politics. But these tensions taken together began to stretch the iron bonds of unity that had been put in place after the Civil War of 1861–1865 and had held the country together ever since that time.

This is the story of how those bonds broke.

braham Bellamy stood silently on the trampled battlefield of Manassas and smiled. He could see dead and wounded soldiers, both Union and Confederate, scattered before him all the way to the horizon. The stench of blood and rotting flesh filled his nostrils. Smoke from cannons and muskets lingered heavily in the air. But his smile gave expression to the joy and pride of every Confederate soldier in his unit, indeed, of every unit on the Rebel side. They had routed the Yankees who, filled with hubris, had been sent to extinguish the light of the rebellion before it got going. Pride goeth before the fall, he thought.

Bellamy was from Georgia, and he answered the call to arms as soon as he heard it. He had great respect for what he heard about the men leading the Confederate campaign, and he hurried to enlist, as did many of his friends and relatives.

He spotted his cousin Hank lying twenty yards off to his right. Hank waved. Abraham sauntered over to him and looked down at his cousin's young face, which also had a smile on it.

"We did it, Abe. By gosh, we did it!"

Bellamy nodded. It took him a moment to realize that Hank's left foot was missing. The smile vanished from his face as he saw the blood draining from his young cousin's body. He looked back at Hank's face and noticed the sweat pouring from his pale forehead.

"Don't worry about me, Abe," Hank said, his voice trembling. "I get to die happy."

For all his joy and satisfaction, Abe could not stop the tears that began to fall across his cheeks. He knelt down beside his teenage cousin and wrapped his arms around him.

"We did it, Abe," Hank whispered again. And then he closed his eyes for the last time.

Abe did not move from his position, and his tears flowed freely. He felt graced by the death of a martyr to their cause. He felt Hank's loss keenly, but at the same time he exulted in the victory they both helped bring about. He wept tears of grief and tears of joy at the same time. He had found his mission.

Abe Bellamy sat in silent disbelief at what was happening in the parlor of the McLean residence in Appomattox, Virginia, a bare one hundred and fifty miles from the first, glorious victory of the Rebels over the Union troops. He had slogged through year after year of war and deprivation, of exhilarating victories and heartbreaking defeats. He believed in the cause of the Confederacy. He had long since stopped thinking of himself as a citizen of any country but Georgia. He had no desire to be a part of the Union.

But reality was reality. He sat under an apple tree a defeated man. He thought of Hank, his teenage cousin who had died on the very first day of battle. He thought of his wife. He could not remember when he last saw her. He wondered about his children. It was hard for him to focus on their names.

Abe looked down at his tattered uniform. There wasn't much left of it, nor of him. He had always been trim, but now he was gaunt. He had gotten so accustomed to hunger that it took little to sustain him. His eyes were sunken in his head, his hearing nearly gone from the din of cannon fire, and he limped badly, having broken his right leg on two separate occasions.

Abe knew he had few choices. He had no voice in what was happening in the genteel rooms of the McLean house. He had no choice about the Southern states being forced back into the Union.

He knew slavery would be no more. He also knew that his farm had been laid waste and his family disbursed to God-knows-where. The life he knew before the war was no more.

He looked around at the still lovely Virginia countryside. God, it was beautiful in the spring, he thought through his misery. He looked at the other men milling around, each lost in his own thoughts, each grieving in his own quiet way.

After what seemed like a long time, General Lee approached, mounted on his white horse. He did not dismount. "Gentlemen," he began. "Tomorrow I shall address you in a formal way. But today I simply want to thank you for your commitment to your country, which is now sadly defeated. The war is over." He turned his horse eastward and left the silent soldiers staring at each other.

It was at that moment that Abraham Bellamy took out his pistol and shot himself in the head.

Part 1

★　★　★　★　★

The Dream

1

The body of Barack Obama, America's first African-American president, lay still in a pool of blood on the white marble floor. His dark skin was a shade paler, and the look on his face reflected the same equanimity it always did, no matter what was transpiring around him. If not for the blood that was pooling beneath his head, one would have thought he was asleep. Sadly for him and for the nation, he was not.

The assassin wasted no time in ending his own life, crying out as he was tackled, *"Sic semper tyrannis!"*—the same deranged cry of a previous assassin who brought an equally insane end to an equally significant historic figure. He clamped down on the cyanide capsule he had in his mouth and was dead before he hit the floor.

Except for the Secret Service agents, whose hyper-alertness to the environment enabled them to swing into furious if belated action, the entourage around the President was in shock. For the most part, they stood there, some in sudden tears, most in disbelief, all in terror. Some fell to the floor out of caution, looking around to see if there were other shooters. The moment was freeze-framed in the minds of everyone present, as it would be to the nation within minutes. The moment seemed to linger, despite the frenetic activity of agents and medics who arrived within a short time.

The medics acted as if the President were still alive, pushing and pulling, injecting fluids and cosseting his body. They wrapped the wound and loaded him on a stretcher. But everyone within ten feet of where the President had been standing knew that the shots were fatal. It is possible that Mr. Obama did not know what hit him.

Law enforcement agents were suddenly everywhere. Since this happened in the Capitol Building, the Capitol police cordoned off the area. The Secret Service had set up a perimeter, but within ten minutes the FBI relieved them by setting up a larger one. By the time the feds arrived, Mr. Obama's body was halfway to Walter Reed. A perfunctory if needless trip, but such was the custom.

The activity level exploded. Media, tourists, government workers: all converged on the Capitol Building; all sensed that something important, maybe even momentous, had occurred. In that belief they were correct.

Vice President Joseph Biden got the call before the body was removed from the scene. He was in his office in the West Wing, and he had just finished watching his boss meet with congressional leaders in an effort to forestall a movement that had grown to worrisome proportions. The meeting was broadcast over a secure intranet used exclusively for such meetings, and Joe was able to watch Obama in action. He was once again awed; he once again was able to savor Barack Obama as the man of the hour, one of few men who were possessed of the intelligence, perspective, broadness of vision, presence of mind, and sheer persistence that could keep this country together and move it forward. Especially in light of recent events. Joe, accustomed to a lifelong pursuit of office that involved always looking for advancement, did not envy his boss's job.

Talk of secession had, since the first Civil War, been relegated to fringe groups, nutwings for the most part. Guys who liked to dress up and go shooting on the weekends, pretending that they were "training" for their country. The survivalists, the isolates, the mostly rural reactionaries. But recently, loudmouthed media types—Glenn Beck, Rush Limbaugh, Ann Coulter—were mentioning it from time to time. As if they knew something. As if they wanted something to change. It wasn't a drumbeat, or at least most people didn't think so. It was as if these talking heads were floating the idea, seeing how it would play. Joe did not think these guys had a single conscience among them: they would do whatever they could to aggrandize themselves, to sell the brand that they had become. Genuine concern about the country or the common welfare or shared problems: these things were further down on their lists. Way down.

Now the common good was up for grabs. Joe held the receiver in his hand long after the Secret Service agent who called had told him that the President had died and that he was now in charge. He was still holding it, staring into space, when his own Secret Service detail entered the room and the team leader walked up to him.

"Mr. President," Jamie Jackson said. He said it in a low tone. He did not want his voice to crack. He almost succeeded.

Joe did not move at first. He was praying. He was trying to muzzle his rage at God and beseech Him at the same time. For all his habituation to power, he did not want it at this time, under this circumstance. It was all wrong.

Jamie cleared his throat. "Mr. President," he repeated, this time a little louder.

Joe looked up at his team leader. He liked Jamie. He was from Scranton, as Joe was. Son of an immigrant laborer. Honduran, Joe thought. Fluent in both Spanish and English. Hardworking, reliable as the sun; there was little about Jamie that Joe didn't like. But just now he didn't want to be bothered.

Yet Joe Biden was nothing if not dutiful. He turned to Jamie and asked, "What now?"

"Chief Justice Roberts is on his way over to administer the oath, sir," Jamie said. "He should be here within the half hour."

Joe nodded. He wanted more time. He wanted time to pray, to weep, to rage against this violent and outrageous act.

The door opened. In place of the Chief Justice whom Joe and Jamie had been expecting, a stone-faced Secret Service agent walked quickly over to Jamie.

"What?" demanded the former vice president.

The new agent, who had leaned over to whisper into Jamie's ear, turned toward him, keeping an eye on Jamie, who nodded in Joe's direction.

"Mr. President," the young man said, "the Chief Justice has been shot."

It took Joe Biden all of a half second to realize what was happening. He got it just before bullets started flying at the windows.

"Get down," he yelled.

He knew the windows were bulletproof, but he also knew they wouldn't hold out indefinitely.

"Jamie," he yelled. "Get your men into secure positions."

Jamie was already talking into his wrist microphone, barking orders in a clear, low voice. "Check in," Joe heard him say. Jamie listened intently. Joe saw his eyes narrow almost imperceptibly twice. Two men down, Joe thought.

Joe looked out from behind the desk where he had taken cover. He saw that the shots were coming from a single-engine Cessna flying perpendicular to the White House. All of a sudden, it burst into flames and disappeared. Joe looked at Jamie. Jamie nodded. The guys on the roof had done their jobs. One for our side.

Joe slinked back down onto the floor.

It's happening, he thought.

2

Joe Biden woke with a start. He was sweating. He had just had a dream he hoped and prayed was just a dream. Was that even possible? he wondered. He got up to get a drink of water. As he did so, he looked at the clock: 4:00 a.m. No more sleep tonight, he thought idly.

Of course it's possible to kill a president, he replied to himself. It's been tried on half a dozen occasions, most of them fatal for the intended target. It's easy to kill a man; it's a lot harder to protect one. After he was finished in the bathroom, Joe walked into the kitchen and started making coffee. He knew there was talk in some states about seceding from the Union, something that had been unheard of since the Civil War, but it was only talk. His tendency was to dismiss it out of hand, but he had to admit the country was seriously divided. Polarized even. And pretty much it was split along state lines: the Northeast was liberal, the Southern states conservative, the West Coast states liberal, the other Western states conservative. The Midwest, of course, was in the middle.

Joe was well educated. He knew that these terms—liberal and conservative—did not begin to capture the cultural and philosophical differences between the polarized groups in the US. He also knew that liberal and conservative sensitivities and preferences evolved over time, sometimes changing to completely opposite positions. It was, after all, the Republican Theodore Roosevelt who first proposed national health insurance. It was the Democrat Bill Clinton who reformed and restricted welfare. Nonetheless, the differences were deep and strong. In this era, old-time, reverential religious sensibility reflected the yearnings of those on one side; progress and secular values were preferred by the other. One looked backward for a model of how to be; the other looked forward hopefully. It was a fissure that had existed since the founding of the Republic, but in the emerging government of the new nation it wasn't much of a problem. It was a relief to embrace secular values back then. No one seriously questioned religion as such. The culture was stable. Change was slow. That was a long time ago, another era. In the twenty-first century, questions abounded and change was fast. This puts some pressure on the direction people want to go and on the politics they choose.

Joe pushed these complicated thoughts out of his mind. Only a fool would take the breakup of the United States seriously. He poured himself a cup of coffee before the carafe was completely filled and walked into his study, a small room in the front of his house. He loved his study. No matter how he got there—even when he was awakened by a nightmare—walking in the small room and sitting at the desk calmed him. He put his readers on his nose and looked at the papers on top of his desk. Anything would be better to focus on than the content of that dream.

The origins of the second American Civil War lay deep in the roots of American culture in the latter years of the twentieth century and in the early years of the twenty-first. Several trends were notable.

Conservatism as a late-twentieth-century movement arose in different areas of American life. On the pundit side, William Buckley blew the horn for slowing down liberal policies. His goal was to "stand athwart history and yell Stop!" as if that were a realistic possibility. In the political sphere, it was with the nomination of Barry Goldwater in the 1960s that radical conservatism first made itself felt in American politics. Not since 1932 had a conservative agenda been mainstream in US politics. Goldwater did not win a single state.

But by the election of Ronald Reagan in 1980, conservatism began to flower. It became popular to denigrate the role of government in American society. Reagan ran on an avowedly anti-government platform. One of his campaign slogans was as follows: "Here are the words you do not want to hear in a crisis: 'I'm from the government and I'm here to help you.'" He was fond of saying "government was the problem." It was in part a reaction to the liberal policies of the preceding fifty years, when Franklin Roosevelt saved capitalism from itself, saving liberal democracy in the process.

Liberal policies had such primacy in the sixties and seventies that few questioned them. Richard Nixon, a lifelong Republican, would in the eighties and nineties be considered far to the left of Bill Clinton. But there were problems with liberal policies. The country was learning that simply throwing money at social problems seldom solved them. The way the laws were structured promoted unintended consequences, such as contributing to a permanent underclass. There was growing discontent with race relations. The American city was largely recast with a decaying inner core and booming suburbs. Mr. Reagan played on those challenges to get himself elected president.

Mr. Reagan was a principled man. He believed in core American principles of fairness and equality. When the first crisis of his presidency presented itself in the form of an illegal strike by unionized air traffic controllers, he fired them all. He did this not out of spite but out of principle. He later reflected that if management had done something equally illegal, he would have fired them instead. In general, his policies were moderate.

But the seed he planted grew. Just as the butterfly flapping its wings on one side of the planet is said to cause a hurricane on the other side, his principled objections to liberal thinking sowed the seed for anti-government attitudes that grew senselessly into something like a religion over the next thirty years.

Along the way, government protections that had been woven into the fabric of our society began to be dismantled. Welfare as it had been practiced for decades ended in the Clinton administration, as did the Glass-Steagal Act, enacted in the Thirties to prevent another depression. Corporate greed escalated in an explosive, unprincipled search for profits, as exemplified by the Enron corporation and in the wildly extravagant salaries paid to top executives, along with golden parachutes that made their departure for whatever reason hugely profitable for them, no matter what happened to the company, much less to the common good.

Government, which for generations had been the sole barrier to unbridled capitalism, was weakened because of the tenor and tone of this emerging trend.

But the most insidious development was that myth and hype replaced rational discourse. Myths arose in the US that were simply untrue; these served as the basis for the worship of greed and for the consolidation of greed among the wealthy classes. Such axioms as "Taxes should never be raised in a recession," "The government is unable to perform tasks in an efficient manner," "The government should get out of the way of private business," and "Regulation is an enemy of business" became mantras for many. The call to sacrifice that characterized the American response to major world events such as World War II gradually morphed into the pathetic exhortation of George W. Bush to help the fight against terror by "going shopping." This degradation of discourse promoted deep fissures in the American mind: as one side got more stringent, the other side saw no alternative but to dig in and match stridency with stridency. In the process, the willingness to discuss and compromise, and thus the common good, was ignored. This was a boon for those at the top of the economic ladder; it was a disaster for those at the other end of the spectrum; it was portentous for those in the middle. Loud and belligerent talk substituted for reasonable discourse; God was invoked as a reason for argument; science and empirical knowledge were rated on par with fanciful ideas such as creationism. These developments delighted the wealthy few who saw their profits increase and their taxes decrease. For them, the rise in inflation or in housing prices was a minor concern; they commanded an ever-increasing percentage of American wealth. Even so, popular sentiment seemed to be turning against them. The accompanying anxiety compelled them to action. Ultimately, it was this group that determined that the time was ripe for an escalation of hostilities and an outright dismantling of the United States of America.

Abner Bellamy stood silently in front of his favorite monument in St. Louis. It might be his favorite monument in all the world. It stood in Forest Park, a huge urban park that dwarfed Central Park in New York. The monument was off the beaten path, not quite hidden, but not in the center of anything either. There was nothing about its setting that would draw attention to it. Abner noted that it was majestic nonetheless. It was a twenty-foot granite column with a bronze relief of a Southern family offering its only son to the Confederate cause. On the back of the column was an inscription in large block letters that he had long ago committed to memory:

TO THE MEMORY
OF THE
SOLDIERS AND SAILORS
OF THE SOUTHERN CONFEDERACY,
WHO FOUGHT TO UPHOLD
THE RIGHT DECLARED BY
THE PEN OF JEFFERSON
AND ACHIEVED BY THE
SWORD OF WASHINGTON,
WITH SUBLIME SELF SACRIFICE
THEY
BATTLED TO PRESERVE

THE INDEPENDENCE OF THE STATES
WHICH WAS WON FROM
GREAT BRITAIN,
AND
TO PERPETUATE THE
CONSTITUTIONAL GOVERNMENT
WHICH WAS ESTABLISHED BY THE
FATHERS.
ACTUATED BY THE PUREST
PATRIOTISM
THEY PERFORMED DEEDS
OF PROWESS SUCH AS
THRILLED THE HEART OF
MANKIND WITH ADMIRATION.
"FULL IN THE FRONT OF WAR THEY STOOD."
AND DISPLAYED COURAGE
SO SUPERB
THAT IT GAVE A NEW AND
BRIGHTER LUSTERE TO THE
ANNALS OF VALOR.
HISTORY
CONTAINS NO CHRONICLE
MORE ILLUSTRIOUS THAN
THE STORY OF THEIR
ACHIEVEMENT,
AND ALTHOUGH
WORN OUT IN
CEASELESS CONFLICT
AND
OVERWHELMED BY NUMBERS,
THEY WERE FINALLY
FORCED TO YIELD.

THEIR GLORY ON BRIGHTEST PAGES
PENNED BY POETS AND BY SAGES
SHALL GO SOUNDING DOWN THE AGES.

For Abner, this was more than an inscription commemorating a past event; it was at once a prayer, a summons, a call to action. It was also an indictment, a declaration that something was amiss, something that no one was acknowledging, much less addressing—something no one was taking care of. In the hundred and fifty–plus years since the War Between the States, the cause had languished. No hero, no movement; not even talk. The Unionists had enshrined their interpretation of power into the legal system like a cancer, disemboweling the very heart of the Constitution as the Founding Fathers had envisioned it. A union of free, sovereign, and independent states. That's what they signed on for. That's what they lost in the War Between the States.

Abner thought about his great-great-great-grandfather, Abraham Bellamy. The story was never far away during his upbringing: how Abraham left Georgia to fight the war; how he lived through many, many violent engagements; and how heart-broken he was when Lee's army was forced to surrender. Some of his relatives said it killed him. Others just looked away. Abner figured there was more to his death than the adults were willing to tell the children. Nonetheless, they were as proud of him as a family could be. He stood for their values. He died for them.

Abner came to this monument as if to a sacred burial ground before every important event that touched upon his mission to resurrect the cause. Tonight he was meeting with a group of men he had painstakingly assembled over the previous ten years to address this singular problem. The monument was his touchstone; it reminded him of a mission he never forgot for a single second. It gave him strength. It connected him to those who had gone before him.

The event this evening was critical. He felt his heart pound in his chest for pride at what he and Providence had accomplished so far. Tonight was the first meeting of the entire group in one place. Abner thought it apt that the group was meeting in St. Louis, technically a Union state but one full of Southern sympathy. It was Abner's job to do what Robert E. Lee with his mighty and devoted army could not do: to reassert the rights of the states that made up the United States, to reassert the right to self-determination on which this government was based. To restore the federal government to its proper place. And in the process to put an end to the status quo, where the needs of the people were ignored because of imperial politics.

Abner looked around. The park was lovely as it always was, and there were a few cyclists and joggers about a hundred feet away. Chances were they didn't notice this monument, he thought. He turned and walked slowly back to his car.

It was in St. Louis that Abner first conceived his plan. Missouri was a divided state during the Civil War. It was officially Union but also allowed slaves. It was claimed by the Confederacy but never formally seceded. There were battles here between the opposing factions. The St. Louis Police Department had its Board split, with control residing not in City Hall but at the Missouri State Capital a hundred miles away. This arrangement was still in force right up to the present.

Just like this country, Abner thought. Nothing settled; everything up for grabs. So why not reestablish the United States the way it was originally? The way it was supposed to be. He got worked up when he thought this way, and, in the midst of these thoughts, he picked up his cell phone and speed-dialed a familiar number. He wanted to calm himself down.

"Hi, darlin'," he said in his native but rarely used Southern drawl. Abner had studied at Yale, and his most comfortable accent was at least Northeastern American, the kind that was closest to highbrow British. But he was talking to his girlfriend, a native of Georgia.

"Hi, sweetie," Judith drawled back. "Been missing you."

"You'd better be missin' me," Abner said. Just talking to Judith aroused him, and arousal quelled his excitement. "You know what tonight means to me, honey," he said softly. "You've been really important to me in all this." Abner paused. "I couldn't have done it without you. I'll be by soon. I'll make this all worthwhile."

"You'd better," Judith teased. She didn't mind his being away. She and Abner had been together for a number of years, but their relationship was anything but conventional. They shared a deep and enduring devotion to a cause they had both nurtured for years. In addition, Judith was genuinely fond of Abner, but he was a demanding man, devouring all her attention when they were together. His visits were usually short, and she prized her time alone. She found in Abner Bellamy a man who fit her desires perfectly: there when she needed him; otherwise, they lived apart, even in different cities. When he was with her, he was attentive, intelligent, and just plain fun. When he was away, she got to rest, work, and do whatever else she wanted. The issue of marriage never came up. Not once in the years the couple had been dating.

That was okay for Abner too. As smitten as he had always been with Judith, as beautiful and sexy a woman as she was, he preferred that their connection be a real one and not one dictated by marriage or any other institution. He adored her. He loved being with her whatever they were doing. But he had been down the marriage route, and he was sure it wasn't for him. Even though he was still technically married, he couldn't be happier with Judith and her independent ways.

"See you soon," he whispered into the phone. He clicked off.

Abner got into his car and started driving across town. He passed the architecture that had become so familiar to him and that he appreciated probably more than the local inhabitants of this classic midwestern city. The stately homes along Forest Park, the older buildings east on Lindell. In the distance he saw the famous Gateway Arch looming against the skyline. Funky monument, but Abner liked it. He liked almost everything American. Except the federal government.

He was headed to the location of tonight's meeting of the twenty-two men he had selected, groomed, and prepared for the special mission he had conceived. He was a couple of hours early, but Abner valued nothing so much as being prepared. He headed downtown to Preservation Hall, an old building on the near south side that offered all the privacy and anonymity he required. It was a great find.

As he drove, he thought of the first days of his plan. He was living in St. Louis at the time. Bill Clinton had just been elected president, and Abner was enraged. He saw the man from Hope as a traitor to the Confederate cause, a pseudo-Yankee turncoat who was smooth-talking and smart but who otherwise had a high tolerance for even more federal government. It was during that fit of outrage that he found himself wandering around the city, driving aimlessly, then walking, then driving again. He found himself at the foot of the monument he had revisited today, and it was at that moment that he thought: Why not?

Why not resurrect the Confederate ideal? Why not resume the war? Just because the Confederacy lost did not mean its cause was not just. Plus, he knew the election of Bill Clinton spelled trouble for the country. He also knew that it would not be enough to work hard in the midterm elections to deprive the Democratic president of a majority in Congress. Even if that effort succeeded, as it did a couple of years afterward, the problems of the federal government were just too deep.

But he also recognized in those days that something was fundamentally wrong with American politics. It was too big, too expensive, too imperial. He ran across a prescient quote by Robert E. Lee that said it all: *The consolidation of the States into one vast empire, sure to be aggressive abroad and despotic at home, will be the certain precursor of ruin which has overwhelmed all that preceded it.*

It was then that the idea began to take shape in his mind: maybe he could pick up this long-defunct cause. He began looking around. He was amazed at what he found: a huge amount of discontent with the federal government, groups in a dozen states that labeled themselves secessionist, sympathetic listeners behind almost every door on which he knocked. He was astonished that so many people felt the way he did.

He found something else. People were tired of the status quo. The federal government was all but run by big companies that paid millions in lobbying fees to buy whatever policies they wanted from the legislature. Elections were mostly fractious, fact-avoiding quarrels that had more in common with a junior high brawl than any reasoned discussion of the issues. People were so polarized politically that major elections hung on the whims of a tiny sliver of the populations, the so-called independents, who were just uncommitted hard-to-get players. It was a sickening charade of civic process.

Abner believed, on the other hand, that local government could not afford the hyped-up extravagances of the federal system. The closer government got to the actual people it represented, the more effective it was. Each state was in a better position to decide for itself what it wanted and needed.

He was circumspect in those early days. Circumspection came naturally to him, fastidious as he was. But as he continued to investigate the cause of the Confederacy, he began to realize that the flame had not died, that many people both in the Old South and in the newer, western states had ideas about forming their own countries. One conversation stood out especially in his mind. He was talking to Senator Donald Colby from Idaho. They were sipping whiskey on the veranda of this man's country estate, which covered several hundred acres of beautiful grass and woodlands. Senator Colby was nobody's fool; not the type to shoot off his mouth. Abner and Colby had been talking about American history. Abner thought he saw an opening.

"Senator Colby," he said somewhat gingerly. "You were born in the South—Mississippi, wasn't it? What do you think of the Confederate ideal?"

Colby didn't even flinch. He looked Abner straight in the eye and replied: "It was the authentic ideal of America," he said. "It was what the states had signed up for." He took a sip from his glass, thought for a minute, and then went on. "Prior to the Civil War," he said, "nearly every state assumed that it was sovereign. The name, the United States, was plural: The United States *are*. Even when they saw some early court decisions go the other way. That John Marshall—he was responsible for the America we see now. The Union version. But it was never meant to be that. It was meant to be more a confederacy than a federation. More a group of equal partners rather than a bossy central government and subservient states. The role of the government was to provide a forum and to facilitate compromise and reconciliation among the sovereign states. It has specific purposes: a common currency, a common defense." He took another sip of whiskey. "Now the states are just regional administrative bodies. More like provinces than states. Now, the 'United States' is singular: The United States is." He gazed over the lush landscape. "Damn shame, if you ask me." He looked back at Abner.

Abner was speechless. He might have expected this kind of talk from some drawling Southern politicians at the end of a night of drinking, but not from a sitting US senator in the middle of the afternoon. And Donald Colby was not an ordinary senator. He was born in Mississippi, but he was educated at Yale, as Abner was, and was a Rhodes scholar. He served in several important government agencies in high-profile jobs before getting himself elected to the

Senate from Mississippi. When he moved out to Idaho, most people thought he was taking early retirement. But the sedentary life never appealed to Colby, and it took him just a couple of years to jump into the fray of Idahoan politics. He emerged once again a senator, now from Idaho. He was in his third term. Tall, lean, silver-haired, and ramrod straight in his mid-seventies, Senator Donald Colby was a force to be reckoned with on the Senate floor. But he was also a man who didn't really give a hoot about ideology and was always available to work either side of the aisle for something he believed in. An unusual political specimen, especially in those days.

Abner did not respond to Colby that day. He gently shifted the conversation toward more general things: how well the South was doing, the beauty of the landscape where the pair was sitting. But Colby's thoughts stoked the fire within his belly to do something, something powerful, effective, and historic. To dismantle the current structure, to reassert the power of the states. To bring America back to what it was supposed to be. To reestablish a Confederacy of Southern States. This was a role he relished taking on. He wasn't quite clear yet, but he felt the first powerful stirrings of destiny.

bner Bellamy had always been a conflicted and passionate man. He grew up in Georgia, a state scarred more than most by the Civil War, a state where the wounds of the war were still felt, even after a century and a half had passed. Abner's great-great-great-grandfather fought through the entire war and died on the day of the armistice. He knew he had other relatives who lived on in musty books of grainy, sepia-toned photographs in his parents' attic.

Abner's father had been a police officer in Macon. He was witness to the civil rights movement in the mid-sixties, and he was unafraid to speak his segregationist mind, something he regarded as his rightful heritage.

"Those niggers will be the ruination of this country," his father was fond of saying. "If you give them equal rights, pretty soon they'll be demanding full equal treatment." He snorted to punctuate his diatribe. Clarence Bellamy clung to a past he believed in, one where the natural state of things was that the white man was the caretaker of poor black souls. He didn't hate blacks exactly; he just felt they were, by virtue of their color and history, inferior humans. It was his job as an enlightened white man to guide them, direct them, and keep them in their place.

That job was underscored by his position as assistant police chief of Macon. He wasn't the top dog, but he was close enough to the top to make sure his views mattered. And he was friends with the chief, a friendship that went back to when both were in high school.

"You mark my words, Abner," he often said to his only son. "If we don't draw the line here and keep the blacks in their place, there will be no peace in this country." He snorted again.

Abner loved his father. He was proud of him, both for being a man of importance in Macon and for standing up for his views. But he thought his father was flat-out wrong about his views of civil rights, and he knew from his reading that his father was on the wrong side of history. Abner didn't believe in keeping anyone in his place, especially himself. He believed in education, in studying a subject until you understood it. He believed in advancement, and he saw that as the American ideal. And he wanted a reward for what he knew. That's how he was. He didn't confront his father. He just kept his opinions to himself.

Not that Mr. Bellamy ever asked. He loved his son and wanted to raise him right. He wanted to be sure he thought correctly, acted correctly, and believed correctly. To that end, he lectured him daily. Not for long periods of time, but consistently. Like Chinese water torture. A little every day, so as to make sure that Abner was on the right track.

Abner never thought about opposing his father, much less rebelling against him. In addition to the affection he felt for him, he was as much charmed by his father's daily lecturettes as offended by them. His father was also careful, it seemed to Abner, to conduct this daily ritual without an audience—that is, with no one but possibly Abner's mother in attendance. He never regaled Abner in front of his friends or embarrassed him in any way. This kind of respect was something that Abner always associated with his father and with his father's ways, his culture, his heritage. He had enormous respect for it.

So on the day before Abner's fourteenth birthday, in 1968, when a crowd of seemingly well-behaved Negroes turned on the police who were trying to guide and direct them and killed his father,

Abner was shocked. He had thought in his heart that his father was well-meaning, that, even if what he said was old-fashioned or even loathsome, Clarence Bellamy actually believed he was doing the right thing by keeping the blacks in their place. Abner was so shocked he couldn't speak for a week.

No one took it well. When the police realized what was happening they called for backup. When they saw their assistant chief on the ground, they started shooting and beating any black person within range. They killed nine people that day. Nine black people. No one in midcentury Macon had seen anything like this. And no one who was white saw anything wrong with the carnage or the retribution.

Nor did Abner's mother take it well. When a uniformed officer arrived at the front door and knocked respectfully with his hat in his hand, the blood drained from her face. She dried her hands on her apron and walked trembling to let Mickey Campbell in. Mickey was trembling as well. Mrs. Bellamy went through the protocols of Southern hospitality: "Please come in, Officer Campbell," she said. "Would you like a cool drink?" Her face was blank and her tone was monotonic, but it was what one did.

Mickey did not reply to her questions or offers. "Andrea, please sit here," he said, motioning to the couch. He sat next to her. "I have some fearful news."

Andrea Bellamy started to cry. Officer Campbell took her hands into his.

"Your brave husband was hurt in the line of duty today," Mickey said. He was working hard not to let his voice crack. "We tried to save him, but . . ." He looked down into Andrea's hands entwined in his. "But we weren't able to." And with that he burst into tears and wrapped Andrea Bellamy in a big bear hug that was as much for his solace as for hers. "I am so sorry, Andrea."

Andrea froze. Abner was watching from across the room and understood exactly what Officer Campbell was telling his mother.

That his father, his beloved, strong, and brave father, was dead. Tears streamed down his face. It was at that moment that he stopped talking.

What he did was grieve. In his silence he raged and wept. He did not speak to anyone because there wasn't anyone to talk to. His mother had fallen equally silent. She went about her routine: she cooked and cleaned and looked out the window as she always had, hoping her beloved Clarence would come walking through the door as he always had. But no amount of looking or cooking or cleaning or acting as if things were normal could change the tragic arithmetic of the household: where there had been three people there were now two. Two silent, bloodless, angry, sullen humans who could not make any but the most formal connection with each other.

Even on the day of the funeral, which was attended by what seemed like half the population of Macon, there was mostly silence. The crowd felt sympathy for the Bellamy family, of course, but there was an unspoken feeling of dread in the room, as if the cultural supports they were accustomed to were being knocked out from under the good white people of Macon. And, of course, they were.

There were more riots, more killings. It was made worse a few months later when Dr. Martin Luther King was killed, and the rage of black Americans, so long ignored, so long suppressed, burst onto the national scene with a vengeance. Cities across the nation were burning, but Macon burned, it seemed to Abner, the hottest. The legitimate rage of the African American community was met with equal outrage on the part of the entitled whites who felt betrayed by people they thought were their friends or, if not their friends, at least people who owed them deference and who were expected to be cordial to each other in an effort to sustain public tranquility and the Way Things Were Supposed To Be.

The week after Dr. King's assassination, Andrea Bellamy turned to her only child and said, "Abner, I need to talk to you." At this point, Abner still wasn't talking much, and he thought maybe his mom was going to tell him to open up or talk or do something. Or maybe he just wasn't keeping up his chores or something. He didn't know. He was lost in a land he couldn't describe.

He nodded to his mother.

The two lost souls sat on the divan in the front room, one at either end. Both were ramrod straight. "Abner," his mother began slowly. "I know your father's death has been an affliction for you." She looked down at her clasped hands, joined so that her trembling would not show. She was, after all, a respectable woman who hated any intimation of weakness. She took a breath and plunged ahead. "I have decided that you should spend the rest of the summer with your Aunt May and Uncle Hubert in Atlanta." She wasn't looking at Abner when she spoke these terrible words.

Abner's eyes widened. He was reaching for words, but his throat was rusty for lack of use. He didn't know what to say. He wanted to scream, but he could hardly breathe. Then the only words that mattered escaped his mouth. "Mama, nooooo," he finally wailed, and he threw himself across the divan and into her arms.

Andrea held her son for a moment. She loved him; she knew that. It was not an issue. But he reminded her powerfully of her beloved Clarence, and she could barely stand the sight of this hairless replica floating around the house when the real one was gone. She had made up her mind.

So after a minute or less, she pushed Abner away as gently as she could. "It will be better for you," she said, knowing all the while that it had very little to do with Abner and everything to do with her inability to bear the horror of the event that had been thrust upon her. Andrea Bellamy was not a stupid woman; nor was she deluded. She was a woman who recognized her limits when she saw them.

No amount of gentleness, real or feigned, could have lessened the pain Abner felt that dreaded day. As soon as he resumed his place on his side of the divan, he knew that his mother's decision was final and that there was no recourse. He felt horrible, but his feelings, well, they would just have to wait.

Abner became a man that day. He knew his aunt and uncle and did not dislike them. But he knew he had lost two parents in a period of a few weeks, no matter that one was still living and breathing. He knew that he would never set foot in that house or in Macon again. This was partly rage—a decision to foreswear any involvement with the woman who rejected him—and it was partly practical. It was clear to young Abner that his mother was not up to the task of completing his childhood. In his mind, she was a broken woman, a woman who could not or would not finish what she had started. He did not give a damn about the reasons. She was his mother, and her job was to stay by him, to be there for him, to finish raising him. But she chose another path. And he hated her for it.

Though only fourteen years old, Abner Bellamy never saw his mother alive again.

5

All those painful memories seemed a distant background to Abner's life in the present. As he drove on to the meeting on his schedule this evening, he gripped the steering wheel with that rage that was so familiar to him. Even after all these years, forgiveness was not in Abner's vocabulary. Not for his mother, not for the black men who killed his father. He was not—he refused to be—that defenseless and frightened boy he had been. He spent his adult life being a man who was filled with confidence and purpose. He did not care what weighed on him; he was a man on the move, and had been since age fourteen.

He completed his high school in record time, taking only the courses he absolutely needed to procure a high school diploma in the state of Georgia. As he was finishing up, he applied to schools everywhere, so long as they were in another city, and preferably not in Georgia. He loved the South but wanted distance from his mother and from the stench of racism that had killed his father and nearly destroyed his hometown.

He managed to attend Yale. It was there that he shed his Southern accent and ways of speaking and acting. He was a mannerly boy, and that never left him; but after six months he walked and talked like a Yankee. He only pulled out his Southern persona when he needed it—mostly with young women who found some charm in those drawling cadences.

Beyond sex and a little pickup basketball, the only thing Abner thought about at Yale was getting a degree and getting to the next step. To that end, he outworked his classmates and did not let up. He had decided on a career in the ministry. Yale had an outstanding Divinity School, and it seemed to the young Abner that ministry would provide him with a large audience for his prodigious talent and for his ambitious goals. So it was off to Divinity School, followed soon after by ordination to the Methodist ministry.

Abner saw the megachurch trend sooner than most. He had a feeling that secular values could not stand up to the rigors of being human. He knew people longed in their heart for something solid to hold on to, for belief in goodness, for belief in God. Even if they had to abandon their own good sense in the process, Abner felt in his gut that people would choose the path of belief rather than the path of reason. He wasn't sure why that was; he just knew they would.

And his early years in ministry confirmed this. People longed to believe; they longed to pray. They believed the sermons and the reassurances that came in Abner's carefully crafted words. Abner had mixed feelings about belief in God. He didn't think the concept of God made much sense, but that was a private thought. He recognized power—Power—when he saw it, and he saw it in religion. So he learned the language of religion and set about building an expanding congregation. Not for him the outlying communities. He went straight to godless Manhattan, where he headed up the First Methodist Church as his first call.

It wasn't long before his sermons began drawing increasing numbers to his church. And more people meant more money, which began to increase, slowly at first, but then into an ever-widening stream. He was eloquent on the pulpit and fawned shamelessly outside of worship services. He flattered everyone, assured everyone, promised everyone his love and his prayers. The unspoken price was greater financial support for his expanding ministries and, along the way, for him.

For five years, he worked this way. He took every opportunity in that thriving borough to schmooze with the rich and famous. He didn't care about fame much, but he discovered that fame and wealth were commonly found in the same enterprise, so he chose to contend with both. It was the wealth in which he was interested.

Abner lived frugally. He saved money, invested it, and watched as his trove grew. He knew there was something big coming, but he wasn't sure what. He just knew he wanted to be there when it happened. He wanted to be ready. His congregation flattered him in return for his fawning over them, and he easily believed what they told him. He was headed for greatness. He could move the world. Idle talk, perhaps, but it filled Abner's young head with pride and promise.

After a few years, his agenda was bearing more fruit more quickly than he ever imagined. He began to find Manhattan irritating. It was heady, to be sure, but he was from small-town Georgia, and the hustle and bustle of the overbuilt island grated on him. He longed for a more peaceful place. Somewhere where he could write and preach and relax a little. Someplace that had the advantages of civilization but less of the intensity that was so inescapable in New York. He had saved his money and figured he could live on his savings for at least a couple of years. In the meantime, he could find part-time work. He wanted a slower pace.

He found St. Louis.

He left First Methodist Church to the tears and dismay of his congregation and moved west to St. Louis, where he established an office in his small apartment and hired himself out as a sermonizer. He wrote a couple of books that were well received in the Evangelical community. He plugged them relentlessly and was pleased and excited by the profitable response. It was during that first year in

St. Louis he met his wife, Charlotte. Charlotte came from a quietly wealthy family that had deep roots in the St. Louis community. Old money. Old Warson Country Club, Huntleigh address; her family kept horses and a house staff. Charlotte had everything. Or thought she did, until she was swept off her feet by the dulcet words of the published preacher from New York.

Abner knew an opening when he saw it, and he courted Charlotte as no one before had done. In turn, she introduced him to her circle of old-money friends, who welcomed the handsome young preacher into their homes, hearts, and bank accounts. Abner was pretty sure this was heaven.

That lasted a few months, and Abner began to realize that both Charlotte and her family wanted more of a commitment from him. They didn't come out and say it, but Charlotte hinted at the long term the way expectant young women often do, and her parents began to be just a notch less relaxed in his presence. The way they looked at him seemed to indicate that they wanted more than his charming company. They loved their daughter and were not going to abandon her to a life that appeared in any way dissolute.

So Abner, not one to shy away from a challenge, proposed to Charlotte on Valentine's Day of the following year. He planned his proposal down to the detail. He spent Christmas looking for the perfect ring, something expensive but not ostentatious. He mapped out the sequence of events. He knew he had to talk to Charlotte's father before he proposed, so he called him one afternoon at his office in Clayton.

"Mr. Weatherby," he began respectfully. "There is something I would like to discuss with you at your earliest convenience." He paused and took a breath.

Mr. Weatherby waited before he responded. "What is it, Abner?" he asked.

Abner was not about to show his hand over the phone. "It is a personal matter in which you might have some interest, sir," he said.

"And I would like to discuss it in person. Could we meet?"

Abner figured that Mr. Weatherby knew what Abner was getting at and Mr. Weatherby figured that Abner was getting at what he was getting at. He smiled to himself and said warmly, "By all means, Abner. Why don't you meet me after work at Cardwell's?" He took a breath. "We'll have a drink and discuss whatever is on your mind."

Abner had no misgivings about talking to Charlotte's father. It was a game, a strategic move, part of the plan. He got to the venue early and found a quiet table in the bar. He ordered a martini, but he didn't touch it until Charles Weatherby arrived. He also ordered the bourbon he knew Mr. Weatherby liked. He only had to wait a few minutes after the drinks arrived. In the meantime, he recited the twenty-third Psalm to calm himself.

Charles Weatherby arrived precisely at the time Abner thought he would, and he stood up to greet him with a warm handshake.

"Thank you so much for meeting me, Mr. Weatherby," Abner intoned. Mr. Weatherby nodded.

"Mr. Weatherby," Abner continued softly, "I will get directly to the point." He cleared his throat and adjusted his tie in a deliberately self-conscious way. "As you know, Charlotte and I have grown very fond of each other over these past months. She is a wonderful woman, and I know in my heart I will never find another woman who could come close to filling her shoes." He looked down at his drink, then slowly returned his gaze to Mr. Weatherby. "I love her," he said with just the slightest tremor in his voice. "I want to marry her." Another pause. "And I would like your permission and your blessing." He looked at Mr. Weatherby expectantly.

Mr. Weatherby's naturally sober countenance bored a hole into Abner's soul. For a single heartbeat, he thought maybe he had overplayed the moment. It occurred to him that maybe this was not something Mr. Weatherby wanted or anticipated.

But then the slightest grin appeared on that craggy face, and Mr. Weatherby extended his hand across the table. "Abner," he said, taking the younger man's hand in his, "I would be honored for you to marry my daughter. I have never seen her so happy. You have my permission and my blessing." He raised his glass in a toast. Abner did the same.

"To marriage," Mr. Weatherby said.

"To marriage," Abner replied.

"And, by the way," Mr. Weatherby said, "please call me Chuck."

The relief that spread throughout Abner's body was enormous. His whole body relaxed, and he took a gulp of his martini. "Thank you, Chuck," he said. "I'd be honored."

This simple meeting triggered a major change of tone. Chuck called his wife, Amanda, to tell her the good news. Amanda suggested she join the men at Cardwell's for dinner. Chuck looked over at Abner who nodded enthusiastically. Another martini later, Amanda showed up, and the three spent the evening eating, drinking, and doing initial planning for the wedding.

It was Abner who, humbly he thought, brought up the possibility that Charlotte may not say yes when he pops the question. "Nonsense!" exclaimed the increasingly intoxicated Chuck, who was growing fond of the idea of having another male in the family. "She's crazy about you!"

Amanda concurred. "Yes, she is," she said, almost slurring her words. "Women know these things."

Abner wasn't really worried. He and Charlotte had hinted around at the long term, along with the M-word, often enough for him to feel confident that her answer would be an immediate yes.

So the very next day at a prescheduled dinner at one of the finest dining spots in the city, Abner, armed with the ring in his pocket, sat waiting for the precise moment, the moment of greatest drama.

It occurred just after the drinks arrived and Charlotte was complaining vaguely about her mother. "She can be such a busybody,"

Charlotte whined. "Just today she was hinting around about your 'intentions' as if it were any of her business."

"Intentions?" Abner asked, feigning indifference but also hiding his irritation that Amanda may have spilled the beans.

"Yes," said Charlotte. "She wants to know way too much about my business."

"Your business?" Abner said softly.

Charlotte looked at him with an impish grin. "*Our* business," she said. She reached across the table and put her hand on his.

To her surprise, Abner grabbed hold of her hand with some force. "I have some, um, business to take care of," he said, looking directly and deeply into her eyes.

Charlotte's eyes widened. She had never seen Abner like this.

Abner reached into his jacket pocket and pulled out a little velvet box. "I have a confession to make, Charlotte," he said. "I met with your father yesterday to discuss a matter of some importance. I asked for his permission and his blessing to ask you to marry me."

Charlotte inhaled sharply. While this was on her radar screen, it wasn't something she was at all expecting just then. She took some time to exhale.

"Charlotte Weatherby," Abner said formally, still holding her hand and dropping to one knee beside the table. "Will you marry me?"

Charlotte's face turned several shades of crimson and she blurted out "Yes, yes," as much out of surprise as out of nuptial desire. "Of course I will, Abner. I love you."

Abner breathed a sigh of relief. He knew that nothing was certain until it occurred, and he heard the final piece of his plan click into place. He smiled broadly, leaned over to Charlotte, and kissed her deeply in front of God and everybody. "Thank you," he whispered.

The wedding plans went into high gear. The engaged couple selected a June wedding at a large suburban church and a Mediterranean honeymoon offered by the bride's happy and relieved parents.

Abner was also happy. He felt he had taken an important step. He found himself about to be wedded to one of the wealthiest families in the Midwest as well as to a beautiful young woman. He felt this gave him some flexibility in his life moving forward. He found himself fawned over by Charlotte's parents, and he loved that. He felt special.

The wedding was the social event of note that year—all subsidized by the bride's family. It was followed by two weeks of luxurious boating in the Mediterranean. Abner felt he was in the perfect place at the perfect time at the perfect age.

These feelings lasted until a few months into their marriage. Until he woke up one morning with a powerful desire to flee.

He looked over at Charlotte, who was as lovely asleep as she was awake in her carefully manicured and expensively coiffed attire. And he felt nothing. Nothing but deprivation and monotony and an overwhelming urge to go hunting for other women. Of course, on the surface, he continued to display the courtesy and solicitude that Charlotte had come to expect, the kind that so pleased her and her family. But on the inside, he knew that this was not what he wanted for himself. He was born for something greater, for something more far-reaching, for a Special Mission. He just knew it.

But he still didn't know what that Special Mission was exactly. He continued to preach and to write some, although even those profitable activities gradually lost their appeal. Fortunately, he traveled a good bit and was able to escape the monotony of family life. He dreaded the prospect of having children and saw potential offspring as a threat to whatever his mission was to be. He had to be ready. He could not be held back by something so ordinary as a family with children.

Abner was angry. And it was during those private rages that he vowed never to be tied down, not to Charlotte, not to a church, not to The Way Things Were. He wanted to be a man of the world, accountable to no one. It was also during this time that he resumed sleeping around.

Greed had always been a part of American culture. Early in the development of the white settlement of North America, survival reigned as the guiding principle. As the country expanded, however, the abundant natural resources of the continent combined with a pioneering spirit of hard work and exploitation to generate huge profits. In the 1980s, Michael Douglas's portrayal of Gordon Gekko became iconic. "Greed is good!" he declared without embarrassment to an auditorium of well-off Americans. That speech captured the spirit of an age that was dawning. Little else mattered in the national conversation so much as the presumed sacred right of wealth and the prerogatives that came along with it. Not poverty, not homelessness, not health care, not peace, not charity, not belief: nothing attained the crowning importance of wealth. So much so that the masses, most of whom were comfortable but certainly not wealthy—identified in 2011 as "the 99%"—refused to levy additional taxes of the wealthiest Americans, believing reverentially if erroneously that any tax increase would forestall recovery from the recession that was plaguing the economy.

This way of thinking had a precursor: the 1920s, when land speculation, stock speculation, and an underground economy suddenly became chic. That experiment in excess contributed directly to the Great Depression, an echo, a harbinger, and a warning of what was to transpire in the mid-2000s. The wealthy elite dismissed these events as normal fluctuations in the "business cycle," a theoretical term that was devised to explain inexplicable slowdowns in economic activity. In fact, the definition was simply a tautology, as the structure, exigency, and reality of a business cycle have never been identified.

But this was a matter largely for academicians. The cultural impact, the cultural ethos, was governed by the spirit of the age. And the spirit of the age was wealth no matter the means. The focus was on advancement at any cost, a focus that fostered a generation of moneyed narcissists.

No more stunning example of the power of greed and narcissism exists than the story of Enron, a company that flaunted its wealth and assaulted the common good of the country with abandon, even as it lied about its numbers and moved forward on the basis of fictional accounting. Enron manipulated power supplies in California, creating an artificial crisis that jacked up power prices, and the company's profits, to astronomical levels. Even with huge inflows of cash, however, the company was so reckless with its investments that it folded over a matter of days. The life savings of many of its investors vanished. While some company officers were prosecuted, many were not. Even the ones who were prosecuted never seemed to comprehend that they did anything wrong.

6

That Special Mission came to Abner in a very personal but undramatic way. He was sitting in a coffee shop having breakfast, reading his paper. It was a few years into his marriage to Charlotte. He was intent on keeping up appearances until such time as his mission became clear to him. He spent a lot of time in coffee shops alone, reading the paper, writing to himself, or just people-watching. He was only half paying attention to the words he was reading. He was restless. He was edgy. He wanted something to happen.

In the midst of his agitation, a young woman entered the little shop and walked up to the counter—a young woman of uncommon beauty with pale skin and blond hair. She was tall and slender, and when she spoke, her voice was loud, distinctive, and Southern. For a moment, Abner was back at home in Macon, back with his mother and father, back at a time when he trusted them completely, when he admired his father and loved his mother beyond words. That sound, that accent, struck a chord deep in his soul. It awakened something inside him.

Not only was this lovely young woman Southern and Georgian to boot, she was strong. Her presence demanded attention; it was impossible not to notice her, not to defer to her. The world was hers. Abner thought this was what the early Christians must have thought about the Virgin Mary. It was as though this young woman was, by virtue of ordering a cup of coffee, taking possession of the entire establishment. It was inconceivable that anyone could resist her. Abner certainly couldn't.

She sat down at the table next to his. He looked up from his newspaper, which by then he wasn't even pretending to read, and turned to her with a smile and said exactly what was on his mind. "You sound like I know you." He said it in such a perfect Georgian accent that he surprised even himself. It was a voice and a self he had long put aside but clearly had not forgotten. The girl smiled in return and said, "Augusta."

"Macon," Abner replied, and his smile deepened. "My name's Abner. Abner Bellamy." He bowed slightly and did not extend his hand. Very old school.

"Judith," the young woman said without a moment's hesitation. "Judith Mayfield." She flashed Abner a ladylike grin. "Pleased to meet you, Mr. Bellamy."

"Please call me Abner. What brings you to St. Louis?" Abner asked, not wanting to let the conversation end.

Judith looked at him softly and said, "The Washington University Medical School."

"You're a student?" Abner asked.

"No," Judith replied. "I was hired as an associate professor."

Smart to boot, Abner thought. There was another thought trying to surface, but Judith spoke first.

"I miss Georgia already," Judith said.

And then the thought broke through to the surface in Abner's mind. "I do too," he said. "Every day."

For the first time in months, Abner did not want this casual contact to turn into a casual sexual encounter. He saw Judith as a prize, but more importantly, he saw her as a symbol and as a sign. She was obviously beautiful and, judging by the absence of any rings on her finger, unmarried. But she stood as a symbol of his heritage, one that he had worked hard to ignore but one to which he felt immediately reconnected. And she was a sign, a sign that his mission was about to be given him. It was breathtaking. He wanted to go home. To Georgia.

But he did not want to go home as a helpless and aggrieved fourteen-year-old whose father died tragically and whose mother rejected him. He wanted to return home triumphant, a shining example of Southern power and manhood.

It was when he and Judith were walking in Forest Park a few days later that they happened to run across the Confederate Memorial. They both spotted it at the same time, from the back, where the long inscription written by a Confederate soldier was carved in huge block letters. They read silently.

When they finished reading, Abner and Judith looked at each other, both with solemn expressions on their faces. "Wow!" Abner exclaimed. He had just caught a glimpse of his future, of his mission.

Judith was no less moved. She slipped her arm around Abner's as they walked to the front of the memorial with the relief of a Southern family sending their only son off to war. A tear fell from her cheek. "My grandparents told me stories about this," she said. "They were too young to know about the war, but their parents weren't. They knew. Many of their relatives—my relatives—were killed. It's a grief that's still with our family." She gazed again at the statue. "After all those years."

This was how Abner made the short trip from an ambitious but unhappily married man to a true believer, from being a man with a vague if not forgotten purpose to being a man surfing on an ocean of vision and resolve. He knew at that moment what, he thought, should have been self-evident all along: he would take up the cause of Confederate independence. It made perfect sense to him. It was his heritage. It was the policies foisted upon Georgia by the Yankee government that killed his beloved father and destroyed his mother and his family, sending him into exile. Judith's mere presence in his immediate space was testimony enough to the superiority of white Southerners. He was captured.

As he continued the conversation, Abner's mind was multitasking. He kept the conversation going, but in his heart, for the first time in years, he felt a powerful desire to return to the land of his youth, the land he had abandoned when he first left for college. He always knew he was a Southerner, but he downplayed it; he put on the accent only for effect, and that was seldom. For the most part, he spoke like a Boston Blueblood. He even spoke that way to himself.

But a triumphant return to Georgia would take commitment, planning, and resources. Abner did not doubt that he had the personal resources, the strength, energy, determination, and willingness to work hard. He had some money of his own, but his lifestyle was presently dependent on Charlotte and her family, who did not fail to lavish on the young couple the many rewards of her father's hard work. The money part did not bother him overmuch. He figured that if he felt this way, there were plenty of other Southerners who would gladly forsake their humdrum lives to resurrect the Confederate States of America.

He had found his mission.

7

This evening would be the culmination of his efforts over the past ten years, the first time the group he had assembled would all come together.

Prior to this, Abner had met with individuals and with small cells—two or three people at the most. But tonight was the night when all the individuals, all the cells, would be represented for the first time. The meeting was scheduled to begin at 7:00 p.m., but it had no scheduled end.

He parked on the street in front of Preservation Hall. He got out and looked around. It was an old building on an old narrow street. Parking was difficult, but all the men at the meeting would be arriving by unmarked chauffeured cars, so that wasn't a problem. Abner walked up to the front door and let himself in.

He saw a crew setting up tables and chairs in the middle of a large room. It looked as if it could have been a church or some other venue that accommodated large groups. As he had requested, the windows were covered, the table was arranged in a square so that everyone could see each other. Individual microphones sat in front of each comfortable chair. There were individual water pitchers and ice buckets. Those would be filled just prior to the men arriving. There were also ashtrays available for those who smoked. Few smoked cigarettes, but some of the men enjoyed their cigars, and the room was equipped with a smoke-eating machine so that no smoke would linger. He had also arranged for the meeting to be recorded, but surreptitiously, so that none of the participants would know. And he had arranged for white-noise machines, so that any other efforts to eavesdrop on the conversation would be thwarted. Abner prided himself on attention to detail.

As Abner was surveying the room, Jack Waller entered through a rear door. Abner had known Jack since coming to St. Louis and trusted him as much as he trusted anyone. Jack was in charge of the arrangements that Abner had stipulated. It was Jack who worked with the staff at Preservation Hall to implement the specifications that Abner had made. Jack nodded to Abner when he spotted him.

"Hi, Jack," Abner said.

Jack nodded again and walked over and shook Abner's hand. "Hi, Abner."

"How's it going here?" Abner asked.

"Great," said Jack. "Everything is exactly to your specification." His voice dropped to a whisper. "The recording equipment is state of the art. There is no way it will be detected by anyone here. I am the only person who knows where the actual equipment is located." He chuckled.

Abner smiled and walked around the room, trying to spot anything that others might think was suspicious. He couldn't find anything. One of the nice things about older buildings was that they seemed to accommodate anything.

Just before seven, people started arriving. There were twenty-two of them, two from each state of the old Confederacy. They all either knew each other or knew of each other, but the relationships were mostly casual. Primarily what they had in common was a close relationship with Abner and a shared vision of a free and unencumbered nation that was the state of their birth. Each person was selected by the secessionist cell system in his respective state. Each one knew what he was doing was illegal and even treasonous. And every single one of them was proud to be there. The all-white, middle-aged men were mannerly, soft-spoken, and had a hidden but potent and steely resolve to see their vision of the Confederacy reawaken.

Precisely at seven, Abner strode to the podium placed in front of the tables and the assembled members. Abner thought of this group as a kind of revived Continental Congress. If his plans came to fruition, the legislative body of the new CSA would devolve from the group assembled in this room on this evening. And he wanted each one of them to know it.

"Gentlemen," Abner said in his most authoritative voice. "Thank you for coming." He looked around to make sure every man at the table was looking at him. "We are here to take the next step in our journey. These past ten years have involved a lot of planning, a lot of hard work, and a lot of risk for you and for the people you represent. But tonight we come together for the first time to work out the next steps."

Abner looked around the room, square in the face of each man present. "We are not here," he continued, "to destroy the United States of America." He paused and looked them in the eye again. "We are here to transform the United States of America, to return it to what it was originally conceived to be. We are here to reestablish our country.

"And we are going to do it the way our forefathers did it. We are going to start by declaring our independence from the tyrannical federal government that has grown so big, so dominant, so imperious as not to even consider that they are dealing with sovereign, independent states. We are here to draw up a new Declaration of Independence.

"This document will serve as the basis of all our future activity. It will also explain to the world and to the current government what we are doing and why we are doing it." Abner paused for effect. "It will look a lot like the declaration our forefathers drew up over two hundred years ago, a copy of which is at your place, as is a copy of the new version, which I propose to use as a starting point for our discussion."

Abner began to read the new version, interpolating changes as he saw fit.

IN CONGRESS Assembled, JULY 4, the day of our Independence

The unanimous Declaration of the eleven Confederated States of America

When in the Course of human events it becomes necessary for one people to dissolve the political bands which have connected them with another and to assume among the powers of the earth, the separate and equal station to which the Laws of Nature and of Nature's God entitle them, a decent respect to the opinions of mankind requires that they should declare the causes which impel them to the separation.

As our forefathers did, we hold these truths to be self-evident: that all men are created equal, that they are endowed by their Creator with certain unalienable Rights, that among these are Life, Liberty and the pursuit of Happiness. — That to secure these rights, Governments are instituted among Men, deriving their just powers from the consent of the governed, — That whenever any form of Government becomes destructive of these ends, it is the Right of the People to alter or to abolish it, and to institute new Government, laying its foundation on such principles and organizing its powers in such form, as to them shall seem most likely to effect their Safety and Happiness. Prudence, indeed, will dictate that Governments long established should not be changed for light and transient causes; and accordingly all experience hath shewn that mankind are more disposed to suffer, while evils are sufferable, than to right themselves by abolishing the forms to which they are accustomed. But when a long train of abuses and usurpations, pursuing invariably the same Object, evinces a design to reduce them under absolute Despotism, it is their right, it is their duty, to throw off such Government, and to provide new Guards for their future security. — Such has been the patient sufferance of these States; and such is now the necessity which constrains them to alter their former systems of

Government. *The history of the present Government of the United States is a history of repeated injuries and usurpations, all having in direct object the establishment of an absolute Tyranny over these States. To prove this, let Facts be submitted to a candid world.*

It has refused to allow States to create their own Laws without the approval of the federal government, such Laws being the most wholesome and necessary for the public good.

It has forbidden us to pass Laws of immediate and pressing importance, unless suspended in their operation till its Assent should be obtained; and when so suspended, it has utterly neglected to recognize or respect them.

It has refused to recognize that conditions differ across different States, and that what is wholesome for one may be a burden for another.

It has declared its own legislative bodies superior in every respect to our own. It has kept its own records at places not readily available to us for the sole purpose of forcing us into compliance with its measures.

It has ignored Representative Houses repeatedly, for opposing with manly firmness the continuing invasions on the rights of the people.

It has prevented us from establishing Churches of our choosing and ignored the pleas of our Christian citizens to grant churches the protections of law.

It has endeavoured to prevent the population of these States from recognizing those persons we would grant citizenship and those we would refuse. It has required that we accept anyone they permit to travel to our lands.

It has obstructed the Administration of Justice by declaring its own Court superior to our individual high Courts.

It has made Judges dependent on its Will alone for the tenure of their offices, and the amount and payment of their salaries.

It has erected a multitude of New Offices, and sent hither swarms of Officers to harass our people and eat out their substance.

It has kept among us, in times of peace, Standing Armies without the Consent of our legislatures and it has declared the right to nationalize our militias.

It has affected to render the Military independent of and superior to the Civil Powers residing in our respective States.

It has quartered large bodies of armed troops among us:

It has protected them from punishment for Crimes which they have committed among the Inhabitants of these States:

For cutting off our independent Trade with all parts of the world:

For imposing Taxes on us without our Consent:

For declaring our militias federalized without our consent:

For arbitrarily allowing new States to form under the same tyrannical conditions to which they have subjected the original ones:

For ignoring our Charters, ignoring our most valuable Laws, and altering fundamentally the forms of our Governments:

For bypassing our own Legislatures, and declaring themselves invested with power to legislate for us in all cases whatsoever.

It has stolen our assets, ravaged our coasts, neglected our needs, and destroyed the livelihood of our people.

In the face of these Oppressions We have periodically Petitioned for Redress in the most reasonable terms: Our repeated Petitions have been answered only by repeated injury. A Government, whose character is thus marked by every act which may define a Tyrant, is unfit to rule a free people.

Nor have We been wanting in patience with our federal cousins. We have warned them from time to time of attempts by their legislature to extend an unwarrantable jurisdiction over us. We have reminded them of the circumstances of our formation and settlement. We have appealed to their native justice and magnanimity, and we have conjured them by the ties of our common kindred to disavow these usurpations, which would inevitably interrupt our connections and correspondence. They too have been deaf to the voice of justice and of consanguinity. We must, therefore, acquiesce in the necessity, which denounces our Separation, and hold them, as we hold the rest of mankind, Enemies in War, in Peace Friends.

We, therefore, the Representatives of the Confederated States of America, in General Congress, Assembled, appealing to the Supreme

Judge of the world for the rectitude of our intentions, do, in the Name, and by Authority of the good People of these States, solemnly publish and declare, That each of these States are, and of Right ought to be Free and Independent, that they are Absolved from all Allegiance to the Federal Government in Washington, DC, and that all political connection between them and the Washington government, is and ought to be totally dissolved; and that as Free and Independent States, they have full Power to levy War, conclude Peace, contract Alliances, establish Commerce, and to do all other Acts and Things which Independent States may of right do. — And for the support of this Declaration, with a firm reliance on the protection of Divine Providence, we mutually pledge to each other our Lives, our Fortunes, and our sacred Honor.

Abner looked out onto the room. He had only felt this kind of silence on one other occasion, and that was when he met Judith, when he received in his mind his sacred mission. In this silence as in that one, the rest of the world, the part outside his field of vision, simply vanished. Nothing mattered but the weight of the moment, the sublime sense of clarity and purpose to which every person in the room was irretrievably committed.

The twenty-two men broke into applause.

During the time Abner Bellamy was thinking of secession or working toward it, he was hardly alone. Two brothers were talking as they sat around on sumptuous leather couches at a plush hunting lodge in Vermont. It was evening, and the two men had spent the greater part of an especially resplendent autumn day hunting moose in the glorious Vermont woodlands of the Northeast Kingdom. They were relaxing before dinner, sipping on their favorite cocktails. The combined net worth of these two men exceeded the annual income of the state where they were hunting. They knew about money and they knew about power. And they intended to use both.

"It is shocking to me," began George Blinder, the older of the two, "that a Democrat is still sitting in the White House." He paused and gazed out the window. "After all those years of failed policies. When we were so close." The words came out in a tell-tale Texan drawl, true to the origins of both of them.

George's brother David knew precisely what George was talking about. He and George had had this conversation countless times. It wasn't that he didn't welcome it; he just knew that his elder brother often preferred to complain rather than to take action. David was the opposite: there was no problem he had ever encountered that he could not find a solution for. And if one didn't strike him immediately, he would grapple with it until the solution arrived. It wasn't often long.

The two brothers had been working for decades to undo the reforms that began during the first half of the twentieth century. They were especially hostile to the accomplishments of Franklin Roosevelt, whom they saw as a sort of political Antichrist. It was he who had instituted many of the policies they detested. It mattered little to them what other people thought about him; they had their private version of history. Instead of acknowledging that Roosevelt was the man who saved the very system they cherished and thrived in, they manipulated every form of media to attribute the positive developments of his term in office to factors other than his efforts. It was, in their view, the Second World War that ended the Depression; Social Security was a blight on the economy and an abrogation of individual responsibility; various government-funded projects, such as the WPA, were a waste of taxpayers' money, etc., etc., etc. They believed that their relentless, magnificently funded, decades-long media blitz had finally tipped popular sentiment in their direction.

They seldom questioned these attitudes or beliefs, in which they were schooled by their father, Silas Blinder. Silas was a self-made millionaire when a million dollars was a significant amount of money. He lived through—even thrived in—the thirties and forties. He had two serious objections to the federal government. The first was that the government had no business handing out money to anyone except the few bureaucrats, soldiers, and politicians needed to run an efficient government. Social Security was to his mind an outrage, and the thought of government paying people's medical bills, a development that occurred toward the end of his colorful life, was a final insult. The second was regulation. To Silas's mind, any infringement on the free pursuit of capital or resource exploitation was similarly outrageous, and he often lectured his boys about this violation of natural law. Silas determined to use his money, his power, and his children to turn back these obscene developments and return America to its roots and, in so doing, to its manifest destiny of ruling the world.

Silas witnessed how the United States of America saved Europe twice, and while he wasn't a fan of war, he was a major fan of profit and of power, and he saw the opportunities that war provided. Given the vast resources of the North American hemisphere and the can-do attitude of most American citizens, he did not see why America couldn't endure as the ruler of the world.

Silas felt strongly that the social programs begun under the New Deal would sabotage this agenda, and he instructed his two boys daily in the evils of social welfare and regulation, the need for self-reliance, and the hypocrisy of religious or ethical values. To Silas's mind, the world belonged to the most aggressive, a belief that blended nicely with his obnoxious but determined temperament.

So for the balance of his life and for the duration of the lives of his prized sons, Silas Blinder's agenda to roll back what he saw as socialist reforms and return America to its former glory were all consuming. And, in fact, great headway had been made. By pouring money into media, the Blinders, *pere et fils*, were part of a larger movement to cast liberalism as a pejorative and government as the enemy of freedom. Fortunately for them, these beliefs helped their many businesses to thrive, as they contributed to the reduced tax burden for the rich and changed the financing of government from one of pay-as-you-go to one of living on credit. It was by design unsustainable.

Plus, only a few years before, no less prominent a courtier than Karl Rove predicted a "permanent" Republican majority in government. The two brothers, as well as all of the friends and acquaintances who made up their social circle, believed that a Democratic president, especially an African-American one, risked bringing their long efforts to naught. They believed that a permanent Republican majority would consolidate the gains made in wealth and property accrual. It would consolidate the grip on power that the rich enjoyed more and more but wanted to finalize. They wanted to seal the deal, making it permanent. It was no small loss when a liberal Democrat won the presidency. Especially for a second term.

David frowned a fastidious little frown and said what had become clear to both brothers in recent years. "We are at an impasse," he said, not looking directly at his brother. "Despite all our efforts, and despite the fact that we have been able to change the minds of half the population, there are still those stubborn independents who lack the fortitude to do the right thing."

George looked out the window as the snow began falling. "This is a fluke," he said. "If Hillary had run last time, or some other Democrat, they would have lost in a landslide." He took a sip of his Maker's Mark. "The country got carried away with that mixed-blood charmer from Chicago." He chuckled softly to himself. "Who'd have thought the country could be snookered by somebody from that corrupt hellhole." He took another sip.

David was not deterred. "But he *was* reelected, George," he said. "I think we could have lived with one term, but this second one is a real setback. They've got momentum; they could turn things around. They could postpone the Plan," he said. "They could even derail it." He looked over at his brother. "This guy is determined. We have got to find a way to get the Plan back on track." He was drinking scotch and watching his brother puff on a Cuban Cohiba. He looked over at his brother through a cloud of smoke. "We don't just have forever, you know."

George nodded. He knew what his brother was saying. They were both comfortably in their seventies now, and they had made a promise to their father and to each other decades before that they would see the "socialist" policies of the New Deal reversed in their lifetime. It had been going smoothly ever since Reagan was in office, and even under Bill Clinton they were able to make steady headway.

In George W. Bush, a former Texas governor whom they believed they controlled completely, they thought they had someone who could close the deal, but his administration was thrown off course by the events of September 11, 2001, and the subsequent wars.

Not that the pair objected to war as such. Their father had taught them that it was a great way to get industry moving and increase profits at a breathtaking pace. It also put a lot of otherwise useless lowlifes to good use as foot soldiers. Pruned the population, in their view.

George and David sat looking out the window; both were focused on the same unspoken thought. *Something needs to happen to get things back on track.*

But another thought lurked in the back of David's mind. They hadn't spoken about it for some years, but it was his ace-in-the-hole for their financial empire and the wealth of their family and the families of their friends.

David looked up at the high ceiling. "There is that other option, George," he said softly. "It would take care of several problems at once." He lifted his glass and looked through the amber liquid. "It would give us the kind of control we've been working for. It would allow us to set up new ground rules from the beginning rather than working with this albatross of a government bureaucracy." He took another sip. "And did I mention control?" He grinned in a way that could easily have been mistaken for a cynical if not evil grimace.

George did not say anything at first. He puffed on his contraband cigar a few times before he spoke. "Biggest problem with that is the same problem we've always had. The military. Nothing in this country is so powerful, so disciplined, so respected, and so bent on keeping the power they have." He puffed on his cigar. "And that means that the military will support the federal government. No matter what."

David did not hesitate. "It looks that way now, but you know, George, blood runs thicker than water. I'll bet when push comes to shove and it's decision time, a lot of those guys in the military—maybe most of them—could be persuaded to see things differently. Remember what happened in the original Civil War: most of those men chose kin and heritage over some vague idea of a country that they couldn't relate to or was far away. I bet that, if given a choice, the military could see things our way. Especially when the country is in the mess it's in now. Maybe all they need is a little education." He glanced over at his brother. "And a little incentive."

George looked at his younger brother. He knew David to be the man of action he was. "You've been busy?" he said.

David looked his brother right in the eye. "I have," he replied.

The wealthy interests of the country had long resented bigger government. In the early decades of the twentieth century, the fortune of John D. Rockefeller was greater than the US Treasury. It was an era of unparalleled amassing of money by private individuals. No matter that the "lower" classes were kept in virtual poverty or had little access to power; what rights or privileges they did have were seen as indulgences of the wealthy to a lower type of individual. It was only by steady unionization, labor movements, and the enfranchisement of women during the early decades of the twentieth century that "the masses" started demanding—and receiving—humane treatment and a greater share of the abundant wealth that was being created across the United States, demands that were given only grudgingly and under duress by the moneyed classes.

Even in the midst of the Great Depression, the wealthy classes, who were relatively unscathed by it, saw the solution as a simple business proposition: sell, sell, sell became the watchword. All that selling did little to alleviate the suffering engendered by the unbridled pursuit of private capital.

For the wealthy conservatives, Franklin Delano Roosevelt was an unmitigated disaster. Born to privilege himself, Roosevelt saw the need for greater government action. He was supported in this belief by the work of John Maynard Keynes, a British economist who pioneered the role of government in economic affairs. He directed the Executive Branch and the Legislative Branch of government to work on these matters. It was during this time that public works boomed.

It was also during this time when certain rights and protections were initiated that later came to be seen as basic. Social Security began during this period, as did the notion of worker's rights becoming enshrined in law. The minimum wage, the right not to be coerced by employers, and the right to bargain collectively were all enacted in legislation driven by the Democratic president and supported by a Democratic Congress. Up until this time, the courts largely supported the wealthy upper class. Even the National Industrial Recovery Act signed by President Roosevelt was declared unconstitutional by the Supreme Court. It was replaced by the Wagner Act two months later, however, and the basic rights it accorded workers were guaranteed.

To the wealthy owners' class, these steps toward basic human fairness were egregious departures from American tradition. But conservative voices were in the minority during the thirties and forties, and their influence gradually lessened. The decade of the 1950s was one of general prosperity and economic boom for large numbers of people.

While the influence of wealthy capitalists was on the wane publicly, they continued to nurse grievances within their private domains. Board meetings, private club gatherings, and exclusive outings were venues to grumble about the deteriorated state of affairs and gradually to plot a return to ascendancy. It was during the Reagan administration that they hit upon the vehicle to increase their influence and reverse their fortunes. It was also during that time that they associated themselves with the Religious Right, a group that had hitherto been seen as rigid, backward, and generally resistant to the march of progress.

A t about the same time that George and David were sipping whiskey in the Northeast of the country, another man was mulling not unrelated thoughts in the Midwest. Unbeknownst to George, this man was contemplating the unthinkable, something he would have virulently opposed just a few years before. This man regarded himself as a patriot, as a stalwart proponent of the American Way, which he believed with all his heart and soul was the way of God. His religion told him so, his friends told him so, and his heart told him so.

Daniel Keenan was praying. Not aloud, but in the privacy of his heart. His wife was putting the children to bed and settling the household before she joined him for the end of the evening. In his prayer, he was considering the path God had revealed to him these past years, a path that modified his unshakable belief in the primacy of the American Way as he had always considered it. Well, not so much the Way, but the way America was now, the current government structure. Daniel had come to believe that the government—his government, the federal government—had turned its back on his values and the values of the nation and had planted its flag firmly in the foreboding ground of secular liberalism. In the process, it abandoned those values that Daniel held dearer than any other loyalties. He held them dearer than his own life.

And those were the values imparted to him as a child: devotion to Jesus Christ, the Lord, the Redeemer, the Savior of mankind, without whom life was nothing. He was raised in a strict Lutheran household, where Duty and the Right held absolute sway, no matter how inconvenient, how distressing to a young mind, or how contrary to desire they might be. He could remember hating his parents for being so strict, but he also had many examples of how that early discipline prevented him from taking wrong turns in life. He never touched drugs; he did not drink; he never smoked. He did not have sex until he was married and then only with the aim of having children. He was a scrupulous, intense man who found compromise with the Truth physically painful.

As an adult he learned to appreciate those values and to inculcate them into the lives of his own children, who now numbered three. He saw his child self reflected in their occasional protests, but he also saw the benefit of his strong personal values over time. He was sure that his offspring would come to appreciate their upbringing as much as he came to appreciate his.

He was talking with his wife, Cherie, one evening and finally decided to share with her what he had been doing. It was shortly after yet another court decision upholding the right of Americans to fornicate without regard to object choice and to avoid the consequences of their actions should a pregnancy arrive unwanted. It made him sick.

"We are going in the wrong direction, Cherie," he said as they were sitting in the living room after the children were in bed. "I think we have to do something. Something more than just preach to our own kind about this."

Cherie looked over at her husband, whose cratered face looked a lot like rock in the soft evening light. "What can we do, Daniel?" she asked. "These things are not in our hands."

"That is precisely the problem, Cherie. They are in the hands of reckless, godless people, men and women who have forsaken the values of Christianity, who have lost a sense of common decency."

Cherie did not know exactly how to respond. She knew her husband to be a principled man, a strict but fair father, a hard worker who demanded much of himself and everyone around him, whether here at home or at his job at the university. She loved him, but she felt uneasy about this topic and more recent pronouncements he'd been making about the direction in which he saw the country moving. She turned her face back to the book that was sitting on her lap.

To her surprise, Daniel shot out of his chair. "Don't you see?" he said in a loud and agitated voice, something that was quite unlike him. "Don't you understand?" He stared down at her from above, a threatening angel sent to command her attention.

Cherie wasn't frightened, at least not for her physical well-being; she did not believe that Daniel would ever strike her or lash out at her physically. But she was not immune to anxiety from seeing Daniel get so agitated. She shifted into management mode. "Daniel," she said softly. "Sit down. Take a deep breath." She patted the open seat next to her on the couch. "Sit by me."

Daniel did as he was told. He felt guilty. He knew none of this was Cherie's fault. It wasn't his fault. That was the problem. It wasn't ever anyone's fault. He took a deep breath and sat next to his beloved wife.

"I'm sorry," he said after a moment. He put his arm around her. "I just don't know how much longer I can sit by and do nothing."

The two sat in silence for several minutes. Cherie dared not speak for fear of triggering another outburst from her normally levelheaded husband. Her eyes did not go back to her book, although that was a bit of a challenge. She loved literature and read every evening.

After a while, Daniel looked up into Cherie's eyes. He took her hand and squeezed it. "I have something to tell you, honey," he said in almost a whisper.

Cherie did not move. Nor did Daniel continue immediately. She waited a few moments and then said as gently as she could, "Daniel, what is it?"

Daniel let out a long stream of air. He turned his head away from Cherie and focused his eyes across the room. Across time in his mind; he was looking toward the future.

"You know our little faith-sharing group," he began in a very, very soft voice. "The one I joined at the university a while back, the one that meets online monthly with people from all over the country."

Cherie nodded.

"You know there are many good, solid men, good Christians, in that group."

Cherie nodded again.

In an even softer voice, Daniel continued. "There has been talk."

Cherie did not move.

Daniel did not speak.

Time stood still.

After what seemed like a long time, Daniel began to describe what had been happening in his faith-sharing group.

"All of the men," he began, "share the same frustration I have. They are angry and frustrated. For a long time they have felt help-less, as I have." He continued not to look at his wife.

"A while back, some of the men began to talk about . . . about doing something more drastic than writing letters that nobody seems to read. They got to talking about . . . about . . . about . . ."

"About what?" Cherie exclaimed out of frustration. She instantly regretted it and softened her tone. "About what, Daniel?" she repeated in a softer voice.

Daniel looked down at the floor. Cherie noticed he was trembling. She could barely breathe.

"About a revolution," Daniel whispered and turned and looked at his wife.

10

That ten-letter word hung in the air for a while. It took the breath out of both members of this staid and observant Christian couple.

"What?" Cherie finally said.

Daniel continued in a low voice; he looked directly at his wife. "Some of the men have come to believe that it would be possible to revolt against the current government, to force either a constitutional convention or to simply replace the present structure of the American government. Most think it is the size of the country that's a problem and that it should break up into smaller countries." Another long pause. "And Cherie," he said, the warmth returning to his voice, "I believe I am going to join them."

Cherie wasn't sure she could move, she was so shocked by this completely unexpected announcement. She knew Daniel was not the type to joke, and the tone of his voice and his demeanor all broadcast the serious commitment he had to what he was saying. But move she did: she removed the book from her lap and turned to look Daniel full in the face. "Daniel, this is crazy. Do not do this."

Daniel returned her stern gaze with his own rock hard face. "I will do this, Cherie," he said. "I can do nothing else."

Not once in the ten years of their marriage had Cherie considered divorce. It almost wasn't in her vocabulary. But she too was a principled woman who would not expose herself or her children to some lunatic plot to change history. And, truth be told, her level of religious commitment did not match her husband's. She was observant but not nearly so invested in their churchgoing life. It was mostly just part of the package of being a family. But this pronouncement from her normally affable husband confirmed in her inner heart the worst fears she had about religion. It was dangerous.

The couple spoke no more about the issue that evening, but that was the night when Daniel, wracked by frustration with politics, encouraged by his professional and religious peers, and at the end of his psychological rope, cast his lot with a small group of bright, well-placed men who longed for a government more responsive to their needs and values, a government that would guarantee that the United States would always remain a Christian nation, as God intended it to be. He was sure he was on the right path.

In truth, he had been considering this decision for months. Until this night, he did not have the courage to tell his wife; but nor did he have the fortitude to withhold such important information from her much longer. He never withheld information from her. He loved her with all his heart. But his sense of duty was overpowering. He knew there might be consequences: Cherie had always been a good and faithful spouse, but their relationship had never been challenged before in quite this dramatic a way. It was clear that Daniel's devotion was to the Truth, no matter how it impacted other aspects of his life. He would hate to lose Cherie, but he would hate even more losing his immortal soul to the fires of hell.

11

The actual physical meeting of the group was held in a basement room of the university where Daniel worked. It consisted of about twenty men, all of whom were devoted Christians and prominent in their respective fields. The list of accomplishments of these men was long, and Daniel, who was no stranger to accomplishment himself, felt honored to be in their presence. He was also honored to be given the task of hosting the meeting.

At this gathering, the various subgroups, which had been selected two years before and which had been working in the utmost secrecy for all that time, were to present their findings and determine the next step. The planning was reaching the critical stage. Daniel had not told Cherie the extent of planning. This was partly to protect her and partly because he endured a deep but unmistakable feeling of shame turning against the government of his birth.

This meeting was being held in a windowless basement room of the university where Daniel Keenan taught as a tenured professor of metallurgy. Daniel had been the one who suggested the room, as he figured it was little used by other members of the faculty. It had boxes scattered around, but it also had a long conference table with enough chairs for the twenty or so men who were attending. Daniel had made all the arrangements. True to his nature, he felt the responsibility of hosting the gathering, and he greeted everyone warmly and offered them beverages.

The men mingled for a while. Most had at least a passing familiarity with the others; some had long-term relationships. They were all at the tops of their field.

After ten minutes of subdued socializing, the men took their seats.

A middle-aged man with too-black hair stood up, and the group fell silent. "Gentlemen," he said. "The time has come to act. The federal government has resisted our attempts to build into law the principles that served as the basis of this country and to which we committed ourselves. It has essentially turned its back on our basic values. It has attacked our religion. It has stuck to its secular policies. In the name of separation of Church and State, it has refused to allow moral principles that we all share to be part of the governance of this country." He paused a moment and frowned. "It has rejected the United States as a Christian nation."

Dr. William Schaeffer was referring to a recent Supreme Court decision that, while putting limits on abortion, did not outlaw it outright in all circumstances, as the group had been hoping. And as they had been led to believe it would. That decision came on the heels of several court cases in which gay marriage was legalized in more and more places. It seemed only a matter of time before the "morning after" pill, late-stage abortions, and all the other horrors of the secular world would become legally protected "rights" in the United States, contrary to the teachings of the principal religion of the country. And finally, the Supreme Court of the United States upheld the Affordable Care Act, legalizing a government takeover of health care.

It was time to take the situation to the next level.

"I love this country," he continued. "But all of these things demonstrate that it has gotten out of control!" As he said this, he slapped the palm of his hand on the table for apparent emphasis. He looked around the room, connecting with any set of eyes he could. He shook his head. "We have worked for years to reestablish the religious basis of our society, of our government. We have tried to get the federal government out of our lives. We formulated an intelligent, comprehensive approach that included representatives of all major religious denominations and groups. We made headway in making sure that the government gave a greater voice to our legitimate concerns." His eyes darkened. "But on the central issues which are dearer to us than any, the ones that have defined our movement, the federal government has slammed the door.

"So now, we have a government that is not only too big, too expensive, and unwieldy, we have one that refuses to listen to the reasoned voice of the majority of right-thinking Christian Americans. We believe we can do better." He took an eyeball count of the room. "What we need is a new vision of what the USA is, what it means. It needs to mean something besides secular humanist Big Brother, money hog, and nanny state. We need to get closer to the beginning, when consent of the governed meant the consent of those with property and means. And we need to get closer to our Christian roots. If not, the whole country is doomed."

No one spoke for a minute or two. There was a collective exhalation of air that signaled that the middle-aged black-haired man had been heard. No one was surprised. It was why they were there.

During that minute or two, the only sound was the air handler that regulated the temperature in the windowless room. Then Daniel spoke.

"I don't think there's anybody here who would disagree with you, Bill," Dr. Keenan said. "We know the list of grievances. We know that Washington doesn't give a damn about what most people in this country value. We know that Congress is debating right now how to 'level the playing field.'" He paused and looked down for a moment. "We all know what that means: it means that, once again, the religious values we hold so dear will be under assault." He spoke with a touch of contempt in his voice. "As they have done time and time and time again!" He had a hard time restraining himself about these issues, even though he had planned to keep a lid on his temper.

Daniel paused a moment to collect himself. This wasn't just drama for the sake of the attendees at this meeting. He felt real heat when he thought about how the government was drifting further and further away from the culture he prized, the one in which he was raised, and the one in which he raised his own children.

He was also resentful of taxes. He knew that half the people in the country didn't pay federal income tax, and they received most of the government dole. Keenan held four patents and did consulting worldwide. He was a man of considerable income. And the government just took what it wanted. And threatened to send you to jail if you didn't pay! This, along with the complete denial of Christian values, enraged him. But he knew he had to calm down, to stay focused.

"We all know," he continued more slowly, "that the real problem is that the liberal government has corrupted the morals of the country. They have legalized immoral acts. Like infant stem cell research. Like abortion. Like . . . " and his face screwed up in a look of particular disgust, ". . . gay marriage." He paused. "They have nationalized health care and put themselves in the position of dictating to everyone what they can and cannot do with their health care dollars."

Keenan looked around the room. He knew the buttons to push. He knew that every single man in the room was wealthy beyond the dreams of most princes and devoutly pro-life, anti-stem-cell research, and pro-marriage as that state describes a union of one man and one woman. He continued.

"We are here for action. We are here to put an end to this charade of a government. We are here to take back control of the United States. As it was originally intended to be: a confederation of sovereign, free, and independent states. Our committee has determined that the way to prevent these kinds of developments is to transfer greater power to the states. On a state level, many of the federal reforms would not stand. Most states that have held referenda on gay marriage, for instance, have voted it down. Even California!"

Heads nodded around the table.

"Giving power back to the states would also mean greater flexibility in taxation and in health care. There are movements across the country where people are recognizing that the money sent to Washington can best be spent on the home front. Even New York would not have a budget shortfall if all that money went to state rather than federal coffers."

More head-nodding around the table.

"So what's the plan?" asked an older man with a cratered face. His voice was deep.

"I'm going to let Dr. Smitherin talk about that in a moment. But first, I want to stress the importance of unanimity here. We have to make sure that everyone in this room is on board. What we are about to embark on is a holy and terrible task; second thoughts will just hinder our success." He glared at the group, hoping his stare was enough to shame people into agreement. "So if there is anyone here who is hesitant, who thinks we should wait, who wants to try to negotiate or otherwise treat with the government, let him say so now." His tone brooked no indecision.

There was silence in the room. Each man, who had been as carefully vetted as was humanly possible, feigned a look of passivity. Some stole glances at the others, but furtively, as if they didn't want to be seen caring what the others thought. As if there were no ambivalence alive in the room.

Keenan waited a minute longer. "Okay, then," he said. "We are now going to hear from the committee chairs. Let's start by talking about the plan. Dr. Smitherin?"

"Thank you, Daniel," Aloysius Smitherin said, nodding to Daniel and walking to the front of the room.

"First," he began, "I remind everyone that we are here because we have all come to the conclusions that the status quo is no longer viable and that decisive and drastic action is called for." He looked around the room; all eyes were on him. He continued: "And if we are going to take action, it needs to be sudden, powerful, and decisive. It's going to take planning, but we have determined that, for all its complexity, government relies on key people: the President, the Chief Justice of the Supreme Court, the House Speaker, and the president and majority leader in the Senate. There are others: heads of departments, the Joint Chiefs. Then there is the issue of succession in office; once we get down to the cabinet level, things get much murkier. There is a succession protocol, but it's never happened that a president wasn't succeeded by his vice president. So if we take out the President and the Vice President and the next in line, it will create a lot of helpful confusion.

"But those actions alone will not guarantee success in our mission." Smitherin bent down to pick up the half-filled glass of water on the table near him. "The other element that is required is general turmoil. A crisis that will terrify the whole country. This must precede taking out key people." He took a sip of water.

"Finally," he continued, "we will need to coordinate with the legislatures and/or the executive branches of key states to formally secede from the Union, to declare their militias inviolate and unavailable for nationalization, and to increase the alert status of those militias.

"Then division is for all practical purposes an accomplished fact. Then the federal government will be helpless to stop the process."

He looked around the room. "Most of these elements are in place," he said.

Eyebrows shot up around the table.

He put his glass back down on the table and sat down.

The silence in the room was reverential. What these men were saying was both a declaration of war and an act of consecration:

it was holy and dreadful and profoundly empowering. That it was treasonous was lost on none of the men present. No one looked up for several minutes. Some thought of a similar meeting in Philadelphia two centuries earlier; some wondered if it could possibly work.

Gregory Manfield stood up. "Our committee was in charge of the economic impact of the war and the management of that. In our work, we have determined that the only way to provide a stable basis for the new economy that will follow the end of the current government structure is a return to the gold standard." He looked around. "We are going to take possession of Fort Knox in Kentucky and build a new economy based on the gold that is there. We are no longer willing to let money be tied to nothing, as it's been since Roosevelt."

The men in the room looked surprised. This was a new angle. No one had thus far spoken of taking over a military installation or the role of gold in all this. But the idea had great resonance among the wealthy men around the table.

Manfield continued. "We will, of course, use some of that gold to finance our operations. As founding partners of the new order, we will also make sure our individual positions are solid. Once things settle down gold will be enormously valuable.

"There are some other things we need to think about, strategic principles that will guide our actions. We cannot avoid a period of economic turmoil, but we can do things to minimize it. Surprise is essential. The government must not know what hit it. Second: The secession must follow this turmoil quickly and decisively, in response to the breakdown of public order of a kind never seen in this country. Each state that agrees will simply and solemnly pull out of the Union in a manner legal in that state, either by a declaration from the governor or by a vote of the legislature or both. Along with the declarations of secession, each state will cease all payments to the federal government by its citizens. In the near term, those dollars will be redirected to state coffers to fund operations. This was one of the most appealing elements of the plan for most of the people with whom we've been in contact.

"This will be the critical time. If the federal government attempts to react with military power, we will be ready. In that case, there will be blood, and there will be heroes.

"Third: The government must be pulled apart all at once, and in separate directions. That means that the regions that are with us will secede from the Union all at the same time as individual entities and form new nations immediately. No one wants fifty different countries to replace the federal government. We believe Washington and Oregon will join California in declaring independence, the Commonwealth of California. The original Southern states will secede as a unit, just like last time, but without Texas. And they will use the same name: the Confederate States of America. Oklahoma will join Texas to declare the formation of a separate United Republic of Texas. Vermont wants to be its own country." He paused for a moment to make sure everyone was following him. "Then we'll see what the rest of the West and the Midwest does. I believe once they see these big states secede, they will have no choice but to form independent nations. There won't be enough left of the original USA to hold together."

"And just how are we going to pull all this off?" asked the man with the cratered face.

Manfield did not flinch. "We have been working with strategically placed members of the military and civilian command structure on both the state and federal levels. Decision makers. Leaders. People who can make other people do their bidding. They are preparing as we speak." He raised his head slightly, as if to highlight the exquisite accomplishments he had just described.

Daniel Keenan leaned forward in his chair. "We have also been working quietly in each of the states and territories mentioned." He paused and looked around. "We found a lot of people who have been thinking along similar lines."

"What about the nukes?" asked a tall, silver-haired man with a deep bass voice.

Keenan was ready for that question. He looked at the man evenly. This was a key question, and the most esteemed man in the room was the one to raise it. Keenan was waiting with his answer. "There are two considerations here. One, the US has a policy never to use atomic weapons on American soil, so we don't have to worry too much about them using them against us. It would be lunacy: if they did it, it would prove our point as to how dysfunctional the government really is, and that would further our cause. Second, we have a plan in place to secure the nuclear codes. That way, the threat factor comes from us. We do not want to use them to invade any of our new nations, but nor do we want to be intimidated by them. The point is, they won't know what we'll do with them."

The silver-haired man was undaunted. "You think you can get hold of the most secret codes in the entire United States? Do you understand how complicated the nuclear chain of command is?" There was more than a small note of disbelief in his voice.

"Yes, I do," Keenan replied. "And I assure you: we have the necessary tools to make this happen, to acquire those codes, and at least neutralize the chain of command if not control it outright."

The silver-haired man sat back in his chair and looked Keenan up and down. "That would be quite an accomplishment, son," he said, a touch of reconciliation in his voice. "Quite an accomplishment."

The smile Keenan felt did not make it to his face. He was in the spotlight, in control. But he knew he had Adam Wilson on his side completely. He couldn't wait to call Blinder.

The focal points of unrest came down to these: cultural divergence, greed and the emergence of a permanent wealthy class, and nostalgia among the majority of the population for things that no longer existed. These were not

strictly separate factions: each factor played a role in different proportions in the different groups. The cultural warriors were arrayed along liberal and conservative lines; the greed warriors were out to maximize profit beyond the wildest dreams of most people; and the nostalgics yearned for a time that was free of the many stresses of life in the new century. Each of these groups had elements of the other two, but each one also had its principal features. And they began communicating among themselves.

It was the moneyed interests that led the way. For most of the latter decades of the twentieth century, this group had grown in power disproportionately to the general population. It was not inappropriate for the Occupy movement to call themselves "the 99%" because so much money and so much of the resources of the nation were increasingly in the hands of the very privileged 1%. This was the group that had the resources to render radical change in the political situation. Because greed spawns greed, this group set its sights even higher. They wanted the oligarchy that was for all practical purposes running the country to be designated as the group that would forever be in ascendance. Their success at amassing great wealth contributed to the feeling that anything was possible, and it intoxicated even the most sober-minded person of means. They assumed the mantle of leadership because they believed it was rightfully theirs.

Part 2

★ ★ ★ ★ ★

arie LeBrun hated waiting. She wanted to do things, and she thought waiting for something or someone else was just an enormous waste of time on this planet. She was meticulous to a fault, and that kind of perfectionism takes time to master and to implement. So she used her time in Max's waiting room to the best effect she could: she made lists.

She did this mentally. She wrote things down on occasion— well, she didn't exactly write things down on paper, as people used to do. But she had certain encrypted computer files on which she kept lists, and she kept these in a secret place on her person at all times. If the worst should happen to her—and, in all fairness, the worst could happen to her—the flash drives on which she kept her data were in special cases that were designed to self-destruct either after a given time or by entering the requisite code. That way the likelihood of their falling into unfriendly hands was minimized. It wasn't foolproof, but Marie had learned long ago that nothing was foolproof. The best-laid plans . . .

She was waiting for Max, her handler at the Central Intelligence Agency, to brief her on a new assignment. Marie was a contract worker, a person with whom certain governmental agencies contracted for specific tasks, usually tasks that could not be successfully accomplished under the exigencies of prevailing legislation. Max never told her to break the law directly, of course; but there were times when crossing over the line was possible and even helpful and the task was of such moment that it was worth having the extra flexibility available in a way it was not to your typical State Department employee.

That's where Marie and people like her came in. Marie started in government work. She had joined the CIA right out of school and had trained for field work. She loved it. She was not a reckless woman, but nor was she easily frightened. She was trained in weapons, hand-to-hand combat, encryption methods, and electronic surveillance. She was conversant in four or five languages, including the French and English in which she was raised, but also in Arabic, Russian, and some Mandarin. She had to admit that the Chinese dialect was tough.

She left the CIA after about six years. She wasn't burnt out or unhappy with her work—her assignments were more often successful than not—it was just that she got to feeling a little too comfortable, a little too I-can-do-this, a little too complacent. She yearned for a challenge. She also wanted to make more money than the CIA pay scale allowed. The pay wasn't terrible, but Marie felt she gave her job everything she had, and she wanted to reap a greater reward for that level of commitment. It wasn't every agent who was so fit or so thorough or so demanding of self, but they were all paid the same. She wanted more.

So she struck out on her own. At first, she thought she would start her own consulting business and contract with various governmental and nongovernmental agencies. But her early work came from some contacts she had in the Agency, and she started landing government jobs. This was an area of government expenditure that was fuzzy, that for all practical purposes had no fixed limits. She was pleased to learn that contract employees made considerably more than their salaried counterparts and that results mattered. The more success she had, the more work came her way and the more she was able to negotiate in payment. This worked for her without the headache of an office and overhead and all the aggravation that comes with running your own business out of physical office space.

Max was her contact and handler in the Agency. She had worked with him on numerous occasions, and he was the first person she told about going out on her own. To her relief and somewhat to her surprise, he was completely supportive. Also, he was the first one to call her with some work after she left. Max was a devoted bureaucrat, a thinker, and a worrier. He always wanted things to go right and would stay up all night in order to see his projects through. He also cared about his people. Marie did not know how old he was, but she pegged him to be in his mid-fifties. Old enough to have good experience, not so old to be locked in. Also just old enough not to be a romantic interest for just-turned-thirty Marie. That always entered into the equation.

So they worked well together.

The door to the waiting room opened, and Max stepped out, extending his hand.

"Hi, sweetie," he said, shaking her hand. This was an indulgence that the otherwise straightlaced Max would never allow himself with any of the women who worked for or with him; that is, he would not under any circumstances use this little endearment with his coworkers. He had been thoroughly briefed on the dos and don'ts of acceptable office behavior, including the perils of sexual harassment, and he steered clear of any hint of transgression. But the rules and regulations did not apply so strictly to contract workers, and he was sincerely fond of Marie. He ushered her into his office.

Marie also had a warm spot in her heart for Max. She associated him with those early jobs. Max not only steered work her way, but he was also always available for informal consultation about the ins and outs of government, something with which, as a lifelong government worker, he was very familiar.

Instead of sitting down as Marie expected, Max grabbed his jacket. "Let's go for a walk," he said, and he ushered her out the door. Marie didn't question this. She trusted Max. She noticed an iPad sticking out of his jacket pocket.

They walked out of the building, got onto the elevator, and headed for the first floor. As soon as the elevator door opened, Max gestured Marie toward the front door. He did not look around him. He acted as if this were normal behavior. As soon as they were outside, he directed Marie to a small park across from CIA head-quarters. Marie played along, but she was on alert. It was so unlike Max to do anything but talk to her in his office. She had never seen him outdoors before.

When they got to the park, they found an open bench, and Max gestured for her to sit. Then he sat down next to her and pulled out the tablet. He also took out a small electronic device with a single switch and flipped it on. "Creates a block to any surveillance mechanism," he said casually.

As his computer was booting up, he turned to his former employee. "Marie, what I am about to tell you is, as usual, highly classified. But it's also dangerous information, and I want to make sure you are crystal clear about how important it is to keep this to yourself." He paused a moment. "I also want you to think a while before I proceed."

Marie harrumphed internally at the thought of any indiscretion with information. She could hold secrets better than anyone she knew. It came to her naturally: she was a secretive person. Probably no more than three people, counting her, knew where she lived. And one of those was her landlord. She nodded.

Max took that nod as agreement and continued: "A few weeks ago, we got wind of a conspiracy. Of course, we get wind of these things all the time, and usually they are schemes that the lunatic fringe dreamed up. Not much substance. Not much of a real threat, either." He paused a moment and brought his hands together before him, as if he were sitting at his desk. "But this time, the players are not nutcases. They are serious and substantial people. Men such as Adam Wilson. . . "

At the mention of that name, Marie's eyebrow raised ever so slightly. Adam Wilson! She knew that name. Almost everyone in the country knew that name. Not only did she know the name, but she knew the man. He was an economics professor when she was an undergraduate at Georgetown. He was a "talking head" on news shows, a regular on Fox News. Marie also knew that he was more than a professor and pundit—he was a sexual predator who had targeted Marie probably the day she walked into his class. She was embarrassed to think that there was ever a time when she was so naïve, so gullible, so easily manipulated. She felt disgust in the pit of her stomach.

All these thoughts and reactions took less than a second, and all Max saw was a slight increase in the elevation of her left eyelid. He continued. ". . . and men such as Daniel Keenan, a professor of metallurgy at Rolla School of Mines in Missouri." Max glanced down at a paper on his lap. "There are a half dozen other names, but the point is that this is not your typical lunatic fringe conspiracy. Something is going on at higher levels." He paused again and looked at Marie. "Something serious and something big."

Marie found herself growing impatient. "What is it, Max?" she said.

"These people are plotting to overthrow the government of the United States of America," Max said.

13

That last sentence hung in the air for several moments. Of all the variations on assignments Marie could imagine—murder, bombing bridges, taking down government buildings—she had never considered the possibility that serious people—hardworking, successful, well-balanced American people—would work to break up the most successful nation on earth. One with a long tradition of justice, fairness, equality, and all the other Enlightenment virtues that her countrymen took very, very seriously. One with viable and long-lived public institutions that were respected the world over, even by people who hated certain government policies. She was, unusually for her, at a loss for words.

"Really?" finally dropped out of her mouth.

Max nodded. "Really," he said simply.

Marie tried to reengage her brain. "And you think these people—including the likes of Adam Wilson—seriously want to destroy the USA?" She was still trying to wrap her mind around this idea.

"Not only do they want to dismantle it, they appear to have decided that they have to do it by force." Max's tone was even.

Marie felt comfortable with Max, and she thought that she wasn't doing a very good job at masking her reactions, so she decided to stop trying. "Holy shit, Max! What's wrong with these people?" Then: "How do they think they can get away with it?"

Max looked at Marie with perhaps greater fondness than was appropriate. "As to real reasons why, I don't know, Marie. Probably the usual suspects: money, greed, power, control," he said. "The cable guys"—Max's term for loudmouthed commentators who held forth on mostly cable stations—"have been working up anti-government sentiment for years. It may just be coming home to roost." He paused for a moment. "But their ostensible reason, the one they talk about, is that they feel that the United States has become dangerously secular. One of the things these people have in common, besides the fact that they are almost all at the top of their respective fields, is that they are devoutly religious to a man." He paused a moment. "Whether that's a cover, whether they are being manipulated, whether there are other forces at play: we just don't know that right now. The how, on the other hand, is beginning to look like this: There is evidence of secret placements of operatives in each state capital. These people are forging relationships with key members of the legislature; they are preparing for an eventual secession of the states. These have been going on for some time. We believe that this group, the one I am about to show you, has been operating under the radar for several years. Their deliberations seem to have accelerated a few months ago. Prior to this, they met in small groups, but last month a group of we think about twenty or so people met to finalize a plan. They gathered from all around the country. At least one of these meetings has taken place in a university. A few weeks back, we got wind of a meeting from a student who stumbled across it while he was working on a computer project." Max reached down and clicked a button on his netbook. "He sent us a video." He turned his monitor so both he and Marie could see it.

"Turns out he was practicing setting up surreptitious surveillance for a class and happened to pick the room where these guys were meeting. He forgot about his project for a couple of days, and, when he retrieved it, he found this." Max double-clicked the play button. "His system was triggered by voice or movement, so he got the entire hour and a half on video. No commercials."

The two watched the screen. Marie instantly recognized Wilson, and her cheeks reddened a bit. She recognized one or two other men at the long conference table also, but she could not put names to faces. She listened intently.

" . . . so we think the public will be on our side on this," an arrogant, black-haired man was saying. "Not the liberals, of course, but all the conservative groups we polled discreetly showed an openness to a new system of governance. And most preferred regional entities." He paused a bit. "Especially the states out West. They are just tired of faraway Washington telling them what they can and cannot do." He smiled a small smile. "And the South, well, they've been ready ever since Appomattox." The black-haired man leaned back in his chair.

Marie's eyes widened. Here was a group of supposedly sober, successful, and respected men talking like a bunch of drunken frat boys about carving up the country. She was beginning to think that maybe Max was putting her on. She looked over at him with a quizzical expression on her face.

"Okay, Max," she said. "What's the punch line?"

Max looked back at her with a sober expression. "No joke, Marie," he said. "These guys just look like bull-shitting college kids. But they are deadly serious."

"How do you know?"

"Keep watching," Max said gently.

He had fast-forwarded the video to a section he had marked earlier. He pushed the button.

" . . . and to Dr. Sanford's question," a new voice was saying, "we have to start with decapitating the DC bureaucracy." The slender man paused and looked around. "All of it," he said. "All at once."

There was silence in the meeting room. No one moved. Marie thought that the recording mechanism had frozen the action in place. Just as suddenly, it started up again.

The twenty or so men around the table started looking at each other, as if they had just taken a big step that was steeped in risk and uncertainty. There were a couple of muffled coughs. Then a short, middle-aged man stood up and began to speak. "I know we decided about this last time," he said somewhat tentatively. "But are we sure we cannot do this without outright violence? What about mass protests? There must be some other way to produce an orderly dissolution of the current governmental structure. Give the DC bureaucrats a chance to resolve this peacefully in our favor? Give them an option they are powerless to oppose?"

"That would be great, Hank," replied the new voice, "but we discussed this last time and agreed that peaceful dissolution is out of the question. They will just not do it. We have that on the best of the many authorities we consulted about this issue. The DC bureaucracy is sacred in US law. No state has a right to secede. No allowance is made for any entity to question the existence of the federal superstructure."

The short guy frowned. "So violence is the only answer?"

"The only answer."

Silence again descended around the room.

"So, Max," Marie said. "Why not just go and arrest these guys? Isn't this conspiracy to overthrow the government?"

"Yes, it is," Max replied. "And I would be happy to have these guys arrested." He paused for a moment. "But for one thing."

Marie waited.

"They have disappeared."

"Disappeared?" Marie repeated.

"Disappeared," Max replied. "Between the time we got this video and the time we reviewed it, each of the twenty men at this meeting has vanished. And many of them were in high-profile positions. I know you are familiar with Adam Wilson: Professor at Georgetown, nationally recognized pundit. Gone. That other guy, Daniel Keenan, professor of metallurgy at Rolla School of Mines. Also gone. No forwarding address, no trace of any kind. These people simply melted into the background. Their assets and most of their families also vanished. And get this: Each of them was quickly and quietly replaced." Max shook his head. "I think they either got wind of the fact that we had this recording and had contingency plans for being detected . . . Or . . ." He paused and took a deep breath. "Or the implementation of the plan has begun." He looked directly into Marie's eyes.

"And I think they have somebody inside the CIA who is feeding them information."

An air of discomfort fell over the twosome as they both pondered the implications of what Max was saying. They both felt the chill that betrayal brings. They both knew that the betrayer or the betrayers could be anybody. They both beheld in their minds the complexity and the sheer technical challenge of pulling off vanishing acts for high-profile politicians, academics, lawyers, and corporate chiefs. They both knew the task before them was both daunting in its complexity and bewildering in its scope. They were struck dumb.

Max finally spoke. "Marie, I asked you to come in today because I trust you. I've been chewing on this since yesterday, and I can count on one hand the people in the building I trust." As he said that, his voice cracked slightly, and he averted his eyes to regain control.

Marie knew that Max loved the Agency. He loved the United States. He was an unapologetic patriot, a devoted public servant, and a perfectly responsible man. Treason made him sick.

Max continued, his voice almost a whisper. "This is why we're out here. Even though my office is a 'safe room' and is swept for bugs and surveillance equipment twice a day, I can't be sure that internal security hasn't been compromised. But if I am right and whoever gave these bastards information about this video is in the building, internal security is compromised. So we can't be too careful." He looked over at Marie. He looked directly into her eyes.

Marie could not think of how to respond.

14

While the momentarily speechless government workers were pondering these developments, the theocrats were assembling in an obscure corner of Wyoming. They brought with them piles of papers, advanced computers, mountain-moving faith, and steely determination. However, it was not lost on the group that one of their number was missing.

Daniel Keenan had long been a central force in the group of believers who got themselves to this point, and his absence was noticed immediately. As they gathered in the central meeting room of the compound, all heads turned to Adam Wilson, the most prominent member of the group.

"Where is Dr. Keenan?" ventured William Shaeffer. He looked sternly at Wilson.

"I am not sure," Wilson replied in an innocent-sounding voice. "My last contact with him was two days ago." He turned to the others. "Has anyone else been in contact with Daniel Keenan?" he asked.

No one spoke. They all shook their heads.

"Well," said Wilson. "Daniel knew the rules. He had to be here by today. If he doesn't show up by this evening, we will have to assume that he's been compromised somehow."

Serious head nodding all around.

For a man of profound religious belief, Adam Wilson's relationship with the truth was strikingly tenuous. Beneath his unctuous facial expression, he reviewed his behavior over the past few days step by step. Secure that he had missed nothing, he let himself relax.

ergeant Daniel Cooper stood at parade rest staring out the window of his office at Fort Leonard Wood, one of the oldest Army garrisons in the United States and one of the largest munitions depots in the US system. Most people were familiar with Leonard Wood as a training facility and even a maneuver support command, but only a small group of people knew about the extensive cave structure underneath the fort that was used to store weapons of every type. The caves were lined with natural salt formations, so the humidity in the caves was very low, and moisture was much less of a problem than it was for even above-ground, temperature-controlled warehouses. Sergeant Cooper smiled inwardly at all this: the intelligence of it, the secrecy, the good sense it made. He was proud of his command, proud of his state, and proud of his role in the US Army. It was his job to keep all this stuff safe, secret, and dry.

He was watching a group of inductees marching up and down the field outside his office, but his mind was elsewhere. He was pondering an e-mail communication granting access to the cave structure to one Harvey L. Winkelstein, a civilian who had, according to this e-mail, been cleared by the higher-ups to inspect the FLW facility.

Cooper was skeptical. He knew the names of each person with clearance to enter the caves, and there was seldom an addition. On the rare occasions when the list was expanded, it was usually communicated by special courier from the Pentagon. He had printed out the e-mail because it did not feel right; he thought it might be bogus. That e-mail also said that Mr. Winkelstein would be arriving tomorrow to exercise his newly granted right, and Cooper was directed to show him every courtesy. If Sergeant Cooper were the muttering type, he would have muttered something like "Over my dead body."

Instead, he stood staring out the window contemplating his options. He knew he had to verify this e-mail. He would also verify the existence and requested prerogatives of Mr. Winkelstein. But the communication itself was uncharacteristically vague about the protocol for that, and Cooper wondered who this guy could be.

He turned and walked over to his desk and booted up his computer. Then he thought better of that and pulled out his smartphone. Harder to trace. He googled Winkelstein's name. Only a couple of entries showed up: one on Facebook with no picture; the other a reference to a Harvey Winkelstein at NYU. A professor? He went to the NYU website to look further.

While waiting for his hand-held device to respond, Cooper chewed on what felt to him to be a breach of protocol. He was an Army man and was accustomed to taking orders. But he was also an intelligent man, and he wanted to make sure that these particular orders were valid. The sense that something was amiss was not diminishing.

After a minute or so—a long time in this interconnected world—he was looking at the NYU website. He entered Winkelstein's name in the search box, and it came up quickly. B.A., Alabama State University, 1975, M.A. and Ph.D. in Physics, University of Pennsylvania. Fifty-five years old, married with four children. There followed a long list of publications about obscure topics, no doubt related to his major field, which seemed to have something to do with explosives. Cooper scanned the list. Most of his work was in the physics of high explosives, but a lot was also about nanotechnology, the science of making things smaller and smaller. Smaller explosive devices? Cooper asked himself. Electrons were, of course, invisible to the naked eye. This résumé did nothing to assuage Cooper's deepening suspicion.

Cooper decided to go ahead and confirm the communication by replying to the original address. He booted up the laptop on his desk and entered the required codes. He got an immediate response. Communication confirmed. The confirmation gave a code that he could cross-check with the manual he kept in his briefcase. He did exactly that, and it matched up perfectly. He had his orders. He didn't like it.

ax and Marie were walking slowly back to CIA Headquarters. They were speaking in a whisper. "What do we do now, Max?" she asked.

Max did not respond right away. "I am going to run a check through the path this material took to get to me. I will search out every person who had access to it. I will record my findings and keep them in a secure file."

"What can I do to help?" Marie said.

"Marie, I trust you. I've known you for almost ten years, and I would not in a million years doubt your patriotism or your dedication. You've been vetted on at least a dozen different occasions, several times by me. We have worked together." He paused for a moment. "Nor do I doubt your intelligence, tenacity, or skills," he said. "I will copy everything I find and upload it to a secure website. We will arrange a signal for modifications to the site. I want you to have as close to real-time information about this as you can." He looked over to her. "I want to use you for backup. In case something happens to me."

The fact that Max was concerned about the possibility that harm might come to him from inside the government was sobering to Marie. She inhaled deeply as she considered what this meant. "Max," she said, "you know you can use me in any way you need to." She touched him lightly on the shoulder. "I can protect you," she said quietly.

Max looked at her, noting her sincerity and youth. "No, you can't, Marie," he said. "That's the problem. I'm going to be doing some deep snooping and may be asking some very uncomfortable questions of people with a lot of power. Enough power to eliminate me if they so choose. I just need you to have access to what I am thinking, to know what I know. As this plays out, we will work out a plan of action. But again, I want absolute transparency between us on this."

Marie thought about this for a while. "Anyone else in on our side, Max?" she asked. She knew to argue would be pointless.

Max nodded. "It is best if you do not know that at this point, Marie," he said.

So much for absolute transparency, Marie thought. But she held her tongue. She could see that Max had a lot on his mind. She also knew one person who was definitely in on her side.

arvey Winkelstein was a busy man. He had just gotten off the phone with David Blinder, and he already had his transport arranged to travel to Fort Leonard Wood. Winkelstein had never been to Missouri—it was never on his radar screen, and he didn't relish the prospect of traveling a thousand miles to some Midwestern backwater. He did think that maybe it was close enough to Eastern seaboard civilization as to be recognizable. He was pretty sure they spoke English there, even if they did so in whatever rustic twang they devolved from the language of Shakespeare.

Harvey knew he was a snob. Ever since he got tenure at NYU, his natural haughtiness flourished; indeed, it became his trademark. Harvey had no friends in the sense that most people think of friendship, but he knew a lot of people. He got the attention of the people he targeted by being smart, by knowing his stuff, and by being insufferable and persistent. He casually referred to contacts and acquaintances he collected this way as "friends."

His targets and his taste ran to the wealthy strata of society. He accepted every invitation to attend the parties and lavish events of the rich and famous. He could barely tolerate opera, but he had been to more gala celebrations at Lincoln Center than most sopranos who worked there.

Not that he cared much, but Harvey suspected that most people did not relish being approached by him. The word on the street was that, if Harvey wanted something you had, be it information or connections or a physical object of some sort, you would most likely give it to him just to get rid of the obnoxious, loudmouthed, pushy, real-life New York stereotype.

Of course, there were people who could use Harvey as much as he used them. And that was why, when he approached David Blinder at a fund-raiser for the New York Public Library, David, who was practiced at avoiding people he did not want to see, allowed him to invade his personal space.

"Mr. Blinder," said Harvey, almost shouting above the din of the invited guests. "Harvey Winkelstein. It is so nice to meet you." He stuck out his meaty hand in an aggressive gesture. The Blinders were known to be private, and Harvey thought spotting David was a stroke of pure good fortune.

David, who never liked to touch anyone, gently put his hand atop Harvey's. He did not want a death-grip handshake. "Likewise, Harvey," he said sweetly, removing his hand at the very earliest opportunity. "I've heard a lot about you."

Harvey beamed. This was the kind of reception he hoped for but seldom received. David, it seemed, was someone who knew what he was capable of, someone who could use him, someone who was, in Harvey's mind, a kindred spirit.

That the spiritual orientations of Harvey Winkelstein and David Blinder could not have been more different was completely lost on Harvey, precocious child that he had been and intellectually distinguished adult that he currently was. Even genius has blind spots.

Harvey's specialty was guns. He knew everything there was to know about munitions, ordnance, the geometry of high explosives; he held in his memory an encyclopedia of information about their physical and chemical properties. He had a Ph.D. in physics, which he made sure everyone who would even be remotely interested knew about, and he refined his practical knowledge at every opportunity. He liked to blow things up.

Harvey also had a side business in addition to his meager teaching duties at the university: he ran guns for shadowy guerrilla movements and miscellaneous covert operations sanctioned by the likes of the CIA, but also including, unbeknownst to that secretive organization, other covert operatives around the world. Not only was this obnoxious pariah practiced at procuring weapons, but he was a master of secrecy. This was, even to his scheming mind, an unlikely blend of talents, but an exceptionally profitable one. The Internet provided the perfect tool for encrypted communication that would require massive effort to locate, much less decrypt. Harvey marveled at how easily the processes of dissimulation came to him.

He ran across David Blinder's name through a "friend" who intimated that Mr. Blinder might be in the market for someone with Harvey's particular skills. There was a small circle of people who had some idea of what Harvey was up to, but no one person knew the extent of his involvement with marginally legal or outright illegal weapons sales. But key contacts had some idea that, if information about the physical properties of guns or the procurement of them were called for, Harvey might be able to help. He could at least point someone in a useful direction. And "useful direction" typically meant that Harvey would construct a deal in which he had both the responsibility and a profit at each stage of the transaction through a series of shell companies, obscure drop sites, and mythical companies with even more mythical personnel. The point of this effort was to make money, and this entire scheme meant a lot of money for Harvey Winkelstein.

So it was with no small measure of excitement that Harvey allowed his hand to be patted by one of the richest men in America. He didn't give a damn how daintily David Blinder shook his hand;

he simply noted what he thought was the fragile if not effeminate physical contact the famous Mr. Blinder the Younger exhibited. In his mind, this equated with weakness.

He was wrong about that.

David Blinder knew more about Harvey than Harvey would have preferred. David had access, by virtue of his money and his own contacts, to the services of no small network of clandestine investigators. Spies, as he thought of them. And that is exactly what they were.

He had targeted Winkelstein because he knew that any revolution required military backup; otherwise, it would just be, at most, a popular protest. He knew that, if he was serious about the option that he and his brother had worked out a few decades earlier, he was going to need access to military hardware and troops to go along with them. He was building a private military network, a private army.

David got directly to the point. "Harvey," he said softly, steering his companion gently into a hall closed off from the other patrons. Harvey hadn't even noticed the door. "I understand that you know a great deal about the military and civilian uses of munitions."

"Yes, indeed, Mr. Blinder," Harvey replied, a little less softly than Blinder would have liked. "I have a doctorate in the physics of explosive technologies. I teach at NYU." He smiled his best superior smile.

"So I understand," Blinder replied even more softly, hoping that Harvey would match his low voice. He had anticipated that he would not like this self-important blowhard, but he had not anticipated quite how much he would find his entire presence and physical and psychological demeanor distasteful. A hint of doubt made itself felt on the farthest horizon of his mind. He shook his head almost imperceptibly, choosing to ignore it. He had long since learned that dealing only with cultured people was not an option if you wanted to accomplish things.

"I was wondering, Harvey, if you could meet with some of my people to discuss our needs in specific detail." He continued the soft tone of voice so that others would not hear. But his look was steady and unflinching. He looked Harvey straight in the eye.

Harvey finally saw that this was an invitation to do likewise. "I would be happy to meet with whomever you like, Mr. Blinder," he said in a similar tone. He did not think of his answer as obsequious as it came off.

David Blinder reached into his pocket and pulled out a small business card. "Good. Please call this number tomorrow morning and make arrangements." He gently tapped Harvey's shoulder and turned and walked away.

Harvey was not at all offended by this curt behavior. He marveled at what he believed was the superior way rich people treated ordinary people such as himself. He promised himself to take lessons.

He glanced down at the card in his sweaty palm. It displayed the name of an official at the US State Department. He turned and reentered the lobby.

18

Harvey waited until 9:00 a.m. the next day to place his call. He had a generally low opinion of government workers, and he did not want to leave a voice mail. He wanted either to be connected directly to Stanley Schindler or leave a message with a real person: a secretary or an assistant.

He had done his homework and had traced the number the night before. He knew it was the line of a Stanley Schindler, a high-level bureaucrat in the State Department. Schindler was the assistant secretary of International Narcotics and Law Enforcement and reported directly to Jack Stewart, the undersecretary for Political Affairs. A good-sized fish, Harvey thought.

He was pleased when, after giving his name, he was put through directly to Schindler. And he was doubly pleased that Schindler was so sprightly when he answered the phone. He had obviously been at his desk for a while, and he was obviously expecting his call.

"Hello, Mr. Schindler," Harvey said. "I was asked to call you by a Mr. David Blinder, a friend of mine. We are going to be doing some business together, and he asked that I call you to meet with some of his people."

Stanley sighed silently. He had been given a heads-up about Harvey's call from Jack Stewart, his boss. Stewart had told him to be nice to Winkelstein and accommodate whatever Harvey wanted. Stewart also told Stanley that he was to arrange a meeting with several of the technical people who reported to Stanley. Stanley didn't think it was a big deal; just another political favor of some sort.

"Yes, Mr. Winkelstein. I was expecting your call. We are happy to do whatever we can for Mr. Blinder. How can I help you?" Schindler had not stopped doing what he was doing and was only halfway paying attention.

How can he help me? Harvey thought. *I was supposed to call him.* He hesitated just for a moment.

"It was my understanding that I was to call this number for instructions."

"I'm sorry, Mr. Winkelstein. That is correct. It is my understanding as well that we are to arrange a meeting between you and some key members of our Task Force for Weapons Assessment." It occurred to Stanley that the reason he was being so obtuse is that he found this "political favor" more than a little inappropriate. He wasn't in a position to override his boss, but he thought Stewart had crossed over the line. He had raised the issue with Jack, who pooh-poohed it. So Stanley was cooperative, but only grudgingly so.

"I see," Harvey said. "How can we proceed?"

"I am going to transfer you to my assistant, who will take your contact information. She will coordinate with you and the other members of the task force. We should be able to arrange the meeting later this week, if your schedule allows."

Harvey thought for a moment. Obviously Schindler had been prepped for his call. Obviously he was bending over backward to help him. On the other hand, Harvey didn't like this meeting being shuffled off to a secretary, glorified or otherwise. But he didn't think this was a good time to push it.

"That would be fine, Mr. Schindler," he said simply. "I appreciate your assistance."

Stanley put Harvey on hold and buzzed Marian McGrath, his secretary.

"Marian," he said. "There is a Harvey Winkelstein on the phone. He's the man I told you about yesterday. We need to arrange a meeting between him and the Weapons Assessment Task Force. Would you set this up? He's waiting to give you his contact information."

"Of course, Mr. Schindler," Ms. McGrath said. "I'd be happy to."

With a bad taste in his mouth, Stanley returned his full attention to the work he had been doing prior to Winkelstein's call. The meeting with the task force fell to the bottom of his priority list. Wasn't his call.

19

David Blinder had a drink with Jack Stewart that very evening. He and Jack had gone to Princeton together in the forties right after the war, and they had a continuing relationship that was something short of a friendship but more than an acquaintanceship. They both knew a lot of other people and had a lot of contacts.

In addition, there was the matter of payback. A few years earlier, Jack found himself in trouble with some pretty major gambling debts. He didn't want his wife to know: they had had previous arguments about his gambling, and the last time she had threatened to go public about Jack's "weakness." It would have ruined Jack's career, and both he and his wife knew it. Melinda didn't care; she had family money and would have been happy to see him squirm a little. Earlier in their marriage, she, or rather her family, had bailed him out on a couple of occasions. She wasn't about to do that again. Jack turned to David for help.

David had always looked upon his relationship with Jack Stewart as a long-term investment: he had nurtured it quietly ever since their college days. David knew Jack to be a bright but lazy student, even as an undergraduate. He knew that Jack's father was also a pampered underachiever, born into wealth that a marriage brought his parents. There was no doubt about it: this line of the Stewart family was bright, resistant to hard work, fond of what money brought, and completely without scruples—just the profile David needed for an upper-level contact in the Department of State. So, for years, he nursed Jack's bumbling career. The two consulted back and forth about various issues, but David used these sessions to tutor Jack in creating a personal style of indifference to any kind of significant activity or any kind of stand. The MO: look interested but never commit. He trained him perfectly.

David also used other contacts to assist Jack's career. Princeton produced an exceptional number of bureaucrats to the federal government: talented men and women whose families were sufficiently well-off so that they did not need to create their own wealth. They could engage in public service and climb the ranks of the powerful easily. It was a sort of system within a system. The vast majority of these contacts were loyal, hardworking, idealistic types. Surprisingly few were jaded about public service, even at this late stage of their lives. David learned early how to pave the way for a malleable pawn like Jack Stewart.

So when Jack came to him in need of money, David was only too happy to oblige. Not only did he eradicate Jack's debt, but he made sure there was no traceable way of proving that he had accrued two and a half million dollars of debt to some decidedly shady characters. Jack didn't know how David did it—in his desperation, he didn't care—but he was forever grateful. He even tried staying away from gambling. For a while. At present, whatever gambling he did was carried out discreetly and was, to Jack's mind, under control.

The payback came a few weeks prior to this visit, when David asked Jack rather casually if he would be so kind as to arrange a meeting between the recently formed Weapons Assessment Task Force and a colleague of his. He gave some vague rationale as to how this was important in his business relationships with allies of the United States. Jack was not just happy to be of service; he was grateful for the opportunity to do something in return for David's generosity. He would do anything he could to help him. The fact that the WATF was "eyes only" mattered not a whit to him.

Jack had no idea of what Blinder was up to; nor did he want to know too much. He had his own narrative in his head about how he had gotten so far in the Foreign Service. There were times in the past when this was a little mysterious even to him. Since he did not know all the facts that contributed to his rise, he was left to make something up; what he made up made sense to him, but it was unknown to anyone else.

Though he was not a political appointee, Jack always felt he had gotten to his rank by not knowing too much. Those Foreign Service officers who knew too much invariably got shot down by their own expertise: they often got so involved with their work that they pushed and pushed. Most often, they pushed themselves right out of promotions.

Jack, on the other hand, knew how to smile, nod, temporize, and weigh and balance every lunatic option that came his way. In his heart of hearts, he felt that, in general, not knowing bestowed more blessings than knowing. He was, after all, now the highest-ranking Foreign Service official in the United States. He allowed himself a measure of pride in this, attributing it, as he did, to his own intelligent if unknowingly incomplete appreciation of the broader picture.

When Blinder asked to meet him after work, Jack did not even consider refusing his friend and savior. Saying yes to Blinder was his role in the belief system that he had developed. It highlighted the wisdom of his profoundly ambivalent behavior and underscored how intelligent his decisions were: to attend an Ivy League school, to enter the Foreign Service, and to maintain key relationships over decades. While his indebtedness to Blinder rippled ever so slightly through whatever conscience remained in him, he believed in his heart that his path was the correct one.

He did not even ask Blinder why he wanted his people to meet with the Weapons Assessment Task Force. In fact, Jack was a little fuzzy as to what that particular task force was up to, why it was formed, or what its mandate was. All he knew was that it existed, was comprised of some of the best military and civilian minds in the business, and was supposed to develop a basis of an entirely new weapons procurement process. It was also responsible to him. He was also aware that it had to do its job within a mandated time frame. Jack would insist that they be on schedule, but he knew from long years of government service that it would not likely be on time. He also knew he had a competent staff of people to fill him in about salient details when he needed to know them. Any other aspects of the process were problems for someone else.

For Blinder's part, he looked to be passing time visiting an old friend. In fact, he was there to feel out any trace of curiosity or concern coming from Stewart, to make sure that his admittedly unusual request would be followed up on with minimal attention drawn to it.

"Jack," he said after the initial pleasantries. "Thanks for meeting me. It's so good to see you. It's been too long." David Blinder had learned that, because he hated physical contact and almost never shook hands with anyone, he had to be more verbally effusive with people to compensate for his standoffish behavior. It was a skill that did not come naturally to him.

"Always good to see you, David. Glad we had a chance to get together."

They talked for a while about Princeton, other acquaintances they both knew, their families. Somewhere into the second round, David looked at Jack with as much sincerity as he could muster.

"Jack," he said. "I am very appreciative of your letting my people meet with the WATF. It will help our work with our allies immensely."

"Glad to oblige, David," Jack replied. "It's the least I could do."

"Good," said David, nodding appreciatively. "I will remember this."

One of the factors that made itself felt in the early years of the twenty-first century was a curious neglect or misuse of expertise. As part of the Republican majority's insistence on wedding right-wing religious ideology with public policy, there developed a priority of litmus tests, or criteria according to which applicants were selected and existing government workers promoted or let go. These included opposing abortion in any form or under any circumstance; opposition to gay rights; a distrust of evolutionary theory; and a belief that marriage was to be defined solely as the relationship between a man and a woman. These issues took precedence over the specific interests or expertise of men and women who spent their lives focused on a particular issue and whose views toward those select social issues were different, unarticulated, or insufficiently enthusiastic.

At the same time and partly as a result of this emphasis on ideology, there developed in the culture a distrust of expertise. People came to believe—or they were manipulated to believe—that truth was a democratic principle, that the truth of a proposition was weighed not by whether or not it was objectively or empirically true but by the number of people who believed it. Thus, evolution was on tenuous ground, not with biologists or the scientifically informed but among the population in general. In 2011, a Gallup poll reported that only forty percent of Americans "believed" in evolution. Of course, the percentage increased in proportion to the education of the respondents, but the matter was far from settled in the public mind.

Fortunately, the federal bureaucracy was home to many experts who knew how to play the system and not get fired simply because they disagreed with ideologically based beliefs. But these people guarded their prerogatives as experts closely. They were aware of their precarious position, but they also felt a duty to deliver the truth to the country's leaders, whether or not those leaders wanted to hear it. It was partly for this reason that the Weapons Assessment Task Force (WATF) was created. It was an interagency committee charged with designing an improved weapons procurement process consonant with the needs and goals of US military leaders in a way that relied on modern principles of economy and the economic conditions of the time, which were daunting. It was a challenging and important task, but the profligacy of the previous decade made even the Defense Department wary of its spending habits. They knew they had to cut expenditures, and they wanted to do it in a way that was least injurious to the security interests of the nation. These men were patriots.

arvey was beside himself on the eve of his meeting with the task force. Marian had given him the names of each of the attendees, their individual roles in the process, and a rough idea of how far their work had progressed thus far. This was information that Jack Stewart had directed Stanley to share with Harvey, and Stanley dutifully instructed Marian to provide it. Harvey was immediately impressed by the easy flow of information that was beginning to come his way.

Harvey knew a thing or two about government acquisition processes. He knew that grand plans seldom translated efficiently into implementation on the ground. He knew that entrenched interests in the federal structure often commandeered even carefully laid plans in many ways: by withholding key information, by delaying compliance, and sometimes by simply ignoring orders. It created a perfect opportunity for knowledgeable charlatans such as Harvey to manipulate the system to follow whatever agenda they wanted.

In Harvey's case, he wanted guns. Lots of them. Lots of different kinds of guns. And explosive devices: cannon, howitzers, shoulder-fired missiles, land mines, guided and unguided munitions—in short, anything that was built to create destruction. And he wanted them in vast numbers. By his connection with this task force, he hoped to learn how much of this sort of thing was available, where it was, and how to procure it, all with the assistance of the Departments of Justice, Defense, and State, which was coordinating this effort. Harvey could not believe his good fortune.

Prior to this, Harvey ran what might be called a mom-and-pop gun shop, running guns in respectable but limited numbers to those desperate enough to pay extortionist rates for high-end, up-to-date firepower. Mostly these were belligerents in small-scale, tribal conflicts who were trying to protect their little plot of earth or who were looking to horn in on someone else's. Definitely small potatoes.

Harvey's hope with this gig was that he would be granted access to all the information that was available to task force members in the normal course of participating in their work, opening up a treasure trove of potential weaponry. He wasn't sure about the details yet, but he believed he would be attending all of their working meetings and, as a result, would be able to collect real-time information about munitions procurement and procedures used to direct it. Especially if those systems were to change. Harvey could hardly wait.

The only fly that Harvey could identify in this ointment was David Blinder's exact agenda. He assumed he wanted guns; he intimated as much when they spoke briefly at the fund-raiser. And, after all, why would he be contacting him if he did not want guns? But Harvey did not have any details. Nor did he have any knowledge about whether Blinder was relying on him alone or whether he had contacted other people who could procure weapons for him. Harvey knew that he was so excited he could be overlooking important details, but this exposure to a nerve center in the government procurement process filled him with such excitement he could not do anything but proceed.

And proceed he did. He was asked upon arrival to the first meeting, which was held, as Stanley had suggested, the very week he called, what he would like his involvement to be. Harvey said simply that he was hoping to be with the task force for some time to assist in their work in any way he could and to liaise—he hated that word—with his colleagues. He was vague enough not to arouse the curiosity of task force members about who those colleagues might in fact be. For all he knew, they may have assumed he was a government bureaucrat.

But even Harvey was unprepared for the rank and caliber of members of the task force that had been appointed for the redesign of weapons procurement. There were several department heads, major contractors and weapons manufacturers, and a liaison from the White House. There were even some independent consultants from old established firms with a long history of involvement in weapons procurement systems. He was relieved about the diversity of the group; paradoxically, it made it easier for him to slip into the meeting without drawing attention to himself.

And the openness and camaraderie of the group also impressed him. He was greeted warmly at his first meeting, and no one asked questions about his background. If he had the blessing of the State Department and of Stanley Schindler in particular, Harvey soon learned, the group felt that he was credentialed enough.

Nor did these men and women stand on ceremony. They called each other by their first names, shared information freely, and asked a lot of questions. That was key for Harvey. He had a lot of questions to ask.

21

After the first meeting with the task force, Harvey went home happy but befuddled. He was pleased his integration into the group went so smoothly, but he had such a limited sense of the big picture. What was David Blinder up to? Why would he want this kind of information? Why would he want guns?

Harvey thought that maybe he knew. He was aware that the Blinder brothers had worldwide operations, and trading in guns was often a matter of course in many countries of the world, where the governments were less stable or were financially strapped. Harvey smiled as he poured himself a scotch. That would be most of them, he thought grimly.

But he recalled Blinder referring to a meeting with "my people." Clearly the task force was not his personal domain. Harvey knew as soon as he saw the number on the card that Blinder had given him that he was to be as much a spy as a collaborator. It was a role he did not mind; he had played it before. But without more information, he wasn't sure what Blinder was looking for.

What he did know was how helpful the information gleaned from this committee would be for his private purposes, no matter what Blinder wanted. Harvey had connections—many of them shady—in the dark world of arms dealing. It was dirty and dangerous business. If he could get a lock on internal US Army operations, it would simplify his life immeasurably, and he would get richer more quickly. This made him smile.

Harvey was not the only one smiling. David Blinder was on his way back home to Texas on his family's private jet. All of his business in Washington, DC, and New York was concluded more smoothly than he could have imagined. He looked out the window of his Gulfstream G650 at the Southern states moving quickly past him. He felt a great sense of pride and exhilaration.

David had long since lost any real sense of allegiance to the United States of America. There were many reasons for this, but the principal one was money. The United States was just too big: it required an enormous budget just to operate on a day-to-day basis; its bureaucracy was the largest of any country on earth. It was true that it provided huge opportunity for money making, but the golden age of that laudable pursuit was, in the minds of both brothers, something that was now in the past, at least insofar as money making was tied to one country. The Blinder brothers had interests all over the world, the same world that was clamoring for what the United States had long ago brought to its people: stability, a comfortable standard of living for the majority of citizens, and the rule of law. But that country—this is how Blinder thought of the US—was on the downhill slide. They were suffering from the twin ills of stability and overreach. They spent more money than they took in, and the country was not growing the way it did throughout much of the twentieth century.

Breaking up the country would instantly address these two evils. It would liquidate the huge debt of the US government, along with all the associated costs. It would generate chaos and turmoil, and in such conditions there was money to be made. The experience of both brothers confirmed this. There would be a period of economic turmoil, but as the states readjusted, they would be able to start off on a responsible economic footing. It was also true that millions of people would find their savings ravaged, but this meant they would have to work harder and longer and for less money. Therefore, the owners of capital and enterprise would get richer and richer.

And since the Blinder brothers were firm believers in this sort of capitalism, they knew that a new set of six or seven nations on the same land mass as the old United States would create a competitive environment of the type not seen since the opening of the frontier. As stability went by the wayside, each nation would vie against its neighbors for a bigger and bigger piece of economic action. Blinder was sure of it.

Any other dislocations that such a breakup might entail bothered David and his brother not a bit. Life was hard. Those who were strong enough or wealthy enough and determined enough to grasp the brass ring were the rightful heirs to the wealth of the world. He did not care if the rest of the world was impoverished or if they entered a state of serfdom. It was his job, and the job of his family, to continue to devote themselves to the accumulation of capital, other people be damned. It had been that way for as long as he could remember. He believed it had been that way since humans began walking the earth.

And the Plan that he and George put together some decades before was now closer than ever to coming to fruition. It was a simple plan really, not so different from a hundred or a thousand other government takeovers or sudden shifts or *coups d'etats* or whatever you cared to call it. A change was coming, and it was coming by force.

For all his ready distaste for Harvey Winkelstein, David knew he was the perfect pawn in the chess match that was about to unfold across a vast board. He was bright, impossibly narcissistic, ambitious, and unflinchingly self-interested. And he would do anything if he thought it would bring him money. This short-sighted profit motive was perfect for the Blinders' plan. Unfortunately for Harvey, he was utterly dispensable once his usefulness came to an end.

David Blinder was especially proud of finding Abner Bellamy. The first time he ran across him was at a church service where Abner was preaching. David did not believe in God or religion—he believed in money and capital—but he attended services from time to time both for the sake of appearances and because it was a way to keep tabs on what the common people were thinking and hearing. Since most hardworking people—that is, useful people with money to spend—were religious, visiting a church occasionally was the best way to keep up with them.

Of course, Blinder's taste in religion ran to the formal and traditional Protestant denominations: Methodist, Presbyterian, and the like. He didn't have much use for the more traditional Catholics or Anglicans, and he had absolutely no use for hysterical evangelicals. He knew that the latter was the expanding portion of the religious body politic in the US, but he figured his traditional Protestant denominations would give him the information he needed. They would, as was always the case among religious organizations, respond to whatever prevailing winds were blowing at the time.

There was something about Abner that he liked. It wasn't exactly what he was saying: he was preaching a fairly traditional theological line about personal responsibility. But the more he talked, the more Blinder sensed an air of righteous indignation in him, something more than the run-of-the-mill kind of shallow outrage many preachers conveyed. Abner's words had teeth. Blinder sensed he was on a mission. He made two references to the South, both of which were favorable. In one, he referenced his father's death at the hands of "liberals" and lamented his exile from his native Georgia because of it. In the second, he alluded to the "still breathing longings for independence" that have been part of America since its founding in the 1700s. Blinder smelled "Confederacy."

There was an impassioned anger in Bellamy's sermon. He wasn't the regular pastor; he had been invited to speak at the Manhattan Church where he had apparently once had tenure. Now he was an occasional visitor. Blinder noted that the church was packed and that the congregation was very favorably disposed to Reverend Bellamy. On the way out, he overheard some members talk about how sorry they were that the good Reverend was no longer their pastor.

Blinder, of course, looked into Reverend Bellamy. He saw that he had written quite a bit: several books and many articles. He talked about the South a lot. Blinder found the absence of a Southern accent curious in one who seemed so devoted to that region. It suggested that Abner spoke in the language of his audience rather than the language of his heritage. Blinder felt a communion of sorts, one manipulator to another. Abner intrigued him.

So David Blinder did what any self-interested man of means would do: he hired Samantha Stranger, one of his favorite private investigators, to shadow the good Reverend and to dig more deeply into his background.

It did not take Ms. Stranger long to learn that the Reverend Abner Bellamy was quite an operator. She dug up the facts about his father's death and the grave consequences it had for young Abner and for his mother, who died of a broken heart just a few years later. Samantha followed his departure to his relatives in Atlanta and then on to the Northeast for a first-class education. She traced his move to New York and then from New York to St. Louis. She documented his ill-fated marriage to the scion of a wealthy St. Louis family. She noted his history of philandering, which he was oddly inept at concealing. Finally, she identified his passion to resurrect the Confederacy.

The Internet was a wonderful invention, especially for those who knew how to use it effectively. It allowed immediate access to basically all the knowledge in the world, and it enabled otherwise painstaking tasks to be done in a matter of hours rather than days, weeks, or months. Samantha was an expert. She cross-referenced and indexed all information about the Reverend. She hacked into his e-mail and Facebook accounts without a trace. She noted that he had been in contact with some fairly substantial characters through-out the South whose common interests included the belief that the War Between the States should never have ended or that it never really did. While it was clear from Bellamy's Internet footprint that he took steps to conceal his connections and his intentions, it was equally clear to Samantha that he was an amateur at it. She exploited his every weakness and was able to report back to David Blinder within a few weeks.

David listened closely to Samantha's account of Bellamy's activi-ties. She had been instructed to put all the information on a single flash drive, but Blinder wanted to hear the details directly from her. This was not a problem because of her prodigious memory. She did, however, have the encrypted file he demanded.

"So in the end," Samantha concluded, "Bellamy is working in secret to resurrect the Confederacy, resume the war that was lost in 1865, and break up the United States." There was no tone of irony or disapproval in her voice. She was simply reporting the facts.

Blinder sat back in his chair and looked pensively up at the ceil-ing. Ms. Stranger had no idea, of course, of the plan that he and his brother had concocted that was similar but far more ambitious than Reverend Bellamy's. He was thinking of the relative merits of approaching Bellamy for some sort of alliance. After all, the Blind-ers already had contacts with a number of secessionist groups across the country. But most of those were fringe outfits largely comprised of middle-aged men who liked to dress up on the weekends and play at military drills and talk about independence. There wasn't a true leader in the lot.

But Bellamy was different. He had an organization; he put it together himself. David looked back at Samantha.

"So give me an idea, Samantha, about how effective Bellamy has been at constructing this group."

Samantha did not pause a second. "He has been exceptionally effective, Mr. Blinder," she said. "He identified men—all men, by the way; no women—whom he felt were both willing and able to take concrete action on behalf of a resurrected Confederacy and who had the means to do it. Several of them are ex-military; a couple are politicians; a few others are religious leaders. Then there are several men of exceptional means." *Not so exceptional as yours, of course*, is what went through her head, but she discreetly left that out.

Blinder did not take his eyes off the attractive investigator. He valued her skills, and he appreciated her beauty. But that was an issue for another time.

"Do you have the details on all these men?" he asked.

"Of course," Samantha replied. She handed Blinder a flash drive.

He raised an eyebrow. "Only copy?" he asked.

"Of course," Samantha lied. She would never be so stupid as to make a single copy of anything.

"Encrypted?" Blinder asked.

"Of course."

"The code?"

"Upon confirmation of payment, as per our usual agreement," Samantha said, raising her eyebrows just a bit to provide professional emphasis.

"Of course," Blinder replied. "You may pick up the information from Audrey on your way out."

Samantha was familiar with the drill. She stood up. "Thank you, Mr. Blinder. Please let me know if I can be of further service." She turned and walked across his large office.

Audrey, Mr. Blinder's personal assistant, handed her an envelope containing codes to an off-shore account as she walked past her desk. In return, Samantha gave Audrey a key to a lockbox where the code for the flash drive was stored. This too was standard operating procedure.

She nodded to Audrey and walked out of the office.

Part 3

★ ★ ★ ★ ★

22

The President leaned forward in his chair as he listened to Eric Holder, the attorney general of the United States, give his report. He was having some trouble taking in what Mr. Holder was saying, as it was so outrageous that he could barely believe it. The thought crossed his mind that his friend and colleague was putting him on.

"Eric, wait a minute," he said with an uncharacteristic tone of impatience in his voice. "Do you mean to tell me that there are reputable people, American citizens, who are actively plotting to break up the United States?" His tone was just on the edge of sarcasm.

Eric looked straight into the President's eyes. "That's exactly what I am saying, Mr. President," he said. "And that they have a plan. And that the plan looks very much as if it is about to be executed." Holder knew this sounded preposterous: he had the same reaction when Bob Mueller, the head of the FBI, presented the same evidence to him not twenty-four hours before. In that twenty-four hours, Holder and his staff had gone into overdrive to confirm what Mueller had told him and to chart a path for an even more extensive investigation. He knew it would take a little while for the President to digest exactly what was coming out of his mouth.

"And you believe this all because of a secretly taped meeting . . . by a student at Rolla . . . who was . . . secretly taping a meeting for a class?" That feeling of being put on did not go away. He almost started laughing, but only the slightest hint of a smile made it to his face.

"As I said, Mr. President," echoing the words and the serious tone the FBI director had used with him the day before, "that in and of itself could have been some kind of enormous prank." The darkness in his eyes deepened. "But the disappearances have gotten everyone's attention."

"I don't get that part, Eric," the President said. "What do you mean, 'they disappeared'?"

"It means that they have abandoned their jobs, their homes, their cities or suburbs; it means that no one knows where they've gone; it means that we cannot find them. None of their passports were registered as crossing any international boundaries, so we think they are either somewhere in the US hiding or they have elaborate methods of avoiding recognition at the borders." Holder was getting a little exasperated himself. He thought of himself as a levelheaded person and definitely did not see himself as a conspiracy guy, even though he was the attorney general of the United States and ran across real conspiracies with some regularity.

The President responded to the seriousness of Holder's expression. He knew Eric to be a serious man; not without humor, but very serious when a situation called for it. And the President knew that Holder felt this situation called for it. The tiny smile evaporated from his face, and he matched his attorney general's serious demeanor, but he didn't speak for a few moments. Holder continued.

"Since this came to light, we have been looking for them. It's a little awkward. We are not certain any crimes have been committed, but if they have they are big ones: treason, sedition, conspiracy, rebellion. Things we as a country haven't dealt with for over a hundred and fifty years."

"'Awkward'?" The President asked. "You're telling me that these men are colluding to bring down the government of the United States by force and you're, what? Afraid of hurting their feelings?"

His impatience was suddenly breaking through. "What exactly have you done to follow up on this?"

Holder responded quickly. "We have mobilized all of our resources to track down the whereabouts of each of the men involved at this meeting. We are questioning the men who replaced them in their respective jobs or positions. We are . . . "

"And what did you learn from the replacements?" Obama demanded.

Holder took a deep breath. "Not much, Mr. President. Each of them had a similar story: they were promoted or transferred with no explanation. Most of them did not have personal relationships with the men they replaced. They do not appear to be lying. They just don't know."

"What about the next layer up? The people to whom they are responsible? If these men disappeared, their superiors or people around them must have known something."

"That's a little less clear at this point. Some of these men were academicians. Evidently one of them, Adam Wilson, informed the dean of his department that he would be away for an unspecified family emergency and couldn't be certain when he would return. The dean, who has a longstanding relationship with him, didn't bother to question Wilson closely. He just made arrangements to cover his classes and his research work." Holder raised an eyebrow. "Wilson is tenured. He didn't tell the dean until the day before he left." As if the culture of academia explained how easy it was for a person to remove himself from the grid.

So how do twenty upstanding—prominent even—citizens just disappear off the radar screen in this highly interconnected world? the President asked himself.

Holder, anticipating this unspoken thought, began again. "We traced their e-mail accounts, their bank accounts, and all their computer-based information sources. It turns out they had manually closed accounts—went to the banks or financial institutions and withdrew cash or cashed in their stock and bond holdings. For some months prior to the day they left, they had already transferred all their assets from these accessible accounts. From the point of withdrawal onward, the money is nearly impossible to trace. All electronic transmission ceased this past Monday morning at 8:00 a.m. There has been no action initiated on any e-mail or website associated with anyone in this group." He paused and sighed again. "It's an impressive coordination of effort," he said with just a trace of admiration in his voice.

Impressive indeed, thought Mr. Obama. "What is your next move, Eric?" he asked, a measure of warmth returning to his voice.

"Right now, we are digging more deeply into the identities of these men. We have feet on the ground asking their friends, neighbors, coworkers, mistresses, accountants, and housekeepers—you name it—for any information that might be helpful. We also put the Eyes Only CyberSquad on potential Internet presences, looking for clues. We have notified banks and financial institutions internationally that any contact from any of these men is reason to alert the FBI on a dedicated number set up just for that purpose." Holder paused for a moment. "But the horse is pretty much out of that particular barn."

The President looked at his attorney general. They both knew they were grasping at straws and that the likelihood of something significant turning up in the next twenty-four to forty-eight hours was slim to nearly nonexistent. But both also knew that this was precisely the path to take.

"Keep me posted, Eric," the President said. "Priority one."

"I will, Mr. President," Holder said. He nodded, turned, and walked out of the Oval Office.

23

On his way back to the Justice Department, Holder began to question himself. He wondered if this was in fact a tempest in a teapot, something that seemed very serious but perhaps wasn't. It could have been sheer coincidence that this situation developed the way it did and came to his attention. He wasn't one hundred percent sure that this wasn't part of some kind of giant practical joke. But he marveled that anyone he had worked with for more than a year, much less Bob Mueller, head of the FBI and a man he had known for close to three years, would believe that he would think this was funny.

But it was clear Mueller had done his homework. According to Mueller, he had been tipped off by a woman who worked closely with Max Grabel over at the CIA, a man in whom Mueller had a great deal of trust. Much more so than in some of the other bureaucrats with whom he was familiar. Mueller knew that Max would operate outside of protocol only under exceptional conditions, and the fact that he used that woman—he had trouble remembering her name—to alert him gave Mueller pause for two reasons. One was that Max did not go through channels, that is, through his immediate superior. The second was that he did not come himself. He knew Max to be an honest but exceptionally careful man, so if he went to these lengths to get the information to him, he must (a) believe it to be credible and (b) see the situation as urgent. After interrogating

Marie—that was her name, Marie LeBrun—and checking out her facts, Mueller went straight to Holder. He also put a tail on LeBrun.

He should have known better. Marie was familiar with the typical reactions of bureaucrats, even highly placed ones, and she assumed that she would be followed once she parted from Mueller, whom she met in an out-of-the-way hallway near his office. She was equipped with the same kind of sound-deadening device Max had with him when they met to discuss this matter initially, and she was sure she took every conceivable precaution to get the information to Mueller as Max had requested and to respond to any questions or requests for evidence that he wanted. Their meeting was brief but intense.

As she left the Justice Department Building, Marie spotted the tail via a small mirror that was encased in a bracelet she wore on her left wrist. Antique technology, she thought, but effective. She got on her BMW K1200S bike and pulled away before the guy was even close to his car. She brought the motorcycle expressly for this purpose: maximum speed and maximum flexibility. Plus, she loved riding motorcycles.

Mueller found the intelligence Marie had shared as bewildering as all of the other people involved. But he knew from long experience that his personal reactions, while sometimes or even often helpful, could not substitute for facts. He confirmed as much of the information as he could, but he did not want to prolong any investigation if events were unfolding as rapidly as they appeared. Time was critical. Twenty prominent men and their families, along with all their on-the-grid information, don't just vanish unless something huge is afoot.

What he was able to confirm troubled him a great deal. He was well acquainted with disappearances among fringe groups: sometimes these types would delight in taking themselves off the grid. Ted Kaczynski was one of the most infamous, and everyone knew what mayhem that deranged character wrought on innocent people. Mueller, of course, knew of other cases. He knew right away that he needed to bring in higher-ups.

But Marie had told him something else that was equally troubling and that complicated the whole situation. That was that Max believed the CIA, and perhaps the Departments of Justice and of State, had been compromised. In fact, Marie told Mueller that Max did not think it was a case of a single mole; he thought it was a systematic infiltration, and he was unsure just how far it had advanced throughout the government. If the résumés of the group of twenty were any indication, it could be virulent indeed.

So when Mueller got to his office to initiate his personal investigation, he had to be very careful whom he told or whom he used. He identified four of his most trusted lieutenants, men and women who had worked with him for years and whom he trusted with his life. Each of these officers had worked with him for a minimum of ten years. He felt sure he could trust each of them. Nonetheless, he ordered them not to disclose the purpose of their inquiries or any substantive information to anyone, even to their secretaries. One of the advantages of being in government service for many years was that Mueller had a sense of where the vulnerabilities of the bureaucracy were. And they were often in places most people would not think about. For instance, secretaries, especially new hires, had access to a lot of information. Many were young, ambitious, and eager to please. They could be and have been seduced, knowingly or unknowingly, and compromised, sometimes for years. Mueller sighed at how suggestible and gullible youth could be. He dismissed those thoughts, assuring himself that he would not let this investigation be compromised because of leaks or mindless oversights.

He also trusted Max, whom he had known for many years. That trust extended to what he knew about Marie, although he deliberately did not pry too much into her. He knew Max trusted her completely, and that was enough for him. He did have her followed, however, just to be on the safe side—as much for her protection as for the opportunity to gain any information—but from what he had heard of Marie LeBrun, the tail he put on her would no doubt soon come up empty.

He was glad to connect with the Attorney General, who agreed to see him as soon as possible after Mueller gave him a heads-up about how serious the situation seemed to be. But Mueller was also a careful man. He grilled his four trusted associates about the strength of their information; he insisted that they double- and triple-check all their facts and provide multiple sources. Mueller felt comfortable working with Holder, but he knew Holder was a straight shooter who did not brook shoddy work.

He met with Holder in the AG's office.

After Mueller finished describing what he knew, Eric Holder was silent.

"And you believe this?" he finally said.

Mueller knew enough about the psychology of humans to appreciate how befuddled most people get with new information that does not fit neatly into their normal belief structure.

He paused a moment before he answered. "I think . . ." he began. "I think this bears the closest scrutiny," he said. Then he added: "I would not blame you if you ordered a psychiatric consult for me, however." He grinned a serious grin.

Holder chuckled humorlessly. He had faith in Mueller's judgment. The two talked for about an hour before Holder was able to wrap his mind around the situation and the two high-level bureaucrats began planning for the next step. Once their roles were settled, Holder looked at Mueller.

"I have to go to the President," he said evenly.

"Yes, you do, Eric," Mueller replied. "Do you want me to go along?"

Holder thought for a moment. "I don't think so," he said, lost in thought. "Not yet, anyway."

arie savored the sensation of air blowing across her face and body as she looped around DC to make sure she wasn't being followed. She was dressed in as nondescript an outfit as an attractive, tall young woman on a BMW motorcycle could be. She also savored eluding the FBI; it was a game to her. One that she was invested in winning. She knew the protocols the FBI used to follow targets.

Satisfied that she had lost the FBI agent, she pulled over to the side of a road and parked her bike under a large leafy cherry tree. She removed her helmet and cocked her head sideways, listening closely for unusual sounds. Then she looked up to scan the sky to make sure there were no other surveillance mechanisms: helicopters, drones, that sort of thing. She closed her eyes and listened even more attentively. Nothing; just the normal sounds of Washington, DC, in motion. She loved that sound. It was unlike the sound of any other city she had ever visited.

She told Max she would contact him as soon as possible after meeting with Mueller. She squatted down and propped her back up against the tree and pulled out her cell phone. She dialed Max's secure cell. After a series of beeps and clicks, he answered.

"Hi, Max," Marie said. "Mission accomplished." She told him about the meeting with Mueller. She recounted almost verbatim the questions he asked. She wasn't going to tell him about the tail, but then she thought better of it and included that detail.

"He had you followed?" Max said with some surprise in his voice.

"He tried," Marie replied. She could feel Max smiling on the other end of the line.

"Are you in the clear?" Max asked.

"I believe so," Marie replied, looking around for good measure.

Out of the corner of her eye, she spotted a man standing behind another cherry tree about thirty feet away. "Maybe not," she said to Max. "I'll get back with you." She clicked off.

Marie surveyed the rest of the area where she was sitting. She could not be sure the man by the tree was watching her, but he seemed nervous, and he was glancing repeatedly in her direction. After a few minutes, she got up, straddled her bike, and replaced her helmet, all the while watching the man near the tree with the mirrors on her jewelry.

As she pulled away from the curb, she gunned the engine and looked back at him one more time.

He was gone.

A chill ran through Marie's spine. She scanned the area of the park where she had stopped. She saw no movement. She decided to loop back around. If the guy thought she spotted him, he may have left in a hurry, but less than a minute had gone by, and he could not have gone far.

As she passed the park she saw a beige Toyota Camry pull away from the curb. It was the only moving car. She circled the park one more time and pulled up behind the vehicle. She made a mental note of the license plate number.

The car began to accelerate. This confirmed in Marie's mind that the guy had been watching her and knew he had been made. She continued to follow him. Did he really think he could outrun a

BMW K1200S, one of the fastest bikes in the world? Small chance.

The driver tried weaving through traffic, but Marie stayed twenty feet back and never lost sight of him. He was heading back into the city. After driving for about ten minutes this way, he pulled into a lower-level garage.

Marie followed. Around the first bend, a car blocked the Toyota's path. Marie pulled up next to the driver's side door. She motioned for him to lower his window.

"Why are you following me?" she demanded.

"What do you mean?" the guy replied. He was nervous; his face was splotchy. Marie was sure he was lying.

"I mean, why were you eyeing me in the park and why did you try to get away when I left?"

The man, who looked to be about thirty, shook his head nervously and then turned to Marie. "Look, lady," he said. "I was just looking. I didn't mean any harm. Please," he continued, "I don't want trouble."

Marie didn't know whether to believe him or not. Truth time, she told herself.

"What's your name?" she asked in a tone that brooked no avoidance.

"Tom," he said.

"Tom what?" she said with more than a little sarcasm in her voice.

When he hesitated, Marie pointed out the obvious. "Look, Tom," she said. "I know your license plate number; I know the make and model of your car; and I know what you look like. You were stalking me. If you think I can't ID you, you are dead wrong." For good measure, she snapped his photograph with her cell phone. She gave him a casual but triumphant shrug. As if to say *I'm holding all the cards.*

Tom looked defeated. "Tom Sanders," he said softly. "Look. I'm married. I have kids. I don't want trouble."

"Do you live here, Tom?" Marie asked.

He looked at her with fright in his eyes. "Yes, ma'am," he said.

Marie almost smiled at the childlike formality. Instead, she leaned her hand casually on the roof of the sedan. It looked as if she were just balancing herself. But as she brought her hand up, she put a small piece of tape on the top of his car. This small piece of tape concealed an even smaller GPS device. State of the art.

"Well, Mr. Sanders," she continued, leaning so that her head was within inches of his, "if I ever see or hear from you again I am going to kick your ass and then tell your beloved wife you're a stalker." She gave him a hard look. "Got that?"

"Yes, ma'am," Tom replied softly. He swallowed hard.

"Good," Marie said. Then she revved her motorcycle and pulled toward the exit.

May be innocent, she thought. Or someone may have selected a wimpy guy to do some grunt work and knew he would fold at the earliest opportunity. Or would look like he folded. Or he was an exceptionally good actor.

After she exited the garage, Marie pulled over to a parking spot on the street. She pulled out her iPad and entered the information Sanders had given her, along with the license plate number. In a few moments, she confirmed that the car was his, that he did indeed live in the building she'd just left, and that he had a wife and two children. She uploaded his photo and sent it to Max.

Marie put her gadgets away and drove to her own apartment, where she redialed Max's number.

"Hi, Max. Me again," She said.

"Marie, what happened?"

"There was a guy stalking me in the park. When I spotted him, I got up to go, and he left. I followed him to an underground parking garage and had a chat with him. Seems like just a stalker, the kind of guy who likes to watch attractive women." She paused a moment. "I got his name, number, and photo."

Marie had no difficulty identifying herself as an attractive woman. It was not a boast; it was simply a fact. It was a fact she had to deal with day in and day out. As much a burden as a blessing, although, in her lucid moments, she preferred to be attractive rather than the alternative.

Max was quiet on his end of the line. "I don't like the smell of this, Marie," he said. "Give me all the information you have on this guy."

"Already done," Marie said.

"I'll get back with you," Max replied. And he clicked off.

om Sanders was shaken. After he found his parking spot, it took him several minutes to calm down, and he did not leave his Camry until his breathing returned to normal. He had been told that Marie might notice him and that he should act innocent, but he didn't like it. He would have refused the assignment if the money hadn't been so good. He and his wife had two kids; they needed money.

Also before he exited his vehicle, he picked up the disposable cell phone the man who hired him had given him. He punched the key for the only number in the phone's memory. A gravelly voice answered.

Tom was nervous. "She saw me, as you said she might," he said. Silence.

Tom didn't know what to say. He listened intently.

Finally the gravelly voice spoke. "What did you observe?" it said.

"She parked near a large cherry tree in a small park on the far side of town. She sat down near the tree and placed a call on her cell. She spoke for a few moments. I think that's when she noticed me."

"Go on."

"Then she got up and left," Tom said truthfully.

"Did you speak to her?"

Shit! Tom thought. He was basically an honest man, and this cloak-and-dagger stuff just didn't sit well with him. He was nervous;

he wanted to get this whole thing behind him. He decided the truth was the best. He described in detail what Marie did and their conversation as he recalled it. He felt a little better.

There was silence for a moment on the other end of the line. Then the voice said, "You did good." And clicked off.

Tom had no way of knowing what "did good" meant. He did what he was told. He felt bad about being discovered. After all, the man who contacted him had told him to try not to be noticed. He couldn't figure out why he was asked to do this. He was too eager for the money involved, and he let it cloud his judgment. At the time he did not believe there was any criminal activity involved. Now he wasn't so sure, although he could not imagine what it could be. He promised himself that would never happen again. He hadn't told his wife, and that bothered him. All he wanted to do was return to his work as a midlevel analyst at the State Department.

ax was staring at the information Marie had sent him. He was thinking. He was also looking into the federal database to collect any information about one Thomas Sanders, a junior analyst at the State Department, where he had worked since graduating in the middle of his class at American University six years before. Not a stellar student; more a workhorse. Took him six years to graduate. Undistinguished undergraduate record, no graduate school, competent job performance but did not stand out in any way. In other words, a reliable, not-very-ambitious midlevel bureaucrat.

Perfect profile for an informant, Max thought.

Max called Stanley Schindler, a man he knew well. The two weren't close, but they had worked on several projects together and both felt respect for the other.

As Stanley listened to Max's description of Tom Sanders, his eyebrows furrowed. One of my people spying? He was getting angrier by the moment. He promised Max he would look into it and get back with him as soon as he knew something.

And he did: Stanley dropped what he was doing and looked up Thomas Sanders on the State Department intranet. He soon found the information Marie had found less than an hour before. He also learned that Tom's immediate superior was Madeline Schumacher, two years younger than Sanders and notably more ambitious. Top ten percent of her class at Bryn Mawr, internship at State, some overseas work; clearly on the fast track. She must run Sanders ragged, he thought with a measure of glee.

Stanley was trying to think if he knew Schumacher. He tried to touch base with the people under him from time to time, but at his level, there were a lot of those people. Still, something about her name and her picture clicked when he saw it on his desktop.

He picked up the phone and dialed her extension.

Madeline answered on the first ring. "Madeline Schumacher," she said crisply, as if she were expecting the call.

"Ms. Schumacher," Stanley said. "This is Assistant Secretary Stanley Schindler. I would like to speak to you for a few minutes in person."

"When, sir?" Ms. Schumacher replied with that same professional crispness that Stanley liked and respected. He knew he had met her before. It may have been at an orientation session.

"How about in thirty minutes?" Stanley said.

"I'll be there, sir," Madeline replied.

They hung up.

Stanley spent the next thirty minutes reviewing the list of peripheral persons who may have had contact with Madeline's department: all consultants, temp workers, other bureaucrats up and down the scale. He had a list of fourteen State Department employees from outside that department and thirteen civilians who had called, visited, or otherwise contacted the department staff.

Then he shifted gears and looked into Schumacher. He was beginning to remember her. It was at an orientation session, and he was immediately impressed by her intelligence, professionalism, and complete lack of hubris. That last feature stood out among the new hires at State, who were ordinarily so proud of being there they couldn't help showing off to each other and, if possible, to higher-ups. She did not. Stanley respected that about her.

He also looked up her personal file, something that was not regarded as a good practice but which everyone did when they wanted a read on how an employee's life was going, how their commitment to State was holding up, and how their patriotism was faring—not things to neglect in the delicate work of the State Department.

Everything seemed in order.

Marian McGrath buzzed Stanley when he was in the middle of these recollections.

"Mr. Schindler," she said. "There's a Madeline Schumacher here to see you. She said you asked her to come."

"Thank you, Marian," Stanley said. "Please send her in."

Stanley rose to greet his guest, shook her hand, and invited her to sit down. He took his seat behind his desk, facing her. She complied. She looked at him expectantly.

"Ms. Schumacher," Stanley began. "I will get directly to the point. You have a man by the name of Tom Sanders who works for you."

Madeline nodded.

"This man was observed stalking one of our contract workers this afternoon. He denied any malicious intent, but he was unable to give a solid reason for his following her. As far as we can tell, no crimes were committed." Stanley looked at Madeline in silence for a moment. He could not tell from the look on her face how this was playing.

"What I want to know from you is this: Is there any reason that you can think of, based on your professional relationship with Mr. Sanders, that he would be following a contract worker from this department?"

Madeline thought for just a moment, shook her head, and said, "No, sir."

"In your experience, have you observed any unusual or peculiar behavior that might raise questions about Mr. Sanders's loyalty or devotion to his job? In other words, is there any reason based on your experience with Mr. Sanders that he would engage in this behavior? Has he ever done anything like this before?"

Madeline's head kept shaking.

"Are you aware of any personal problems on his part that may negatively impact his judgment?"

At that, Madeline stopped shaking her head. She was clearly thinking. There was silence in the room for a few moments.

"I am not sure, sir. Tom, Mr. Sanders, has complained about money lately. Everyone does that, given how expensive it is to live in DC, but his complaining has stood out over the past few weeks." She thought for another moment. "I believe his wife is pregnant again."

It was Stanley's turn to nod. "Do you have any reason to suspect him of, um, divided allegiance?"

"No, sir, I do not," Madeline replied.

Stanley turned and glanced out his window.

"Why wasn't he at work today?"

"He called in sick, sir," Madeline said.

Stanley exhaled a long stream of air. "Ms. Schumacher, thank you for your time. I would appreciate your keeping this conversation and its contents between us."

"Yes, sir," Madeline said. And she got up and walked out of the room.

My kind of worker, Stanley thought. He would soon know if she was true to her word.

Stanley dialed Max's number. Max answered on the first ring.

"This is what I know, Max," he said. He detailed the information he had collected.

Max did not know exactly what this meant, but it felt in his mind to be part of the larger, darkening picture. He thanked Stanley and picked up his cell phone to call Marie.

"You've been tagged," he said. And he hung up.

27

It was not in Marie's nature to get angry the way most people get angry. It was in her nature to get to the bottom of things. Quickly. She glanced at her watch; it was not yet 3:00 p.m. Mr. Sanders was either at home (with or without his wife—it did not matter to Marie) or he was going somewhere in his car. She pulled out her GPS tracker and entered the code for the tiny device she put on his car. Nothing. That meant it was most likely still in the underground garage.

Marie changed her clothes to put on something that would not draw attention to herself but also give her maximum freedom of movement, in the event that she had to make good on her threat to Mr. Sanders. She picked up the keys to a Toyota Prius and left her apartment. Within twenty minutes, she was standing in front of the building where Tom Sanders, midlevel government worker, lived with his wife and children. She pushed the button for the superintendent.

"Delivery," she barked into the microphone. The outer door buzzed loudly and she opened it. She took the stairs up to the third floor and walked halfway down the hall until she was standing in front of the Sanders residence. She knocked but stood outside the range of the peephole. She flipped on her sound jammer in case the apartment was bugged. Within a minute, she heard steps. Tom Sanders opened the door.

Marie did not hesitate. She pushed the door open with one hand and pushed Sanders aside with the other.

"You lied to me, Tom," she said in an accusing voice. "I do not like to be lied to."

She glanced around. "Are you alone here?"

Tom Sanders was suddenly pale. "Yes," he stammered. "My wife's at work. The kids are in day care." He looked at Marie with fear in his eyes. "They'll be home in about an hour."

Marie motioned with her head for him to take a seat on the couch. He complied.

"You were following me for a reason. It was not just some sicko pervert sexual thing. You were put up to this. I want to know who put you up to it and why." Her eyes never left his. "And I want to know now."

Tom was frightened on two fronts. His contact had told him never, ever to disclose any information about their connection. This sinister woman was threatening him with God knows what. His wife was not home to help. He was in a scenario that represented his worst nightmare. He was alone and in danger.

But the contact was not in the room and this dangerous woman was. He decided immediately that the best course of action was to deal with the immediate threat.

"What do you want to know?" he said.

"I want to know every detail of how this came down. *Every* detail," she emphasized.

Tom swallowed hard. "About a week ago, I got a note on my desk asking me to arrange a contact. At first I thought it was from my boss, but then I realized it wasn't. It was handwritten. It told me to call a number. I did." He swallowed hard again. "I got this guy who had a deep, gravelly voice. He said he got my name from somebody I'd never heard of in the department and that he had a business proposition for me. At first I was confused. I didn't know the guy he was referring to, and I'm a government worker: we don't do 'business propositions.' Then I thought maybe it was a prank or something. I mean, I didn't really know what to think. He asked me to meet him at a bar about a mile away from the State Department after work. He said it would be worth my while.

"Honestly, I was confused. When he mentioned the possibility of money being involved, I sort of got hooked. Money's been tight lately, and, well, I don't know; I thought maybe if I could make a few bucks on the side and not break any laws or hurt anything, what would it matter?"

"So you met him?" Marie said.

"Yeah. I went to the Rocket Bar in Chinatown. He said he would find me when I got there. I walk in—I never go to bars; it was really creepy—and I sit down at a small table for two just in front of the bar itself. This short, stocky guy in a hat and huge shades comes up and waves for me to follow him. At this point, I'm freaking out. I almost left, but I thought he might get violent. I don't know; I followed him to a dark corner of the bar. He never took off his sunglasses or his hat. He also had a scarf on, which was a little weird because it's spring, but okay, this was some kind of cloak-and-dagger thing.

"Next thing I know, he pulls out a wad of cash and counts out ten hundred-dollar bills. He lays the money, a cheap cell phone, and a picture of you on the table. He says that if I follow you I can take the thousand dollars and the cell phone. And he says if I complete the assignment he will give me another grand. He also says that he doesn't want me to break any laws and that if I don't want to do it, I can get up and leave the phone and the thousand dollars on the table, no problem." Sanders looked at Marie. "Honestly, it's been a while since I've seen that kind of cash. It was too tempting. I said okay, if he was sure I wasn't breaking any laws."

Tom took a deep breath. This was scary for him, but at the same time he was relieved to tell the story. He was not one to keep secrets.

"Go on," Marie said.

"So I say okay, I'll do it. He says he'll call me when he knows where you'll be. I say, 'Okay.' He says, 'Okay, that's it.' 'That's it?' I say. 'Yeah, that's it,' he says. I take the phone and the thousand dollars, put it in my pocket, get up, and leave."

"So he called you?" Marie said.

"Yeah, this morning. He said today was the day. He told me to call in sick and wait for his call. Then he called me a couple of hours ago and told me to go to the location where you saw me. I don't know how he knew about it. I don't even know who he is. All I know is that he told me to be there and I went there."

Marie could not unburden herself of the notion that something was amiss in this story.

"So he called you this morning before you would have left for work and told you that I would be in this park."

"No," Tom replied. "He told me today would be the day. Then he told me he would call me again when he knew your exact location. He said he would call me on the cell phone. And he did later on, about a half an hour before I found you. That's when you saw me."

"Where's the cell phone?" Marie demanded.

"Right here," Tom said, pulling it out of his pocket and holding it in his trembling hand.

"Give it to me," Marie said. Tom handed it to her.

Marie opened the phone and scrolled through the recent calls. There were only two new incoming calls. The number was blocked. "Was this him?" she asked Tom.

"Yeah," he said, sighing. At this point, he wished he had a number to give her.

"Why did he want you to follow me?" Marie asked.

Tom thought for a moment. "I have no clue. He didn't say. I don't know you; I've never seen you before. He told me not to have any contact with you." Tom thought for another minute. "When he called, he asked me if we spoke, and I told him what happened . . . when you stopped me in the garage." Tom looked scared.

"And?" Marie said.

"And nothing. He just said okay, you 'did good.'" He made quotation marks in the air with his fingers.

Not much of this was making sense to Marie. Why would some nameless guy want her followed for no reason? She was wondering if Tom was telling the whole truth. Then a chill ran down her spine. They tagged my bike!

She stepped away from Sanders and pulled out her cell phone. She mumbled into the phone out of Sanders's earshot about her bike being tagged. Then she calmly clicked off and walked back over to him to continue.

"Did you get the other grand?" she asked.

"No, not yet. He told me I'd get it tomorrow."

"Tomorrow?" Marie said, interrupting him.

"Yeah. I'm supposed to meet him at the same bar after work to collect the other thousand."

Finally, Marie thought. Something to go on. This whole story still wasn't adding up in her mind, but now there was at least a direction.

"Hang on," she said to Tom. She turned away and walked to the other side of the room again. She pulled out her phone and dialed Max's number. When he answered, she quietly and briefly described her conversation with Tom and included the rendezvous that was scheduled for tomorrow afternoon. She also told him she thought her bike had a GPS on it.

Max asked Marie if she felt it would be safe for Tom to stay alone with his wife tonight.

"I don't know, Max," Marie replied. "There've been no threats so far, but my bet is that this place is bugged, and whoever this guy is knows I spoke to Sanders, even with the jammer on."

Max thought for a while. Even though he did not know Tom Sanders, Max felt some responsibility to Schindler, who was Sanders's superior.

"Okay," said Max. Marie knew that within ten minutes a Special Ops team would arrive to check out the place. She also knew they would be ready to remove Tom and his family to a safe location.

Marie walked over to the window. There were views of this apartment from a number of other buildings, although she did not notice anything suspicious. She turned back to Tom.

"I'm afraid it may not be safe for you to be here," she said.

Tom turned a more ashen shade of gray.

28

The Special Ops team arrived a minute before Marie expected them to. They were dressed in civilian clothes. Max thought of everything. There were two men and a woman. It looked like a casual visit until the door closed behind them.

The members of the group nodded to Marie and then to Tom. Then they started combing through the apartment. They quickly found microphones on the phones and in the light fixtures of each room. They double-checked for video cameras but didn't find any. They swept for fingerprints. They took the SIM card out of the cell phone and made a duplicate. One of the agents pulled out a small computer and started typing furiously.

"Got it," she said quietly within a few minutes. She turned the screen so that the other two agents could see and Tom could not. They both nodded. On the screen was a photograph of a man of medium height and stocky build. He had thick black hair and bushy eyebrows. Italian, maybe; his name was Mario LaSalla.

Marie hit a button on the computer that made the face full screen. She waved to Tom to look. "Is that the man you were talking about?" she asked.

Tom's eyes grew big, and he nodded.

Marie showed the female agent the jamming device she was using. The woman nodded approvingly.

All the agents and Marie looked at each other; they nodded in unison.

Then Marie turned toward Tom. She had none of the hardness she had earlier.

"Tom," she began. "I'm afraid you will have to go with these people."

Tom did not respond right away. "Go where?" he finally said.

"They will take you to a safe house. Your wife and children will be there."

Tom's eyes widened. "A safe house? Am I . . . are we . . . in danger?" He was shaking visibly.

Marie told him the truth. "We don't know that, Tom. What we do know is that someone infiltrated the Department of Justice and probably other federal departments as well to gain information. They infiltrated your home. Someone had to enter this apartment to plant the bugs these agents found."

Two tears were streaming down Tom's trembling face. "Oh, my God!" he said. "Oh, my God, oh, my God, oh, my God!"

Marie felt genuine sympathy for Tom, who clearly had no idea what he had gotten himself into. "There's another part of this, Tom. It was not an accident that we made contact. Someone is sending us a signal. We are not sure what it means just yet, but you are being played in a much larger drama."

"Cindy!" he cried. His wife's disapproving face flashed through his mind.

Marie raised her hand. "As we speak, two agents are visiting with your wife explaining what is happening. They will help her collect the children from day care and meet you at the safe house." She paused and looked into Tom's quaking eyes. "We are doing this for your safety, Tom, and as a precaution. We don't know a lot about what is happening. What we do know is that there has been what appears to be a major breach in security. We need to track it down. And we want you and your family to be safe until we know more. I am sorry."

Marie was sorry. So this young guy impulsively agrees to snatch some cash but doesn't have the slightest clue about what he is getting involved in, and the situation blows up in his face. It was easy to describe from a distance; lots of people have gotten in over their heads at one time or another. But it's nightmarish to go through, and this nightmare was just getting started.

Infiltration of US government networks, while not easy, is surprisingly not so difficult as the government would like the public to believe. Given the proliferation of information technology and the rapidly and increasingly sophisticated technology itself, knowledgeable individuals could enter domains previously inaccessible to nongovernment agents.

During the buildup to the Second Civil War, several different groups were attempting to gather information about government policies and resources, looking to degrade performance, especially in military matters, and in general demonstrating to themselves and perhaps to the federal government itself that it had power that could threaten them. For most of the post–World War II Cold War, the concern was infiltration by foreign espionage agencies from the Eastern Bloc: the KGB and the like. As the Cold War wound down and terrorism grew to replace it in terms of national priority, the focus was still on infiltration by foreign nationals. It wasn't until well into the second decade of the twenty-first century that home-grown terrorism threats were identified and were beginning to be understood clearly for the destructive forces they represented. There was some question—and some hope in certain quarters—that this was too little too late. As it is for persons, it is hard for a bureaucracy to change its mind.

29

The only other person who knew where Marie LeBrun lived besides herself and her landlord was Samantha Stranger. The pair met when they both applied for the CIA and instantly connected on many levels. They were both smart, hardworking, attractive women who demanded a lot of themselves. They both left the CIA to pursue independent careers, and both had the know-how and the *access* to know-how to make a success of their lives. Theirs was more than a friendship but not a marriage. They lived separately but had free access to each other's apartment. They did not claim an exclusive relationship or protest other relationships unless they threatened the web of secrecy they had both created; nor did they complain about the pressure or demands imposed on them by their jobs. They were both workaholics, obsessed with detail. They were a perfect fit.

Their main connection was their unspoken ability to understand exactly what the other was saying. This was not something they set out to do; it was something they discovered within minutes of meeting each other and was always present. It was the basis of their relationship.

So they spent a lot of time—of what time they had together—talking. And specifically they talked about their work projects, but only if there was any question of their legality or doability or any threat of exposure. These two women valued their privacy over everything else.

Once Marie saw to it that Tom and his wife and young children were safely ensconced in the safe house and Marie was on her way home, she stopped by a drugstore to pick up a disposable phone. She was uncertain just how exposed she had gotten, and she did not want to risk using her own phone. She called Sam according to a protocol they had previously arranged in the event that their secrecy was or could be violated. It was an old ruse used by many people but a serviceable one: one ring, hang up, redial. Sam answered on the first ring of the second sequence.

"Trouble," Marie said. She proceeded to describe what had happened earlier that day. She omitted nothing.

Sam was quiet on the other end of the line. She was thinking.

"Do you think you're clear now?" she asked.

"I think so but I can't be sure. I switched vehicles. But we need to know if there was a tag on my bike. It was the only way I can think of that I could have been tracked."

"I'll check that out right now," Sam said. "I'm coming up on the garage."

The garage was located several blocks from their apartment precisely for this reason. Even if there was a tracking device on the bike, it would not pinpoint where they lived; it would only identify where some of their vehicles were parked.

"Call me when you know," Marie said. And she clicked off.

Marie initiated a pattern of turns so as to confuse anyone who might be tracking her whereabouts. It only took Sam a few minutes to call her back.

"Yeah," she said. "It's a cheap tracking key under the front fender." Marie could hear her friend sigh. "Clunky but effective. I think you should be at least a little insulted," she teased.

"More than a little," Marie replied. "But I'm more irritated that I didn't even think to check, much less find it." She thought for a moment. "Now what?" she asked, as much of herself as of Samantha.

Samantha did not skip a beat. "I will get rid of this in a way which will seem as if you are riding your bike. Then I'll make sure it's planted somewhere we can keep an eye on it."

Marie felt a twinge of gratitude for the competent and active response on her friend's part. "Thanks, Sam. See you in a bit." She clicked off.

Before Marie parked the Toyota she was driving, she pulled over and did a complete inspection of the vehicle. She had a device that could detect GPS signals, but she wanted to eyeball it just to be sure. Layers of security, she learned long ago, were the most reliable kind.

Satisfied, she drove to the parking garage and left the car.

When she got home, Samantha was not there. This did not worry Marie; she had complete confidence in Sam's skills, and she knew that it took some time to do the tasks she had set for herself. She went over to the refrigerator, pulled out a bottle of white wine, and poured herself a glass.

Marie was trying to make sense of why these people chose to tag her, a not-very-important contract worker for the government who placed a high value on privacy and evading detection. The only conclusion she could come to was that it was to demonstrate a capability that this group had. She assumed it was related to the conversation she had with Mueller and Max and the meeting in Rolla, but she didn't know that for sure. The feeling that she was somehow betrayed was growing; she had that queasy feelings that comes with unexpected betrayal. It was compounded by the disgust she felt because this was all about homegrown Americans. She would have much preferred a foreign attack. But an attack from our own citizens? Sick.

It was in the middle of these thoughts that she heard the key in the lock and saw Samantha walk in.

"Hi, honey," she said, getting up to greet her. The two hugged a warm, lingering hug.

"Hi," Samantha replied. She walked over to the kitchen and got herself a wine glass.

Marie waited until Samantha was comfortably seated before she started talking. The two women each took a sip of wine. "There is something I want to talk with you about," Marie said. "A lot of this, of course, is 'eyes only,' but I need your eyes in addition to my own." She smiled sweetly. Samantha nodded.

Marie then told Samantha every detail of her conversation with Max on the Ellipse. She told her about the video and how it came into Max's possession. She told her about the task Max had given her and about leaks in the upper echelons of government departments. She shared all this information as if it were routine: crisp, professional data.

But then she paused. She was clearly befuddled by the day's events. "Today was different," she began. "Max tasked me with sharing the information with Mueller. He did not want to be seen briefing him himself, but he felt it was vital that Mueller know the information he shared with me ASAP. So I met with Mueller and briefed him. We met in an out-of-the-way hallway in the Justice Department. There was no one within fifty feet, and I had a sound neutralizer active the whole time." She paused and took another sip of wine.

"When I left, I noticed that Mueller had someone tail me. Probably as much for my protection as anything else. It didn't take me any time to lose him. Then I started circling around the city to evade anyone. I stop by this small park on the north side. I call Max." She took another sip of wine.

"Then I notice out of the corner of my eye a guy watching me. At first I thought it was just some gawker, but when I left and circled around, I saw that he left immediately after I did in another direction."

Marie took a deep breath. Then she shared every detail of what happened next: confronting him, talking to Max, getting the story from Sanders, dealing with the Special Ops guys, the safe house. When she finished, she looked squarely in Samantha's eyes. "For the life of me, Sam, I cannot figure out how or why I was targeted. It gives me the creeps."

Samantha listened closely. "Well," she finally said. "It is clear that somebody knows more about you than you think and that you are more significant than you believe."

Silence hung in the air for a few minutes.

"Mueller!" Marie exclaimed. "It must be someone who works for Mueller."

She pulled out her disposable cell and dialed Max's number. He answered on the first ring.

"Max, this is Marie," she said. "It had to be someone working for Mueller."

ario LaSalla was feeling pretty smug about his little cat-and-mouse game with that loser bureaucrat. The guy didn't even bargain for more money, he thought, and he believed I would meet him to dump another grand on him. What a goof. These were Mario's thoughts as he got into his car to drive up to New York to meet with the man who hired him.

Mario did not know who the man was. He met him in the dark corner of a New York tavern. Whoever he was, he spoke softly and did not shake his hand. He drank only water. This man had given him ten thousand dollars just to find someone in the State Department who would follow someone from the Justice Department for reasons that Mario was completely ignorant of. When he asked the mysterious man in the New York tavern, the response was flighty, Mario thought. "We just want them to know that we can do pretty much as we please with them," the man said. "Just to create a little chaos."

This sounded like a lame reason if not an outright lie to Mario, but he would do a lot of things for ten grand, and the money that the guy laid on the table was real. He was sure he could pull it off without a hitch. Mario smiled. Not only did he get the ten grand that dainty guy was paying him for this little curio drama, but he had another thousand that he withheld from Sanders. He was feeling flush.

So much so that at first he did not notice the black vehicles that pulled up to block his car from moving in any direction. He had to shake his head a couple of times before he realized he was the object of attention for the dozen or so men and women who got out of the black vehicles, guns drawn.

He finally got it when one of those men was opening his door demanding that he get out of his car with his hands up. Christ! he thought.

"Mario LaSalla?" asked the unsmiling man who was pointing a gun at him and flashing a badge.

"Yeah, that's me," Mario replied.

"Mr. LaSalla, you are under arrest for intimidating a federal employee, sedition, and espionage." He finished the Miranda warning.

Mario looked at him as if he were crazy. "Espionage?" he said. He wasn't sure what sedition was, but spying? He wasn't spying. "You got the wrong guy," he said.

That mild protestation did not prevent the man with the gun from twisting Mario's arms behind his back and handcuffing him. "We will see about that," he said simply. "Right now, you will come with us."

hen Marie got off the phone with Max after telling him about the connection to Mueller, she turned to Samantha. "It helps me so much to talk to you about this, Sam. I'm sorry if it's any kind of burden."

Samantha was deep in her own thoughts. She could not help thinking that these mysterious goings-on at the State and Justice Departments were related to her recent conversation with David Blinder. She was silent for about five minutes. Marie knew not to interrupt her during these times. Samantha was an introvert who needed quiet internal time to process things.

Finally, she looked back up at Marie. "Something major is happening, Marie. I need to fill you in on another piece of the puzzle." And she proceeded to tell Marie about her recent assignment from Blinder and what this guy named Bellamy was up to. Marie listened attentively.

The two sat in silence for a long time, quietly sipping their wine. The notion that different groups of serious people were plotting to overthrow the constitutional government of the United States was breathtaking for both of these two youngish, hardened, but idealistic women. Neither had any intention of being anything but idealistic. They loved the United States. They had both taken oaths to support and defend the Constitution. There was no doubt in either of their minds that the commitment that oath entailed did not end when they left formal government service.

"This is a very delicate situation, Marie," Sam said. "But we have to do something. I doubt that anyone but me knows about what I dug up on Bellamy. Which means Blinder can track any leak to me."

Marie nodded.

"We'll think of something," she said, and toasted their friendship.

32

Mario LaSalla sat at the interrogation table across from a very serious middle-aged man, presumably some sort of government agent, who was making notes and ignoring him. Mario wasn't worried: whatever he did in the past forty-eight hours paled in comparison to other "projects" he had undertaken for much shadier people. When that guy in New York first approached him, it was hard for Mario to take him seriously. Well dressed, well spoken, a little delicate by Mario's standards, whoever he was did not seem like the criminal type. Of course, since he found Mario, the guy must have had some connections to bad people, but, still, he did not seem at all dangerous or threatening as most of Mario's clients were.

All he asked him to do was find someone who worked for the State Department to track another person who did work for the CIA and then report back. It was not a tough job. Mario had some contacts in the department, and he went through the department directory. He identified Sanders almost immediately: a youngish government worker with a wife and a couple of kids with another on the way. He figured Sanders would need the money, so he lined up a meeting, flashed some cash, and Sanders was hooked. The fact that Mario was not planning on doing the follow-up payment wasn't even on his radar screen. That was Sanders's problem. Besides, being picked up by the feds meant that he had a good excuse not to meet with him and pay him the money.

Mario pretty much figured he would sit around for a couple of hours, the feds would try to intimidate him, and they would eventually let him go because there wasn't much of a crime here. He asked the man across from him for a cigarette.

"I'm sorry, Mr. LaSalla," the man replied. "There is no smoking in this building."

Jesus! LaSalla thought. You can't even smoke in jail.

He wasn't dying for a smoke. He had actually given it up some years before, but every once in a while he would light up just to remember what it was like. It had long stopped being a habit.

Finally, the man stopped writing and looked directly at Mario.

"Mr. LaSalla," he said. "I am Special Agent Wilson from the FBI. Two days ago, you met with a Thomas Sanders and offered him two thousand dollars to follow a contract worker for the State Department."

Mario did not move.

"You provided him with a thousand dollars up front and a disposable cell phone. You contacted him the next day on the phone and directed him to follow the contract worker to a park on the other side of town. You knew where this person was because you placed a GPS device on her motorcycle. You promised the State Department worker another thousand dollars when the assignment was complete."

Mario still did not move.

"From your record, I understand that you undertake various tasks for people on a regular basis. Many of these tasks appear to be against the law and are occasionally violent. You have been arrested on several previous occasions, the last time this past year in May. About ten years ago, you served time at a federal penitentiary for intimidating a government witness."

Hearing about his prison time made Mario wince ever so slightly. On the one hand, it was kind of a badge of courage in his line of work to have done serious time. On the other hand, it was the scariest two years of his life, and he had no desire or intention to go back.

"What I want to know, Mr. LaSalla, is who paid you to spy on our contract worker, who put you up to getting Sanders involved, and why."

Mario could not think of a reason to say anything. He just stared back at the government agent.

The agent waited quietly.

Mario was thinking that, if the agent didn't have anything on him, he wasn't acting like it, but Mario knew these guys to be good actors. They were bluffing. He remained silent.

The agent continued. "You might be thinking, Mr. LaSalla, that there was no crime committed here, or at least not a serious one. That is, not one that is up to your usual standards. However, I am here to inform you that, because the possible crimes here involve national security, you can be held under the Patriot Act indefinitely. And you will be held until you answer the questions."

Mario continued to stare. "This guy's bluffing" was the only thought in his mind.

The agent looked at his watch.

"Here is how we will proceed, Mr. LaSalla. You may talk now or you may think about it. In the latter case, you will be removed to a cell in this building for twenty-four hours. After that, if you are still unwilling to talk, you will be transferred to a federal detention facility along with other potential terrorists. You will remain there until you talk."

"I want a lawyer," Mario said.

"No," the agent replied.

"Whaddya mean 'no'?" Mario said. "I want a lawyer. I know my rights."

The agent remained calm. "You do not seem to understand the situation you are in, Mr. LaSalla. Because your behavior may be seditious and related to terrorism, you can be held indefinitely under the Patriot Act without counsel. If you do not speak, you will rot in jail."

Mario still wasn't sure what *seditious* meant, but he knew enough about the War on Terror to understand that the feds didn't screw around with it. He was beginning to think this guy was not bluffing. He did not want to spend one minute in jail.

He looked around. He had been in rooms like this before, and he seldom made any headway against the clever bastards who questioned him. His confidence began to weaken.

"Okay," he said after a few minutes. "Ask away."

33

David Blinder was wondering how his little drama in DC was going. It was a tad frivolous on his part, but he figured there was nothing to be lost and something to be gained by sending the *federales* on a wild-goose chase, trying to figure out how a low-level criminal could trip up their vaunted security measures. Spying on one of their "confidential" operatives would raise the alarm about vulnerabilities in their system. They would pour resources into trying to patch what they would perceive to be a major security breach. They would question everybody, assuming there was a mole somewhere. They would also try to prevent knowledge of the breach from going public. Blinder, on the other hand, was determined that it would do just that.

That he picked one of the lowest life forms even in the criminal underworld was of little importance to him. As a matter of fact, he thought that Mario LaSalla could, with a little spin, be made to look like a victim of the bloodless and labyrinthine federal system that would abuse him, deprive him of rights, and make him seem like a traitor and a terrorist when LaSalla had no intention of betraying his country. And if he weren't caught, the whole affair would be inexplicable to the affected departments of government, except to those charged with maintaining its security. Those few but very earnest and important people would be forever scratching their heads and looking over their shoulders.

While the real battle began, David thought. He could not stop the rush of excitement every time he thought about that moment, the moment when the guns fire, announcing the beginning of the end of this charade of a government. But that was a ways off.

David turned his attention back to Mario. He had arranged a meeting between Mario and some nobody at State, someone who in fact had never laid eyes on David Blinder. David loved these little dramas, and he believed he was the master puppeteer in the drama unfolding beneath him. He had promised the diminutive hoodlum serious money for a petty thief, and Mario gave no inkling of doing anything but jumping on the assignment. David was sure it didn't matter to Mario what David's motives were. All he had to do was take a cheap GPS and attach it to the motorcycle of a government contract worker and have her followed. Not by himself, but by this guy in the State Department who was equally clueless. David marveled at how simple it was to deceive and manipulate people. Money is power, he thought.

So in the hopeful, according to his view, event that Mario would be detained, he would have nothing to offer the federal investigators. And they would think he was lying and/or withholding information. That's what they typically thought. Then they would likely send him to one of those rendition facilities that were largely unknown to the public but beloved by sociopathic spy types who would stop at nothing to save the Union and protect it from all enemies foreign and domestic. Those are getting to be big numbers on both fronts, David thought.

It would be at that point when David would see to it that Mario's plight would come to the attention of the media. It would not only expose the draconian methods of the federal government; it would also lead to their tightening security. What they did not know was that this effort to clamp down was futile and worked precisely to Blinder's advantage, especially with Harvey Winkelstein's newfound access to the vast stores of American arms. He marveled at how the elements of his plan were coming together.

34

Harvey Winkelstein was so excited, his heart rate shot up the moment he landed at Fort Leonard Wood. He was met by Sergeant Daniel Cooper, who had been assigned by the commanding officer to accord Dr. Winkelstein every courtesy.

Harvey's first impression of his escort was that he was very stiff. He saluted Harvey when he got off the plane and extended his hand in a perfunctory greeting. Otherwise, his speech was clipped and professional. Harvey thought he was just a typical military guy with a stick up his backside.

That Sergeant Cooper's demeanor masked the antipathy he felt toward Winkelstein was invisible to the fort's distinguished visitor. Cooper was one hundred percent military, and he would not allow his personal feelings to interfere with an assignment, no matter what. It was his job to show Winkelstein around, and that is precisely what he would do.

Cooper's tepid welcome quickly became a small matter when Harvey was led into the underground cave structure of the fort. What he saw there took his breath away and elevated his blood pressure even more.

Guns: rows and rows of the latest military hardware. Guns of every shape, size, and caliber. Arms for individual soldiers and arms that required a team of men to operate. The rows of neatly arranged weapons went on and on and on. As they walked through the storage facility, fluorescent lights automatically came on, presumably controlled by motion detectors. Harvey noted the video cameras that kept watch over these stores at regular intervals along the ceiling. He listened attentively as Sergeant Cooper described the computer-based inventory system, pointing out a scannable bar code on each weapon. He noted the system of elevators that allowed for rapid deployment or storage of the weapons, also at regular intervals. It must have taken years to develop this, he thought.

There were a few items with which Harvey was unfamiliar. Mostly, these were large, futuristic weapons that he had never actually seen in person. He had read about some of them and had some appreciation of their destructive power, however, and seeing them felt like a sacred moment. He asked about one in particular. It had a long barrel, an especially shiny metal case, and a round base.

"What is that?" Harvey asked the sergeant, feigning ignorance and trying to act as nonchalant as possible.

"I'm sorry, Mr. Winkelstein," Sergeant Cooper replied. "That is classified information."

Harvey turned to look at Cooper. "Isn't this entire facility classified?" he asked with just enough of an edge in his voice to register displeasure.

"Yes, sir, it is," Cooper allowed. "But I am not authorized to provide specific information about classified systems. You may make a request directly to the commanding general."

Harvey knew he wasn't going to get any further with his escort. He let it pass. He knew what it was and what it was for. It was something that would make even a small group of armed men exponentially more dangerous.

After that short conversation, they walked for what seemed like miles through the labyrinthine cave structure. "How deep is this structure?" Harvey asked.

"A mile down and six miles in diameter as far as we know," Cooper replied. "We only explore it as we need to." He went on to describe the advantages of storing weapons in these dry caves.

Harvey pretended to listen, and in fact he did hear what Cooper said. But in his mind he was cataloging the types and range of weapons stored at this largely secret facility. On another level, he was trying to catch a glimpse of something that came up at the task force meeting he had attended the previous week. It had to do with another entrance to this cave structure. It was a highly classified bit of information, too high, evidently, for his escort to know about. Harvey could barely contain himself, but he knew in moments like this that composure was everything.

He allowed himself to wonder what David Blinder was really up to. Something big, he thought; something really, really big.

35

George Blinder was glad to know that his workaholic younger brother was so busy, but he was impatient for details. It wasn't like David to show his hand unless he had made substantial progress in whatever project he was working on, so George figured that David's admission in Vermont reflected significant movement in the direction he and his brother had discussed for decades. But that was months ago, and he had not heard another thing. He knew his brother to be a fastidious, controlling type who did not like questions. After all these years, George thought, still a stick up his ass.

But finally, the pair was to meet up after David returned to Texas from his last East Coast trip. The plan was to have dinner with their respective spouses before David and George adjourned by themselves to the expansive mahogany-lined library in which both of them worked from time to time.

"Well, David?" George began, once his ubiquitous cigar was lit and his brandy poured. "What have you got to tell me?"

David thought for a moment. He was ready, but he wanted to arrange his information in a way that made sense to his brother, and he wanted to be as clear as possible. There were a lot of players and a lot of details.

"As I mentioned last fall, George," David began, "I have been busy with the project that you and I have been talking about. Three things have happened."

David took a sip of his scotch before continuing. "The first thing is that I discovered independent groups of successful people who were thinking along the same lines, mostly for different reasons. One group is a bunch of well-placed Confederate sympathizers who never quite got over the war their great-great-great-grandparents fought in the mid-nineteenth century. They are ready to do battle.

"A second group consists of devout Christians who are just fed up with the nature of secular government and have come to the conclusion that they are powerless to influence the current government structure. They feel like outsiders even though their influence has been on the increase. They are ready to start again nation building, and they have deep contacts in key state government structures. They are also ready to make war." A slight, ironic smile crossed David's face, reflecting the low opinion he had of these people who were so important to the project under way.

"But, David," George interrupted. "I am sure these are well-meaning people, but we've known about similar groups for years, and none of them had the firepower, the will, or the resources to do much about their grandiose plans. What's different now?" He looked at his brother impatiently.

David was ready. "What's different is this. Not only do we have high-end talent making specific plans for the, um, transformation of the Union"—he took another sip of scotch—"we have an army."

"An army?" his brother said, eyes widened.

"An army," David replied simply.

"And where is this army?" David's brother asked skeptically.

"All around us, George," David replied, smiling.

The pair sat in silence in their air-conditioned, mahogany-paneled room. Even in their minds, war was serious business, easier to dream about than actually do. Beads of perspiration formed on their foreheads.

But George could see that David thought it was also the most exciting prospect they'd had in years.

"Tell me more," George said simply.

David looked at his brother. "What is different from all those fringe groups that we knew about who went out on weekends doing military drills is this: I have discovered that there is a large network of people who are offended in their souls about the intrusiveness of the federal government into their personal lives. Some of these people are religious, but some, maybe most, are just plain folk sick of being taxed to death and being told what they can and cannot do. A lot of what we would call libertarians. But they are much better organized and much better prepared to take action than ever before." He looked over at his brother. "And, George," he said. "A lot of these people are young. Fighting age."

George's interest was piqued, but he was impatient for more information. "What kind of numbers are we talking about?" he asked.

This was the moment David was waiting for. "Best guess?" he said. "Two hundred fifty, perhaps three hundred thousand."

George was speechless. "Impossible!" he finally said. "How could that many people be armed and trained and not be noticed?"

"But, George," David said. "They have been noticed. You have read about them in the newspapers. Terry Nichols was part of this group. You know, the guy who was part of the Oklahoma City bombing."

George looked at David with even greater impatience. "But those people are nuts, David. They could no more mount a real military campaign than the man in the moon."

"Crazy like foxes," retorted David. "It is true that they promote oddball ideas, but that is part of the ruse. In fact, they have been building military-like groupings for almost two decades.

"After Oklahoma City, the movement realized that small acts of terror would not get them where they wanted to be, which was free of federal control. So they had a series of planning sessions, where they decided to ramp up some of the more lunatic rhetoric while secretly preparing real people for real combat."

"And none of this came to the attention of the authorities?" George asked with more than a touch of sarcasm in his voice.

"Only the outer layers, the lunatic part," David replied calmly, ignoring his brother's impertinence. "The government has been watching the Sovereign Citizens for years but have only been able to infiltrate the outer layer." He continued: "You remember those contacts we've maintained in Washington? Well, they have come in very handy. But that's only part of the story. The real story is that the vetting process for new recruits into the second layer is very complicated and very successful at enabling them to fly beneath the radar of the US government. No one gets past the outer layer until they are subjected to a complete background check, a series of personal tests, and a grueling interrogation." He paused and looked down for a moment. "It resembles torture."

"And not a single government agent made it past that?" George said.

"Didn't even come close. Not in fifteen years," David replied.

The biggest obstacle to radical transformation of the federal government structure, besides the ambivalent affection most Americans had for it, was the US military. In recent decades, because of the more or less constant warfare abroad, the military had grown even stronger as well as more respected than ever in US history. The obstacles facing subversive groups loomed large.

But there were weaknesses in the military structure. One was that the international demands of US troops were so constant that manpower on US soil was spread thin. The job of keeping the frontline troops equipped, fed, and housed demanded an enormous chain of support that soaked up more and more resources. So some things had to suffer, and some of those things were new weapons systems that had been conceived originally for larger scale conflicts than the recent ones the military had been fighting. Those were housed in various military installations, including the underground caverns in Fort Leonard Wood in outstate Missouri.

But political discontent also played a role. As late as the last two decades of the twentieth century, secessionist groups, which had always been present in small numbers, remained small. But with terrorist acts on American soil—both the homegrown variety, such as the Oklahoma City bombing, and the jihadist type seen on 9/11—the war on terror weighed on the routine liberties of Americans, drawing them tighter and tighter. Law enforcement agencies were accorded expanded powers, and the CIA as well as the military engaged in behavior that was an abomination to many freedom-loving American citizens. The Patriot Act curtailed traditional freedoms, and people began to feel the press of Big Government. While everyone was concerned about safety, the extent of humiliation routinely demanded at airports and the unbridled rights of the police began to wear on people. Even President Obama's Health Care Reform Act, which was designed to help more people have health insurance coverage, was seen as yet another affront to American liberty. Of course, the Right took up this call, despite the fact that the bill was fashioned after one proposed by Republicans. Nonetheless, additional measures from the federal government were more and more unwelcome.

In the face of this, the underground group began to get itself better organized, adopting many of the procedures and policies government agencies used in their own work: secrecy was key, as was organizational discipline. It was in this environment that the formerly small and disparate groups thrived, growing to significant numbers largely unbeknownst to federal authorities.

eorge puffed and David gloated; both were silent for a long time. It was finally George who spoke. "So, David, you are telling me that there are several hundred thousand . . . troops . . . that are available for an actual ground war in the United States? Is that correct?" More puffing.

"That is correct, George."

"And . . . how . . . is this going to come about?"

"George, this is like a giant jigsaw puzzle. What the Confederates know they need is more than a political statement, a declaration of secession. In fact, they have that already. They know they need more than influential contacts. They have those too. But with only those things, the feds could quash them immediately. They would nationalize the state militias, withhold funds, and demand the states get back in line. They could and would call out the US Army. They could and would take it to court, probably directly to the Supreme Court, which of course would rule in its favor. So the Confederates are ready for battle; they have the political organization, but they need an army.

"Same thing with the religious side. They have no compunction about breaking up the Union and using military means to do it, but they know they need the backup that only a military force can provide." He took another sip of scotch. "Now it turns out that, even though the feds have been unable to penetrate the Sovereign

Citizens, I have been able to make a contact through an arms dealer who has been providing them with modern weapons. He did this piecemeal. He was never sure where the arms were going. He didn't care; all he wanted was to make a profit. So he's met with some of these people. He had and still has no idea how well organized or how well funded they are." He took another sip. "But he's about to find out."

George raised his left eyebrow.

"As we speak, he is visiting a top-secret military installation in Missouri where the US Army stores many of its most recent material. State-of-the-art stuff. Tons and tons and tons of it." David leaned forward. "He can get these guns to the Citizens.

"The point is this: All of these groups have come to a similar conclusion, and that is that there is no insurrection without military force. On the other hand, they also recognize that there is no need for a protracted war. What they all envision is a sudden strike at the heart of the federal bureaucracy that gives the states enough time and distance and leverage to pull out of the Union and to declare themselves sovereign entities. The overall plan involves decapitating the federal structure and grabbing key installations. For instance, taking charge of Fort Knox in Kentucky, where all the gold the US government owns is stored. Appropriating that secret military installation I told you about earlier. Things like that."

George's eyebrow did not go down.

"There are enough Citizen soldiers to keep the forts in the US tied up so that they will not be able to be used against the insurgency. There are lots of military facilities in the US, but most of them are small. The big ones are the ones that matter. Everyone is counting on this being over in a matter of days. And given proper planning, I think they are correct."

David leaned back in his chair and let out a deep breath. He was excited; he was anxious; he saw the scenario in his mind as clearly as he saw his astonished brother's frowning face sitting across from him.

George did likewise. He exhaled a long stream of air. He had not been aware that he was barely breathing during David's presentation. Skepticism, however, was written all over his face.

"I don't know, David," he said quietly. "I just don't know."

David turned to face his brother but did not speak.

George thought for a moment. "You realize," he said in a quiet, moderate tone, "that this is in essence the takeover or the defeat of an institutionalized government structure beloved by millions by a minority of groups with strong but narrow agendas."

George took another puff off his cigar. "Even assuming that victory could be achieved with proper coordination, etc. Then what? We just expect the American people to go along?"

For the first time in his adult life, a disturbing thought appeared on the horizon of David's mind. He realized that perhaps his older brother and he were not on the same page about this issue, as he had always assumed they were. A slight sensation of embarrassment connected with a tiny but growing feeling of irritation made itself felt in his mind. "What do you mean, George?" he said evenly.

George continued: "Let's say this succeeds. Somebody has to go on national television and explain what is happening, why it's a good thing, and what it means for the future of the United States. And that person will have one shot to convince a majority of Americans that breaking up the existing structure is in everyone's long-term interest. This is a very, very tall order."

David did not respond right away. In his mind, he was weighing the possibility that the years he and George had spent in conversation about this topic were a pastime for his brother, not a serious possibility. A game of sorts. It was never an idle pastime for David.

"You may be construing the possibilities too narrowly," David said calmly. "The fact is that there are many competing interests out there, including the groups I've been talking about and ours. And there is a range of outcomes. The primary goal here is not so much to destroy the United States as it is to rethink the structure we have. There is no other way to do this short of military action. The way the government is set up, it is one hundred percent self-perpetuating; it cannot be rescinded. At the very least, an insurrection will force a constitutional convention. At best, it will balkanize the American land mass, providing enormous opportunity for growth and competition. It will turn the continental United States into something like what Germany was prior to Bismarck, an area of the world that shares similar values but which consists of sovereign states rather than subservient provinces, which is what they are now. It will still be a fiercely proud and productive place, just without the drain of a federal superstructure."

David could hear himself lecturing his brother. It was galling, since they had been through all this before. There was no doubt that George had been exposed to the rationale for David's action. He could not shake the feeling that George was capable of betraying him.

ax was frustrated. Mario LaSalla turned out to be a complete dead end. The petty thief did not know the man who hired him, he did not know for whom that man worked, and he did not know why he was hired to do what he did. This was the outcome of hours of interrogation.

He did know that the GPS device placed on Marie's motorcycle was purchased in New York and that Mario had met his contact there, but narrowing down the man who actually purchased the device was a near impossibility.

He called Marie and shared this disappointing news with her. She listened quietly.

"None of this makes much sense, Max," she finally said. "Unless, of course, that was precisely the point."

"What do you mean, Marie?" Max asked.

"This whole thing feels amateurish on the one hand and highly professional on the other. Maybe somebody was just trying to throw us off, to mess with us." She paused for a moment. "It's happened before. But whoever it was did a very thorough job."

Max was torn. Marie was right: it seemed like an almost childish prank, but it was carefully executed. Still, Marie had a point. Sometimes the bad guys just can't help throwing a monkey wrench into the works just to see what happens, to throw the cops off balance, or to create a diversion, a cover.

"Okay, Marie," Max said. "Back to the beginning. Say it's a cover for another operation. We have no data that anything is happening now. There is no major movement of people—"

"Except for those guys who disappeared, Max," Marie said, interrupting him. "Have you forgotten?"

In fact, that obvious and important fact had somehow slipped from Max's normally steel-trap mind. He blushed on his end of the phone. The stress must be getting to me, he thought. Marie sensed that this was precisely what had happened.

"Don't sweat it, Max," she said softly. "It's been an intense few days."

But Max did not know how not to sweat stuff. "We need a plan," he said icily. "And we need one soon."

"I'm all ears, Max," she said, knowing that any further reassurance was wasted.

Max hesitated for just a moment. "We need to find those men," he said.

Marie heard the determination in his voice.

"How, Max?" she said. The preliminary investigation had turned up no leads.

"I'll get back to you, Marie," Max said. And he hung up.

38

Cherie Keenan was more than just uneasy. Daniel had not spoken of revolution in several days. Still, he was withdrawn and irritable, and, truth be told, so was she. It was not like either of them to act like this with each other. It was certainly not like Daniel to play his life so close to the vest, she thought. But then again, she was beginning to understand that maybe Daniel Keenan was not exactly the man she knew. He obviously did keep secrets. Perhaps he kept them very well.

About a week after their initial conversation, Cherie couldn't stand it any longer. She was in her usual spot reading, the same spot she was in when Daniel, who was sitting in his favorite spot, first broached the topic. Daniel was in his chair, also reading. The kids were in bed. This time it was her turn to start.

"Daniel," she said quietly. "I want to get back to what we were talking about last week. About the . . . the . . . revolution, as you called it."

Daniel looked at his lovely wife. "What about it, Cherie?" he said with more insouciance than Cherie thought appropriate.

"I want to know exactly what you are planning," she said flatly.

Daniel took a deep breath. He knew what he was planning; everyone in their group knew. But the time had not come to disclose this to spouses. It had been agreed among the group that the time wasn't right yet.

"I can't say right now, Cherie," he said quietly. He hated keeping information from his wife, but he was pledged to a higher truth. "I promise I will tell you as soon as I know for sure and as soon as the time is right."

"Are you saying that you don't know for sure?" Cherie asked.

Daniel's face flushed a little. "No, that's not what I'm saying. I am saying that I can't tell you yet."

Cherie looked at him as if he were someone else. "What?" she spat out.

"I just can't tell you now," Daniel said in a louder voice. "I will tell you when I can."

"You *will* tell me now," Cherie said just as loudly. "I will not be silent until you do. I will hound you and hound you until you do. And if you don't talk, I will leave you until you do." There was fire in her eyes. Daniel was sure he had never seen his wife like this before. She had never in their entire life together threatened to leave him. This took things to a new and uncomfortable level. He was a little frightened, but he couldn't act contrary to the will of the group. He thought it best to man up.

"You are my wife," he said firmly. "You will obey me."

"You are my husband," she retorted, "and you will not deceive me."

And there you have it, Daniel thought. That is the problem.

So he made a decision: he would tell her, but he would swear her to secrecy first.

Daniel closed his eyes for a moment. He got up and moved over to the couch where Cherie was sitting, sitting right next to her and talking her hand. "I am sorry, Cherie," he said. "I do not mean to deceive you. It's just that, as a group, we decided to act in unison and according to the plan that is being developed." He looked deep into her eyes. "I will tell you, but you must promise me you will share what I am about to tell you with no one."

Cherie was wishing they had just continued escalating a shouting match rather than suffer this sickening feeling in the face of Daniel's lugubrious behavior. This turned her stomach. She nodded.

Daniel continued. "There is a plan among our group to be part of a larger movement that has broken out across the country," he began. "There are apparently several large organizations that, for different reasons, have decided that the current government structure has to go." He looked at his wife askance. "Our reasons are religious, of course," he said. "You know how this secular government has turned against religion, how it has dethroned Christianity from the center of American life, how it has allowed abortion and gay marriage and contraception. . . . There is no end to the indignities perpetrated upon Christian believers by the forces of secular government." He paused a moment. "State governments don't do this, or at least not so much, but the federal government is committed to it. And the federal government insists that all states follow its rules." He looked at his wife. "It's not right, Cherie. It's just not right."

Cherie was silent.

In the back of his mind, Daniel was wondering if this was a wise course, sharing the details of their motives and their plan with his wife prematurely. He thought that it probably wasn't, but he was torn. And he was a little frightened of the strength shown by his normally long-suffering wife and by her threat to leave.

"So a while back, we learned that these other groups are forming leadership structures and developing a militia to take up our cause and the causes of other, like-minded groups. We are planning to revolt against the federal government. And we will do it by force. We have exhausted all other means."

Cherie Kennan could not have been more dumbfounded if Daniel had changed shape right in front of her, which, as she thought about it, fairly described what was happening. Who is this man? she wondered. She could not believe what she was hearing, and she was pretty sure Daniel had lost his mind. But she did not say anything. She waited.

"So the plan is simple: just prior to the beginning of hostilities, we are going to go 'off the grid': we are going to prepare by closing our bank accounts and our Internet accounts. We will pay off all our bills and make sure our money is safe in a foreign currency. We will go to a place that has been prepared that cannot be spotted from the air and that can't be traced by any electronic means. We will wait there until the hostilities cease, and then we will return to help build the new government structure." He sighed. "This is so well planned, we do not expect hostilities to last more than a week."

Cherie finally spoke. "And when will this happen?" she asked.

"Soon," Daniel replied.

Cherie wasn't quite sure where to begin. "And you assume that I and the children will go along with this without complaint?"

"Yes," Daniel said, looking away.

"And you think I will approve of this just because you do?"

"Yes," Daniel said, not turning his head.

"And you—all of you—think that you will get away with overturning the government of the United States of America in a week?"

"Yes," Daniel said.

Cherie was silent.

"Daniel Keenan," she finally said softly. "You are out of your mind."

Daniel didn't say anything. He did turn his head to look at his wife. This was not how he had envisioned the conversation going. He disregarded what she actually said: he knew he wasn't out of his mind. If anything, he felt more alive these past months than he had in years. He was filled with enthusiasm for the plan, and that enthusiasm was shared by other successful men he knew. So he felt he was on pretty solid ground.

He thought maybe he just hadn't explained it well enough to his wife. So he began again: "Cherie, I know this is a lot to swallow all at once. In fact, our group came to this conclusion gradually over time. You have only had a few days to think about this. Give it time. I think when you think it through you will understand just how essential this is for us and for our children."

"Our children!" Cherie exclaimed. "You are laying this cocka-mamie scheme at the feet of the welfare of our children? You think that engaging in violent acts of treason is good for the family? You are truly, truly off your rocker."

It wasn't ordinarily in Cherie's nature to be explosively angry, but she didn't know what else to do. It was a way of trying to reach Daniel before he actually acted on this lunatic idea.

Daniel was quiet for a moment. "Well," he said at length. "Let's just give it some time." He turned to her with a dark expression on his face, something that Cherie had never quite encountered before. "And don't forget your promise," he said in a voice she had never before heard.

Cherie was silent.

39

No more was said about the issue that evening. The next morning, which was Saturday, the family went about their routine chores: They made a grocery list and went shopping. They finalized some plans with their neighbors to get together for dinner that evening. The kids did their appointed chores, although their young ages meant that they didn't do much. It was mostly for discipline reasons: to instill in them a sense of personal responsibility.

But beneath the surface, Cherie was thinking that she needed a plan. She was starting to understand that Daniel was serious about this ridiculous project and that he might be beyond convincing otherwise. She had the welfare of herself and her children to attend to, and she had no intention of going off any grid or going to hide out somewhere like some idiotic religious sect. She was going to care for her children and do right by them, no matter what Daniel Keenan, the man she thought she knew, did or thought. She just couldn't do it with his knowledge. Suddenly, she was no longer sure she could trust him.

It also occurred to her that a bunch of men planning this kind of thing might have taken steps to coerce their reluctant spouses to go along or might get violent with them if they did not. After all, they are, despite their Christian beliefs, advocating violence in the public square. She couldn't imagine that all these men thought all their wives would go sheepishly along with a crazy plot and abandon their lives for a week, a year, or even five minutes. But in these brief conversations with Daniel, she felt his determination, his commitment, and his desire to follow through with the plan no matter what she or anyone else thought. I suppose that's how revolutionaries think, she mused silently.

She was not a revolutionary. She was a mother, and the welfare and safety of her children were utmost in her mind. As was her own.

40

Samantha Stranger had a lot of information about Abner Bellamy. She did the investigation for Blinder; she knew him as well as anyone. But what was happening with Marie commanded her attention and focused her mind. She was especially troubled by the disappearance of twenty prominent individuals and by the fact that someone was messing with her good friend. As she learned more about what Marie and Max knew, her suspicion deepened. Something big was afoot.

She tried to think of how she could help Marie, Max, and the country counter what she was beginning to believe to be a burgeoning and immediate threat. To that end, she went into the small study in her apartment and started putting together intel she had gathered from any source she had.

Most of her information came from her work with Blinder. She had a detailed history for Abner Bellamy, and she also had information on the members of his group. But he was only the most recent of her assignments from Blinder. She had also done other projects for him, and she began to assemble and organize all the data at one time.

She began to detect a pattern. Blinder had her dig up information on a variety of characters, some prominent and some shadowy. Usually, there were organized groups involved. Many of these groups were disaffected Americans who liked to indulge revenge fantasies; most of these were to Samantha's mind grandiose dreams born of some real or perceived grievance or frustration or God-knows-what.

After compiling data on all her Blinder projects, she made a graph on her large computer screen with all the characters she could think of. In addition to Bellamy, there were members of another group, including Daniel Keenan and his wife, Cherie, Adam Wilson, Aloysius Smitherin, and Gregory Manfield. She hovered over the names of Madeline Schumacher, with whom she'd had some casual contact, and wondered if there were some connection between her and that guy named LaSalla who was arrested. She also paused as she considered the name of Judith Mayfield, who, by all accounts, was a bright, upstanding medical professional with a profound love of the South. Daniel Cooper was another name to which she kept returning.

And then she came to Harvey Winkelstein. She knew about his involvement with the Sovereign Citizens movement. She was one of the few outsiders who had an inkling that the Citizens, as they called themselves, were more than their strident and fanatical cover suggested. They were deadly serious; they were well trained; and they were well armed. She knew Winkelstein was their chief supplier of arms, and she knew Winkelstein did gun running around the globe. Most of this was outright illegal, but he was skilled at covering his tracks, at least as far as law enforcement was concerned.

Then she added all the names that Marie had given her in their recent conversation. She did not know anything about the Missouri group before she heard about them from Marie. This got her attention: in the clandestine world, shadowy groups tend to share a common experience and, odd as it may seem, there is a flow of information that gets around within that world, even if most of it never reaches the general public. Like attracts like: paranoids find each other even though, or perhaps because, they are suspicious.

But in the instances of the Citizens and the Missouri group, the information was particularly well controlled.

She wondered if Blinder had any connection with the Missouri group. She scanned the list of names. The last meeting was hosted by Daniel Keenan, a professor at Rolla School of Mines, a successful, highly religious man who did consulting worldwide. He could easily have shown up on Blinder's radar screen or even Winkelstein's. Given the radical religious orientation of that group, she decided to do some checking. That meant checking cell phone records for calls between him and Blinder. It took her less than twenty minutes to determine that Keenan had in fact been in contact with her sometime employer.

Samantha sat back in her chair and tried to get some perspective. If Blinder was in contact with Bellamy and with Keenan and with Winkelstein and through him with the Sovereign Citizens, it was entirely possible that he was orchestrating whatever action was unfolding. Or, if not orchestrating it, at least playing a major role. Knowing Blinder, however, she figured he was doing the directing. Controlling bastard, she thought. But what was the exact nature of this whole enterprise? she wondered. What was the goal, the endgame? Did he really think that he could get these disparate groups of fanatics to coordinate an assault on the federal government? Were all these groups capable of coalescing to pose one coherent and coordinated threat to the federal superstructure under Blinder's direction? This seemed like sheer lunacy.

Samantha knew Blinder to be a conniving, manipulative, and cynical man who believed he could do whatever he wanted with whomever he wanted. He had access to vast amounts of cash, and his grandiosity, in her experience of him, knew no limits. But what was he really after? Why would he do this? Why would he risk his vast wealth and solid standing to take on something so extreme, the outcome of which was dubious at best? Why would he destroy the system under which he thrived?

A lot of questions and no sure answers, Samantha thought. One answer floated across the mental landscape, however. It did not explain everything, but it was not something to be ignored either. The likelihood is strong, she thought, that whatever motivated David and George Blinder was the same thing that has motivated men and women throughout history: power. They were engaging in dangerous enterprises because they thought they could, and they believed their plans would succeed.

Was Blinder grandiose enough to believe he could control events? No question.

Did Blinder have something to gain by tearing down the national government? That was something Samantha couldn't discern. Men have taken risky actions before in the hope of some kind of reward that might not be readily visible to others.

Samantha pushed back her chair from her desk and stood up and stretched. It was getting late; she was tired. But she couldn't pull her mind away from the material she was working on. It was too dangerous, too in-process, and too scary. She forced herself to walk into the bathroom to get ready for bed. But her mind could not stop working.

As she went through her nightly ritual, Samantha realized that Harvey Winkelstein was even now doing some work for David. While David Blinder was an overridingly careful man, Harvey was only as careful as he thought he needed to be. So he had shell companies and encrypted e-mail accounts and the usual safeguards that most people think protect one from scrutiny online and off, but he also suffered from a vanity that clouded his judgment and a sense of invulnerability that had grown in the years he had been selling arms illegally without getting caught. He got sloppier over time.

Samantha walked into her bedroom and stripped off her clothes. She threw herself on the bed and turned off the lamp on the nightstand. She lay staring at the ceiling.

She was thinking about Marie. When Marie told her about the happenings at the State Department—both the disappearance of a group of prominent people and her finding herself under surveillance—her antennae and her anxiety level shot up. This situation was coming to a head much sooner than she thought. She felt a sense of urgency that was all the more vivid because of the amount of information she had at her disposal. Systemizing it this evening made events seem to ramp up even more. The question now was how to best use this information and how to proceed: whom to tell, what to do, whom to mobilize? She was grateful to have Marie to hash this out with. She would contact her first thing in the morning.

But sleep was elusive for Samantha on this night. She realized that at first she thought that David Blinder was just playing rich-guy games with people, getting vulnerable people like Bellamy riled up by playing to their grandiose fantasies, probably in the hope of using him in some other kind of money-making scheme. But she realized over the past six months that this was more than a game to him. David Blinder, and presumably his brother George, were serious, and their serious plans were about to be implemented. These other groups that were coming together: they were also serious. She thought about the chaos these plans would engender across the nation. She felt bile rise in her throat at the wanton disregard for the centuries-old institutions of the United States of America. She thought of the US contribution to the world: first to be of help in a crisis; first to express outrage at violence; dogged in the pursuit of freedom at home and abroad. She found it hard to believe that even outliers such as the people she was investigating could work to bring that structure down for their own petty reasons.

Sleep was nowhere close, so she sat up in bed and turned the light on. She gave herself over to the process she could not derail, not even for rest and recuperation. She kept thinking.

She knew by the amounts of munitions Winkelstein supplied the Sovereign Citizens that their numbers were significant. He sold them thousands of small arms, rifles, and other handheld firearms and offensive and defensive weapons: grenades, rocket launchers, mortars. And he had been doing this for a number of years. Samantha imagined that they were not just a loose, weekend-only collection of disgruntled, past-their-prime, would-be play soldiers. And she had recently begun collecting data to prove it.

She wondered how the Sovereign Citizens were paying for all this. Weapons dealers such as Winkelstein were not known for charitable deals: they were in it for the money because lots of money was to be had. And that money had to come from somewhere.

Tracing Winkelstein's dealings, she found that the delivery sites for the weapons purchased were spread among three separate locations, all remote. One was in Wyoming, one in Montana, and one in North Dakota—in short, the most desolate parts of the continental United States, where significant numbers of weapons and people could easily be sequestered without drawing undue attention.

The Sovereign Citizens were smart. They took delivery of their weapons at remote spots, which were probably not exactly where their other facilities were located. Money was transferred electronically, of course, as soon as the delivery shipment was verified. The route of the money was easy for Samantha to follow. The path of the weapons, however, was more difficult. The Citizens used their own trucks, they inspected every weapon, and they did not depart until whoever delivered their shipment did. No one knew where they went from there. Samantha understood that someone could find out, but that would require boots on the ground and some additional technology and more information than anyone but she had.

Suddenly, Samantha jumped out of bed. Winkelstein was going to Missouri! He may be there now. She couldn't stop herself: she ran into her study and rebooted her computer. She scanned the information she had on Winkelstein's schedule. Yesterday he was scheduled to visit Fort Leonard Wood in Missouri.

She couldn't wait until tomorrow. She decided she needed to talk to Marie about this now. She dialed her number and went through the coded sequence. Marie picked up on the first available ring.

"Marie," said Samantha. "I've been working on this situation all day. I think events are accelerating. Winkelstein's at a military facility in Missouri."

Marie was asleep when Sam called, so it was taking her some time to take in what she was saying. "Okay," she finally said. "What do you think that means?"

"I don't know what it means, Marie. What I know is that Winkelstein is an arms dealer, he's at a large US Army base where presumably there are a lot of weapons, and he is in Missouri, where that meeting you told me about took place. I can also link him to Blinder, to another crackpot preacher/revolutionary, and to a group called the Sovereign Citizens, which he has worked for a lot in the past." She paused a moment. "I think something big is going down. And soon."

Marie trusted Samantha; that wasn't the problem. She just didn't know what to do with the information at 1:00 on a Tuesday morning. "I'm coming over," she said.

41

Samantha placed a very high value on her relationship with Marie LeBrun, and she was relieved when she heard her say she was on her way over. She got dressed and put on a pot of coffee. Marie arrived precisely at 2:00 a.m.

Sam could hardly wait until the coffee was done. She started talking as soon as the door closed behind Marie. "I've been tracking illegal arm sales and shipments by a guy named Harvey Winkelstein, who is, of all things, a physics professor at NYU. I have all the data about number of weapons—and they are huge—and amounts paid. I'm able to track the money easily enough. At least through Winkelstein's books. But when I follow the guns themselves, all I've been able to come up with are some exchange sites in several remote areas of the country, all of which are out West in sparsely populated states.

"I have a hunch that the Sovereign Citizens are going to provide the firepower," she continued, "and the muscle for a couple of other groups who are planning to rebel against the federal government. And I think the guy who is bringing them all together is David Blinder." She paused for a moment. "And I have no proof, but it would not surprise me if Blinder were footing the bill for all this equipment."

Simultaneously, Marie and Samantha sat down on the couch to continue the conversation.

"Marie, this is serious, and I think it's imminent. I have felt that ever since you told me about the disappearance of those guys who met in the Midwest. And I think having you followed was just another way to throw the government off track. I have a hunch that the plan, whatever it is, is in play."

Marie nodded. While this was news to her, it was not far from her own fears.

Sam continued: "There's been some chatter in the e-mails I've been tracking, including Winkelstein's. I think a new shipment is being arranged, a large one. Delivery is set for this coming weekend. I have done what I can do from here. I need to get on the ground to see what is happening and to track these guys. Even better, we could use some aerial surveillance with night vision capabilities. I need your help." She paused a moment. "I may need Max's help as well."

Marie nodded.

aniel Cooper was relieved when Dr. Winkelstein left. He could not believe that this was the guy his compatriots in the Sovereign Citizens relied upon to procure weapons. He had spent the better part of the week fretting about Winkelstein's arrival. He wasn't sure the way they got him into the secret weapons warehouse was legitimate. He did check it out, but he was by nature a paranoid and superstitious man, something that was easy to mask behind a strong military persona.

He knew it was his job to link Winkelstein to the abundance of weapons stored at the Fort Leonard Wood facility. But Winkelstein the man left a bad taste in his mouth: rude, presumptuous, uncouth; this was how Cooper experienced Harvey Winkelstein. It was obviously all about money for him. It was definitely not about freedom or value or religion or any of the things that Sergeant Cooper prized.

So when Winkelstein left and Cooper got off duty, he got into his car and drove toward St. Louis. Outside the city, he was to meet with his contact in the Citizens movement, a man by the name of Winslow Parker.

They met at a small truck stop just south of the city. Meeting in person was the sole way Parker and Cooper communicated. Old-fashioned getting together was something that the feds were not so likely to track unless there were specific suspicions. It had other advantages as well: you could check things out, ask questions, and explore alternatives more collaboratively, all without being tracked online or by satellite or all the other myriad ways the federal government had to snoop into your affairs. Cooper thought it was a simple but brilliant solution to the problem of being discovered. It gave a sense of freedom and solidarity with the other members of Sovereign Citizens who were in this project with him.

"How'd it go?" Parker asked.

Cooper looked at him straight in the eye. "I don't like the man," he said simply.

Parker chuckled. "You've got company, Daniel," he said. "As far as I can tell, nobody likes this guy."

Cooper gave Parker a dark look, as if to say, Then why work with him?

Parker, anticipating the unspoken question, responded. "He's the best at what he does, Daniel. He is a man utterly without scruples. And his motivation is simple: all he really wants is money."

Cooper scowled. As far as he was concerned, this was one of the lowest forms of life, no better than a scavenging rat or some other disease-ridden creature. He felt disgust deep in the pit of his stomach.

Parker continued. "All we really need at this point are the big guns. We have plenty of small arms, thanks to Dr. Winkelstein's efforts over the past few years. Even the most advanced field rifles. What we need now is massive firepower, the MOABs and the M230 Chain Gun. I think that will complete the inventory we need. And you have access to those weapons."

Indeed he did. Within the purview of Sergeant Daniel Cooper's responsibilities was the entire underground munitions depot at Fort Leonard Wood that was so prized by the military. He had lied to Winkelstein when he said he didn't know what was beyond the section the professor toured. He knew every inch of that cave structure, including access points that were unknown even to his military superiors. Cooper guarded this information very, very closely. And even though Parker seemed to think that Winkelstein had a place in their strategy, he didn't see it.

"Why do we need Winkelstein?" he asked after a while.

Parker sighed. "For all his flaws as a human being, Harvey Winkelstein has the best contacts and means to secure and transport weapons in large quantities. He has the trucks and equipment to transfer this stuff anywhere. He has a worldwide network; he has provided arms across the globe to outfits that many people haven't even heard of. And he has done it without being detected. All of his shipments to us have been executed flawlessly." He looked Cooper in the eye. "We need him, Daniel," he said softly, knowing that Cooper did not like going against his instincts.

Cooper was quiet for a while. Then he nodded. "When?" he said.

Parker took a deep breath and let it out slowly. "A week from today."

Cooper looked at Parker and nodded. "I'll be ready," he said quietly.

s Cooper drove back to base, he thought of the plans he and his comrades had made, plans that were now coming to fruition. He had trained a small but elite cadre of six soldiers—US Army soldiers who were also, unbeknownst to anyone but he and the six men, Citizen soldiers—to enter the underground cavern and load select heavy weapons into containers, the same ones used by the US Army to transport arms around the world. These could be stacked on to ships or onto huge cargo planes or even on trains. They were sturdy but flexible in their applications and easy to pack and easy to transport. And since the containers and transport vehicles used by his select team would be the ones that the US military actually uses, no casual observer would notice. It would happen in broad daylight.

Parker had the execution planned down to the smallest detail. He had prepared the paperwork designed to safely transfer munitions and ordnance from base to base—paperwork that was intended to prevent just this type of theft or misappropriation—and he had been over it numerous times. He believed in attention to detail, and this was the most attentive he had been in his entire life. It still galled him that, at some point, Harvey Winkelstein had to take possession of the weapons; it galled him even more that the loutish Winkelstein would profit from this project. But his superiors in the Citizens insisted that this was the only way to safeguard the anonymity of the troops who were doing the loading. In effect, the munitions would simply vanish. The soldiers would load the weapons, drive away from the facility, and transfer them to Winkelstein's waiting vehicles miles away in the sparsely populated Missouri Bootheel. They would then return to their US Army base, and no one would notice—not for months, maybe not for years—that several tons of heavy weapons had disappeared. Even Cooper had to admit it was an elegant scheme.

But he was not privy to the final destination of this shipment. One of the ways the Citizens managed to escape detection was that they were scrupulous about limiting information to a need-to-know basis. And Cooper recognized that he did not need to know where the munitions were going. All he needed to know was how to extract them from their putatively impenetrable underground storage place.

All of this made him smile.

arie called Max, and she and Max and Samantha met later that same day. They deliberately met in a safe house they had used before; each of them took great pains to make sure they were not being followed.

Max knew Samantha, but he had not seen her in a long time. He knew she and Marie were very close; in fact, they had both worked for him from time to time. Samantha greeted Max warmly; he did likewise.

Marie began. "Max," she said. "Sam and I have been talking and pooling our information. I think she can expand our information base about what's going on." She turned to Samantha and nodded.

Samantha proceeded to bring Max up to date on the information she had assembled yesterday. Max listened intently, his brow getting more deeply furrowed as he did so.

When Samantha finished, the three were quiet. Then Marie said, "We think it's a priority to stop those weapons from being delivered."

Max nodded. "Clearly," he said softly.

Max thought for a while. Then he turned to Samantha. "What do you need from me, Samantha?" he said simply.

Sam did not hesitate: "I need rapid stealth transportation to southern Missouri. I need night vision equipment, quiet but fast ground transportation—a motorcycle or something similar. I need state-of-the-art GPS tags that can be affixed to large vehicles without being detected, and I need the Echelon satellite to start tracking as soon as I get these onto the vehicles." She thought for a moment. "I'll also need high-res compact camera and video equipment. I think that should do it."

Max thought for a moment. "We could send in Special Forces to do this," he said.

Both Marie and Samantha shook their head. "Not without broadcasting to all these groups that we are onto them, Max," Marie said, reflecting what both women thought.

"Good point," said Max. "But I'll need a satellite uplink throughout the entire operation." He looked at Samantha. "Will you need guns?"

Samantha shook her head. "I can handle that part," she said simply.

"We're both going, Max," Marie said. "This is not a one-person job."

"Okay," Max said. "I'll make this happen." He paused for a moment. "What else?"

"We need to put very careful surveillance on Winkelstein, on Abner Bellamy, and on the Blinder brothers," Samantha said. "And we need to find those men who disappeared. I don't think it will be a problem on the first two guys, but the Blinders are nuts about security, so that's going to be more of a challenge."

"What do you suggest?" Max asked.

Marie and Samantha both considered this question. "Hard to say, Max," Marie finally answered. "David Blinder has placed himself in a veritable cocoon of protective countersurveillance. We are going to have to give this some serious thought and proceed very carefully."

"We can certainly track their electronic communication," Max offered.

"Not so easily as you would think," Samantha said. "The Blinders sweep for bugs and unusual traffic frequently and randomly throughout the day and night. David Blinder has an entire staff devoted to electronic security."

Max let out a low whistle. "We need to find a way in," he said, as if he were thinking aloud. "I agree: we'll give this some more thought. I'll put a team on it. Anything else I should know about security, Sam?" Max asked.

"Just one minor thing. I have never met George Blinder, but David, who is the one who is more actively engaged in all this crap, is very sensitive about being touched. Almost paranoid; certainly OCD. He extends that sensitivity to everyone around him. It is rare for anyone to get physically closer to him than across a table."

Max nodded. "Thanks, Sam," he said.

"I think we can handle the surveillance on Bellamy and Winkelstein," he said, still thinking out loud. "And probably even Blinder. We have state-of-the-art technology at our disposal. In fact, we're especially good when the bad guys are looking for leaks. Remember Stuxnet? That's child's play next to what we've got now. We won't be noticed, but we'll be doubly careful just in case."

Samantha shrugged and looked at Marie. "Okay," she said. She knew Max would not lie or misrepresent his office's capabilities. She just hoped he wasn't being overly confident.

"One more thing," Marie said. "I think we should keep an especially close eye on that facility in Missouri, Fort Leonard Wood. If Winkelstein was there, it was for a reason, and I imagine it had to do with his procuring some of the toys they have there. In fact, I think that the upcoming transfer may be related. It's possible they have a man inside."

Max nodded. "Got it," he said. In fact, he had already had a conversation about that with his senior military consultant before leaving the office. The Army didn't want those weapons misappropriated any more than he did.

"What about those men who disappeared?" Marie asked. It seemed like a long time ago that Max told her about these people, even though it had only been a few days.

"We've ramped up our efforts to locate them," Max replied. "We may have gotten a lead. One of their wives evidently did not go. She stayed behind with her children. It's not clear yet where she's staying, but she has been in contact with authorities in Rolla. We have a team on the way to talk with her now."

The three nodded silently.

Marie felt for Max. He was not only a colleague; she regarded him as a friend. And she knew, as a friend, the toll this whole subversive stuff was taking on him. He looked haggard. "Take care of yourself, Max," she said, squeezing his hand. "We'll get to the bottom of this."

Max squeezed back, but inside his head, he was thinking that just getting to the bottom of this situation may not happen soon enough.

45

herie Keenan could not believe her husband would actually go through with the lunatic plan he had told her about, and when he came home to inform her that they would all be leaving the next day, she was dumbfounded, even though she had been thinking about little else for days. She felt lost, tired, angry, and pretty much alone. She also felt as if she were living with the enemy.

"What do you mean, tomorrow is the day?" she asked her increasingly uptight husband.

"I mean, tomorrow is the day we disappear, the day we go off the grid," Daniel replied.

Cherie looked at him through narrowly slit eyes. "So what about your job, your consulting, your . . . your life?" Cherie said. She was having a hard time looking at her husband.

Daniel Keenan was getting more and more exasperated. "We will return to our life when it is appropriate and safe to do so," he intoned.

Cherie stared at him for a long moment. She was sure she did not know this man, even though she had been married to him for almost fifteen years.

"You know I have no intention of going anywhere," she said softly.

Daniel had been preparing for this conversation. He had even discussed it with some of his colleagues. He spoke slowly, in a low growl. He did not look at her. "If you do not go, Cherie, you will never see your children again."

Cherie walked in front of her husband's gaze, cocked her head back, and looked straight into Daniel's eyes. "And exactly what do you mean by that?" she said.

"I mean, I will take the children with me, and, when this is over, I will make sure I have sole custody."

Cherie had expected resistance and some kind of threat, but she really hadn't counted on Daniel being quite so unfeeling or so unscrupulous. She thought maybe he or his goons, as she came to think of them, would try to kidnap her or wrap her up in a carpet or have some other goofy, muscle-bound way of getting her to do what they wanted her to do. Her thinking seemed clear to her, but she wasn't sure she could vouch for it against any objective measure.

She believed that Daniel was clearly beyond reason, and she felt she had no alternative but to fight evil with evil and to do so immediately, before this situation got even further out of hand. She searched her mind for an alternative: something to say, something to do. That's when her eyes fell on the large chef's knife in the wooden block on the kitchen counter, where the pair was having this conversation. Half on impulse and half to get his attention, she grabbed a knife from the wooden block. As she did so, Daniel took a step toward her. Without thinking, she lashed out at him and cut a deep gouge in his right arm.

"Ouch!" screamed her surprised, shocked, and now-injured husband. "What are you doing?"

Cherie did not relent. She shoved Daniel back with both hands, and he fell onto a nearby chair. She wasn't a large woman, but she was possessed of righteousness, something she did not often feel. She felt strong and clear and purposeful. She would not allow herself to be pushed around by this man who had obviously lost his mind.

Cherie hovered over Daniel and put the knife to his throat. "If you ever again threaten me with the loss of my children or in any other way, you will not live to see another day." She looked at him with nothing but steely resolve. "You might not see tomorrow anyway," she said with acid in her voice.

Daniel could feel the cold steel of the sharp chef's knife against the skin of his neck and against his windpipe. He also heard a voice coming from Cherie that he had never heard before. He was one hundred percent sure she was not bluffing. He was sweating. He didn't know what to say. He had promised his group that Cherie would comply with their request; now she had gotten the jump on him.

"Get out of my house," Cherie said. She put some pressure on the blade. She stared down at him for a few moments.

Then she moved away from Daniel, but she did not lower the knife. "Now," she said.

Daniel was scared. He had no doubt in his mind at that moment that his beloved wife would kill him rather than comply with his request. Bile and rage and fear and humiliation all rose inside his gut. He took a step toward Cherie, who raised the knife and an eyebrow in response. Daniel took a deep breath. His arm hurt like hell; it was bleeding like crazy. He didn't know what to do. He glared at Cherie and then turned and stumbled out the door.

Cherie waited a few minutes until she heard Daniel's car leave the driveway. Then she went to look out the front door.

He was gone.

She started to shake. She was not normally a violent person. She had no idea she was so angry as she was. She locked the front door and staggered back to the kitchen, where she threw the knife onto the counter and leaned against the kitchen sink and threw up. She was too anxious to cry, too enraged to feel much of anything else.

She did not know what Daniel Keenan was up to; she just knew she had to get out of this house with her children, her sanity, and what was left of her dignity intact.

And in order to do that, she had to call the police.

46

Samantha and Marie went back to Sam's apartment to continue working. Samantha started following Internet and phone traffic emanating from Fort Leonard Wood and the surrounding counties. She hacked into Winkelstein's computer and smartphone. Marie started listing the gear they would need for a trip to the Midwest.

After a couple of hours, Samantha leaned back in her chair. "I think this is it," she said, pointing to her computer screen. Marie looked and saw an official US Army disbursement form describing a shipment of arms from Fort Leonard Wood to Fort Leavenworth in Kansas. It was signed by a Sergeant Daniel Cooper, and it listed lots of heavy weapons, the kinds that require more than one person to carry and manage. The transfer day was Friday. Today was Wednesday.

"Doesn't give us much time," Marie noted.

"Enough," Samantha replied.

"It will take me a couple hours to round up the material on my list," Marie said. "I'll check with Max about transport and the other things you requested."

Sam nodded. As enraged as she was about what they were learning, this kind of adventure thrilled her. She was born to be a field operative. And Marie was the perfect partner for this kind of work.

Marie sensed Sam's excitement. She turned and looked her directly in the eyes. "Let's define our mission," she said simply. "We are going to see if those weapons that are scheduled to depart Fort Leonard Wood on Friday are going to fall into Winkelstein's hands. And from there to the Sovereign Citizens. If they do, we are to track them to their final destination. Is that your understanding?"

Samantha thought for a moment. "Yes, that is our task. But it might be helpful if we could somehow redirect those weapons elsewhere, especially away from the Citizens; maybe back to Fort Leonard Wood." She was silent for a few moments. "It's a big shipment, and it's hard to say how much the actual soldiers who are carrying out the delivery know about what's happening. We don't want any good guys—and by this I mean US Army regulars—getting hurt."

Marie looked at Sam with a mixture of shock and delight. "I wish you didn't get so excited about the prospect of a firefight," she said, only slightly overstating her sentiment. "I don't want anyone to get hurt. Especially us."

Samantha blushed ever so slightly at her glee being exposed. "You know as well as I do, Marie, that these 'surveillance' trips often go in unexpected directions. I am not spoiling for a fight. I just want to be ready if one erupts."

"I got that," Marie said. But she wasn't entirely convinced her good friend was being completely candid.

47

Adam Wilson listened to Daniel Keenan in disgust. He thought every man in their group was strong and in control of their lives, as he believed himself to be. After all, God was on their side. He believed each man would be able to deliver on his commitment to bring his wife and children to the rendezvous spot without a hitch. And now, Daniel Keenan, one of the ringleaders of the whole operation, sat before him wounded and apologizing like a frightened teenager for not being able to control his wife. If Adam Wilson were less sturdy a man himself, he would have thrown up.

After recounting his story to Wilson, Keenan looked at him as if to say, Now what?

"We'll have to go without her," Wilson said at length. "But I will tell you, Daniel: she will hear from one of us about the importance of remaining silent about what she knows." He looked away in a manner that Daniel believed intimated that if she didn't stay quiet she would pay a stiff price. Adam Wilson didn't think much of women, and he saw them as eminently dispensable. He wouldn't think twice about eliminating someone, especially a woman, who stood in the way of his plans.

"Don't hurt her," Daniel said in a weak voice.

In a voice Wilson thought lacked all conviction. Here was a pathetic loser with a large gash in his right arm given him by a woman he is now saying he wants to protect. Wilson gave serious thought to eliminating both of them. He postponed that decision for the present.

Doing so just now would draw attention to the whole enterprise in a way he didn't think they could afford. He would have to settle for taking Keenan along and threatening his wife. He wondered if he should do it himself or if he should send someone. Adam Wilson had a high regard for his ability to manipulate women, so he decided he would do it himself. He was pretty sure Cherie Keenan did not know who he was.

"Daniel," he said to the man in front of him for whom he had lost all respect. "I won't hurt anyone. I'll just go talk to Cherie. You take care of that arm; it looks like it needs stitches."

Daniel nodded and looked away. He felt relief.

Wilson walked out of the room and called David Blinder. He explained the situation to him. He knew that David had been in contact with Keenan and that Keenan thought he was the sole contact. But David Blinder never trusted a single channel of communication, and he had been in contact with Wilson as long as he had with Keenan.

That David Blinder shared his contempt for Daniel Keenan was not obvious to Wilson. Blinder listened intently to what Wilson said, and then he was quiet for a while.

"I concur, Adam," he began, "that we have to proceed without Dr. Keenan's family. At least for now. I take it that you will talk to Mrs. Keenan?"

"That is my plan," Wilson said. "I don't think we can do anything that will raise suspicion at this point."

"Agreed," said Blinder. "I will let the others know. When will you speak with Mrs. Keenan?"

"I will pay her a visit as soon as we finish here, David. I don't think this can wait. So far, I do not believe she has contacted anyone."

Wilson could feel David Blinder nodding over the phone. Wilson knew he had a way with people and could handle any situation that arose. He did not lack self-confidence.

After he hung up, Wilson left the building and got into his car to drive to the Keenan residence. As he pulled up, he noticed that it was deathly quiet. Surely heaven did not approve of Cherie Keenan's actions and had walled off the scene of her outrageous behavior. He walked up the porch steps and tapped lightly. Then he rang the doorbell.

He waited.

After a few moments, he tapped and rang again.

Still no answer.

Wilson looked into the front windows that faced out onto the porch. He saw no movement. He waited for just another moment before he left the porch and walked around toward the back of the building. He passed the garage door. He peered through the single glass panel and saw that there was no vehicle inside.

Cherie had left.

Adam Wilson sighed deeply. Then he pulled out his cell phone and dialed William Schaeffer's number.

"Cherie Keenan has left her home," he told him. "I imagine she has gone to collect her children. We may have to take them by force." He clicked off without waiting for a reply.

In fact, Cherie already had possession of her children. She had left her house within minutes of Daniel's departure. She picked up her children, who ranged in age from two to eleven-and-a-half. She stopped by the day care center first and then the middle school where her two older kids attended. She was now driving them all out of town, north toward the general area of Chicago. She was born in Louisiana and moved to Rolla, Missouri, with her husband. She had no connections in Chicago, but she figured it would be the one direction where the goons would not think to pursue her, especially if she drove the back roads through Iowa. Chicago also had a lot of authorities to contact.

Thank God the kids are young enough to follow me without question but old enough not to need around-the-clock attention, Cherie thought when she picked up the children. She told them there was a family emergency and that they had to leave town for a while. She did not mention her destination; nor did she mention their father. They sat amiably and quietly in the backseat of their minivan. As she drove north, she began to think that Daniel was part of something that was a lot more complicated and treacherous than even he imagined. It began to dawn on her that her phone might be bugged, that her house might be wired, and that she was being followed. She was not ordinarily a paranoid person, but the shock of the past few days cast an uncertain light on her habitual ways of relating to the world. She had run out of the house as quickly as she could after Daniel left.

Cherie was not a big fan of spy or adventure movies, but she watched enough television to be worried about her car being tracked or her credit card transactions being logged. Maybe that was just something the federal government could do, she thought. But as she drove, she got more and more nervous about driving a car that was registered to her. She decided she needed to rent a different vehicle.

She had stopped by the bank before she left town and learned that, fortunately, their savings account was intact. Daniel had mentioned closing all the accounts, but that must be on his list for later. She took all but ten dollars from the account, and placed almost forty thousand dollars in cash in her purse.

As she approached the outskirts of St. Louis, she found a car-rental agency. She ordered her kids to stay put while she went in and perused the options. She selected a Lincoln Town Car. It was big enough for her children, it was fast, and it was a comfortable road car. She thought about how she and Daniel had rented one while on vacation years ago, almost in jest. She pushed those happy, innocent thoughts aside, however, and forced herself to focus on the task at hand. She paid for the rental in cash. She also noticed that the rental agency sold disposable cell phones. She bought one and casually put it in her pocket. She was sure her oldest boy could figure out how to use it.

And of course he did. Once he explained to his mother how to use the phone, including how to block her phone number, she dialed directory assistance to get the phone number of the chief of the Rolla police department. The nice robot on the phone offered to connect her at no additional charge.

She declined. As she and the children drove north, she weighed the pros and cons of making contact with anyone. She had a serious dilemma: the person she trusted the most had just turned on her and became someone she barely knew. She was pretty sure she wasn't ready to trust anyone else just yet.

She knew Chicago was her ultimate destination, but she didn't see any reason to rush to get there. She left St. Louis and headed to Iowa. A more circuitous and harder-to-follow route, she thought. She liked cities and thought they were great places to hide out, but she felt safer and freer and more able to breathe in the open country.

The children didn't seem to mind the drive. They were quiet for the most part. Occasionally they would play road games the way kids do or play with their electronic toys, but mostly they sat silently staring out onto the midwestern landscape.

As evening fell, they found a small Hampton Inn along the highway where they would be spending the night. Again the children followed her lead without protest. They did what they did most evenings: they got cleaned up; they had dinner; and they prayed before watching a little TV and getting ready for bed. Cherie was exhausted.

This went on for several days. Cherie could feel herself being tempted to avoid dealing with the situation altogether. Maybe she could just drive on forever, forgetting that any of this happened. Maybe, she thought as the hours went by, she and the children could just return to Rolla and everything would be as it was before the terrible news struck.

You are out of your mind, Cherie, she informed herself. You will face this and you will face this now as the responsible adult you are. It was then that she decided to use the number the nice robot had given her. On the third afternoon of her journey, she told the kids to stay in the car, she took the phone, and she walked ten feet away for at least a sense of privacy. She dialed the number.

"Chief McAlister," Cherie said. "This is Cherie Keenan. I have a situation I need to explain to you."

Darrin McAlister had the time to listen. Rolla was not a crime-ridden city. He knew Cherie casually and always liked her. Something about her Southern charm had not worn off after all her years in the Midwest. "Shoot," he said.

"What I am going to tell you sounds a little crazy. No, it sounds a lot crazy. But here is what's been happening over the past few days."

Cherie proceeded to tell McAlister exactly what she remembered from the past week: she included everything that Daniel had told her in as much detail as she could remember, which, in this case, was considerable because it was etched so vividly into her mind. She concluded with the events of the day, including what Daniel had told her and her own assault on her husband with a knife that very morning. She explained her decision to take the children and flee. McAlister listened.

When she was finished, Cherie said, "Chief, feel free to check out any of what I've told you, but I think you should notify somebody on the national level, the FBI or whoever deals with this stuff. These people are nuts. And dangerous."

Darrin McAlister did not dismiss what Cherie was saying out of hand, although he wondered who the dangerous player in this drama was. He knew both Daniel and Cherie by reputation: they were both pillars of the community, active in their church, devoted to their children. It did not seem to McAlister that Cherie would be acting this way if she didn't believe the situation was dangerous, and she would not be talking to him if she didn't believe what she was saying. Nor did it seem likely to him that she would admit assaulting her husband.

But he was a police officer and was by vocation and temperament skeptical. He could not let go of the possibility that Cherie, despite her good name, was playing a higher stakes game than she appeared. She could have gone off the deep end. It's happened before, he thought grimly. But he saw no reason to confront her just yet. She was obviously in distress.

What he needed was time to check things out. "Cherie," he said as softly and as professionally as he could. "I promise you I will look into this. How can I get a hold of you?"

Cherie thought for a moment. "I'll contact you, Chief. Right now I'm being extra careful. I'll call you back in the morning." She clicked off.

Chief McAlister called his deputy and explained the broad outlines of the situation to him. He did not reveal anything about a conspiracy; he focused primarily on a domestic altercation between Daniel and Cherie Keenan that had gotten violent. "Find Daniel Keenan," he ordered him. "And find him quick."

Once his deputy left, McAlister put his hand on the receiver of the telephone and pondered whether to call Washington. After a minute, he thought better of it and let go of the receiver. First things first, he decided.

arrin McAlister was also by temperament a careful man. The last thing he wanted was to make a fool of himself with the federal authorities, and he realized that would be a high probability if he contacted them without all the facts.

He put the matter out of his mind and got back to the paperwork he had been doing before Cherie's call. He trusted that his deputy would find Daniel Keenan in short order. Rolla was not a huge place.

But when Darrin didn't hear from the deputy near the end of his shift, he began to get edgy. He called him on his cell phone.

"Any luck?"

"Not so far, Chief," Darryl James said. "It's as if the guy just vanished." He said it with an edge of guilt in his voice. He hadn't thought finding Keenan would be difficult either.

"Keep looking," said Darrin, and he hung up.

McAlister sat back in his chair and glanced at his watch. His shift was almost over, but he could no more get out of his chair and go home than he could deviate from his demanding temperament. He decided to help Deputy James look for Keenan. He called him back. "I'll take downtown," he said.

After checking out all the possibilities that he and Deputy James could think of, the two men met up around 10:00 p.m.

"Something's weird about this, Chief," James said.

Darrin nodded. Something was weird indeed, he thought. "Get some sleep, Darryl. We'll resume this in the morning." He drove home wondering if there was even a crime committed here. But he knew he didn't want to have another conversation with Cherie Keenan with no husband and no other information. So he decided to call Washington first thing in the morning.

The FBI handles a lot of calls on a daily basis, but a call from a major law enforcement official even from a middling sized city like Rolla, Missouri, gets a kind of priority that normal citizen tips do not. McAlister was routed up the chain of command as the details and content of what he was saying revealed more and more red flags. He ended up talking to Max, having been routed through to his cell phone.

"Chief McAlister," Max said after listening closely to what he said, "we have evidence that the situation Mrs. Keenan shared with you is real and, in fact, is in play as we speak. I want you to accord every protection to Mrs. Keenan."

"We don't know where she is," McAlister said. "She wouldn't tell me." Darrin McAlister was, truth be told, more than a little unnerved by this whole affair. He was relieved that Cherie was apparently telling him the truth, but he felt his spine stiffen at the implications of the story, which were confirmed by the FBI. "She said she'd call me tomorrow."

Damn! Max thought. But he kept his focus. "I also want you not to share this information with anyone in whom you do not have absolute trust. Evidently this group has infiltrated several government agencies, and we cannot be too careful." Max was not ordinarily this trusting of people who had not been vetted, but he had a sense about McAlister that he had a level head, and he was pretty sure he wasn't on the side of the bad guys. If he were, he wouldn't have called.

"I can do that, sir," Darrin replied. "Is there anything else I can do to help you?"

"Yes," Max said. "We're sending a team out to meet with Mrs. Keenan. I would like you to be the point person when they arrive. They will help you find her. They are coming out for her protection and because she is one of the few sources of information we have about the specific plans of these guys."

"Okay," Darrin said. He would do anything for his country and for the good citizens of Rolla, Missouri.

49

Abner Bellamy was also in contact with David Blinder. He liked David the moment they met, after church a few years before. David seemed to take a legitimate interest in Abner and his ideas, and he was obviously a man of means. An Internet search after their brief initial meeting gave Abner a sense of just how extensive his means were. It struck him as providential that the two came together.

After the meeting in St. Louis, Abner's group went home to prepare for the next stages of the planned secession. Their task was to solicit as much support for the breakup of the Union as they could as discreetly as possible, expanding their network. Abner knew this would take time. He also knew that they needed more than just a declaration; they needed a timetable and a plan that went beyond identifying sympathetic voices. But he was willing to be patient. Abner thought that David might be able to contribute key components of the influence segment of the plan. After all, David Blinder had access to contacts and resources that members of Abner's group lacked. While his men had influence and some means, they did not have extensive influence, the kind that they would eventually need. They also did not have any military arm, but that was something they would deal with in the future, as their plans came into clearer focus.

However, Abner and David had a subsequent conversation over dinner one evening, a conversation that was forever etched into Abner's mind, down to the last word.

"So I understand you are interested in government affairs," David had said to Abner over cocktails at a high-end Manhattan eatery. They were sitting in a dimly lit corner away from most other patrons. Abner was surprised at David's directness. But at this point he didn't know him very well, so he demurred.

"Well, David," he said. "You know I'm from Georgia, and I think a lot of Georgians, and a lot of Southerners, have a stronger attachment to their state than to the federal government." He took a sip of his drink. "Plus, we didn't like how the war ended." He smiled a slight smile, as if he were joking.

David also smiled slightly. He took a sip of his tonic and lime— he never drank alcohol when he was working—and leaned across the table. His face suddenly grew serious and dark. "I know about your meeting in St. Louis, Abner. I know about your organization. I know about your goal." He leaned back into his chair. "And I am here to help you. I have what you don't have and what your organization needs the most."

Abner looked at David across the table and said nothing. He was shocked that David knew so much about him. Abner was accustomed to acting in the shadows, and he was uncomfortable to be discussing his plans in a public place. The thought crossed his mind that David was bluffing or that he was an undercover cop or that he was trying to hustle him in some way. He remained silent, but his breathing became ever so slightly labored.

"Don't worry, Abner," David said, smiling a little smile again. "I am not here to expose you, or to expose myself for that matter. As I said, I am here to help you."

Abner only had one question in his mind, so he asked it. "And what do you have, David, that you think I need?"

David leaned over to Abner once again and said in a whisper: "An army."

An army? Abner thought. What does he mean, an army? Abner had thought that the militias of the various Southern states would serve as the lead force in a secession, but he had to admit that that part of the plan was a little murky for him just then. It was a down-the-road piece that he was sure would come together at the right time, when he needed it.

David relished Abner's obvious discomfort. "Come now, Abner," he said. "Did you really think you could pull this off without major military conflict? You look shocked."

Abner thought for a moment. "Surprised, David. I'm eager to hear the details."

"And you will, Abner. When the time is right. Now I just want to assure you of my support for your goals. And if you know anything about me, you know that I am capable of substantial support for the causes that are dear to me." Another sip of tonic. "And this one is as dear as it can be."

David and Abner sat in silence for a few moments. Then David said, "I also want you to know that you are not alone in your desires." He rubbed the top of his glass gently. "There are other groups with whom I have been in contact. All of these want what you want."

Abner was quiet. Then he looked around the restaurant. Everyone was doing exactly what they had been doing, but in Abner's mind, everything had changed. He suddenly saw the world in a new light: what had been a dream and a hope took, in his mind, a giant step in the direction of reality. His whole body began to fill with the kind of euphoria that comes along with the unexpected fulfillment of one's dream.

He turned back to look at David Blinder, who had a look of approval on his face. "I don't know what to say, David," Abner said.

"There's nothing to say now, Abner," Blinder said. "Just know that I and many others are on your side. We'll talk more about this when the time is right."

The pair spent the rest of dinner talking about other topics. David felt as if he had just snared a perfect pawn in his scheme, and Abner struggled to digest the fact that he had just been visited by his personal avenging angel.

arie LeBrun and Samantha Stranger landed on a private airstrip just north of Fort Leonard Wood, Missouri. Samantha knew because of movements of Winkelstein's trucks that a transfer of arms was going to take place somewhere in the southern part of the Show-Me State, and she kept an eye on her iPad to track any changes, however slight, in their movements. Marie, on the other hand, tended to the equipment and to the logistics. The first step after disembarking from the unmarked NSA Learjet was to hook up with the motorcycles Max had arranged for them.

They were parked in the hangar. Marie checked the equipment. Each of the bikes had been modified for increased speed, silence, and maneuverability and contained the additional equipment that Sam had requested, plus some extras, such as integrated automatic rifles, small canon, first-aid kits, flares, and other odds and ends that might be useful if a firefight or other dangerous situation arose. Marie nodded to herself as she looked over the equipment.

Marie and Samantha loaded their gear onto the bikes and put on the helmets that sat atop each. These were equipped with secure radio links to each other and to central headquarters so they could communicate with Max in real time. They took a few minutes to test them; they worked perfectly. The two women nodded to each other, started their engines, and drove off. The sooner they got on their way, the sooner they would find their prey.

Samantha had learned that Winkelstein's trucks left Texas the day before. They were headed north through the Mark Twain National Forest, a huge reserve that spanned multiple states, including southern Missouri and southern Illinois. Max had tasked the Echelon satellite to track the trucks visually, so they had real-time data. Marie figured they were two and a half to three hours away from running into them, given that they were headed toward each other.

They drove past the army installation at Fort Leonard Wood itself. They did not bother to stop there, although it held a lot of interest for them, given its vast munitions stores. They continued due south through the National Preserve.

About forty miles south of Fort Leonard Wood, Marie spotted a convoy of Army trucks headed in their same direction: due south. They increased their speed to pass the convoy, counting the trucks as they did so.

Twenty Army trucks traveling toward an oncoming convoy of half the number of trucks that were each twice as large as the Army vehicles. It did not take either Marie or Sam long to do the math.

The pair agreed to race ahead to get some time to plan how to proceed. They didn't want to keep buzzing the trucks and raising suspicion, but neither did they want to lose this opportunity to ID the trucks and perhaps identify what was in them.

About thirty miles down the road, the pair stopped at a peaceful rest area. They removed their helmets and looked at each other. "Where are Wink's vehicles?" Marie asked.

Sam looked at her iPad and did some searching. "Headed due north on Route 67, just south of Bald Knob, Arkansas." She stared at the screen for a few more minutes. "But it looks as if they are separating." She stared harder at her small computer screen. "Yeah, they are splitting up."

"Are there other routes up this way?" Marie asked.

"Yeah," said Sam. "Lots of them. Most of them are small roads that wind through the Mark Twain National Forest and can't be spotted from the air." She thought for a moment. "But they will have to get back together at some point. It won't matter that much, unless our Army friends break out in small groups as well." She stared up the road they had just traveled. "If they disperse themselves to rendezvous at individual points, say, two Army trucks to one of Winkelstein's, and if they do that in the canopied parts of the forest, they are going to be a lot trickier to follow. We need to tag all of those Army vehicles."

Marie took out a small device that looked like a toy rifle. "I think this will help," she said. Samantha nodded.

They figured they had about fifteen minutes before the Army trucks would pass by their location. They locked their bikes and set out to find a suitable location from which to tag the green Army trucks. They found a small clump of trees with an unobstructed view of the highway. Perfect.

Marie settled into preparing the mechanism. It was in fact a type of rifle, one that shot tiny GPS trackers that attached themselves to any kind of surface: metal, canvas, rubber. Tagging all twenty vehicles would allow Echelon to track the trucks precisely through the GPS satellite system and not just visually, as it was watching the northbound ones.

Within a half hour, they heard the Army trucks coming up on their left. The effective range of Marie's launcher was only about one hundred and fifty feet, so she waited until the first truck came within range. She fired.

Samantha was watching the target through a pair of binoculars and saw the area where the tag landed: on the right front fender just above the wheel. Solid contact.

Marie waited patiently for each truck to come into position and fired. The firing mechanism made almost no noise at all, a deliberate refinement. After she tagged the ninth vehicle, she felt Sam tapping her shoulder. Sam pointed at the empty road behind the tenth truck.

"Shit!" they both said softly. The trucks had broken up into two columns and separated. Marie tagged the last vehicle, and the women retreated to their bikes. They didn't notice the tailgate of the last truck open.

"Echelon should be able to track this," Sam said. She pulled out her iPad and made some fast adjustments. She stared hard at the screen. "There!" she said.

The second columns of trucks had broken away about five miles up the road. Without another word, the two women jumped on their bikes and hit the road north as soon as the last of the first column of Army trucks was out of visual range.

Out of the corner of her eye, Samantha caught the movement of a northbound Army motorcycle with a side car attached. Two men were inside heading in their direction.

Samantha signaled Marie, and both women hit their accelerator hard. They thought they could easily outrun the heavier Army bike. Fortunately, the roads in this part of the country were winding, providing some coverage.

Racing northward, Samantha said to Marie, "We're going to have to find a way to lose these guys and get around the second convoy without passing them so as not to raise suspicion." Marie nodded and looked around. "Let's try the most direct path," she said.

Without skipping a beat, Marie pulled her bike into the forest itself and went off-road. Sam followed. The foliage was not so thick that the sleek bikes could not maneuver around them, but their rate of speed slowed as they negotiated the rugged hills and gullies of the National Preserve.

Marie signaled for them to stop. She was the first to spot the Army bike about a hundred yards off to their left. While their bikes were quiet, they were not silent. Both women shut off the engines. When it passed, they started up their bikes again.

About a mile in, Marie noticed an old logging trail that ran north to south. She nodded for Sam to follow. They were able to pick up speed for the next half dozen miles.

Sam spotted the trucks first. They were traveling ahead of them at about fifty miles per hour. They were on a narrower arterial road, and their speed suffered as well. Both motorcycles sped up to get ahead of the column of green trucks.

About two miles ahead, Marie stopped and pulled out her tag rifle. She ran toward the road to find a spot where she couldn't be seen. Sam followed close behind. Sam also pulled out a semiautomatic weapon. Within minutes, the trucks rumbled into view, and Marie started tagging each one.

When they were finished, they lay frozen in their positions until they could no longer hear the rumbling of the heavy Army vehicles. They watched closely to see if another motorcycle would appear. When none did, they rolled onto their backs and breathed long sighs of relief.

Step one, they both thought.

arvey Winkelstein always thought that locating his trucks just south of the Mark Twain National Forest was a stroke of genius. Three seasons a year, the canopy of trees was so thick that visual reconnaissance was nearly impossible from the sky. There were plenty of places to load and unload material, and it was close to major military installations as well as to a large number of groups that wanted weapons. Even South American gangs were willing to send their own vehicles to meet his in that vast green space maintained by the federal government.

Plus, there were so many roads that it was easy for even his largest trucks to take different paths. The drivers were for the most part men from the Ozarks who were very familiar with the terrain. They had the same kind of advantage that the mujahedin had against the Russians and the Americans in Afghanistan: they were fighting on their home turf; they knew the ground, respected it, and used it to maximum advantage. Even a large convoy of ten big semis could split up and rendezvous at various points in the forest.

And, while he was not so fastidious about security as David Blinder, he had a keen investment in keeping his dealings private. To that end, he kept surveillance teams around his vehicles every time they were on the road. He insisted that the Citizens group do the same during sensitive exchanges, such as the one that was unfolding now in southern Missouri. Since aerial surveillance was not feasible, he insisted on placing spotters along the selected routes.

That was how he learned that the current shipment was being tracked by two agents.

His cell phone rang just as he was leaving his office for lunch. It was Parker.

"Dr. Winkelstein," Parker said. "We have a problem. Two people were spotted trailing the Army trucks leaving Fort Leonard Wood."

Winkelstein thought for a moment. "Do you have ID?" he asked.

"Not yet," Parker replied. "They are on bikes—fancy bikes, I might add—and they were wearing helmets. We are searching for them as we speak."

Winkelstein sighed. He hated complications. And he had been lucky; he had had few complications throughout his illicit career.

"Let me know when you've got them," he said, and he clicked off.

Harvey Winkelstein sat back down at his desk. He knew there was no easy way to trace any connection between him and the trucks, either the Army trucks or his own vehicles. Each had been carefully shrouded in a paper blizzard of phony companies, registered to deceased or mythical people, and generally were not easily identified. They had no serial numbers; they had bogus papers; and the drivers knew only that they were to drive them from point A to point B with no knowledge of why or wherefore. He felt okay about that.

What he didn't feel okay about was the fact that two people with high-tech equipment were tracking the Army trucks. They might even be tracking his own. He retraced the whole arrangement in his head looking for leaks in the plan. He couldn't identify any. This could be a coincidence, he thought, but if there was one thing Harvey Winkelstein was not it was naïve. Somebody was onto this shipment. He trusted Parker to make sure those people were found, interrogated, and disposed of properly. He figured he would know by the end of the day what had happened.

Armed with a restored sense of self-confidence, Harvey Winkelstein went to lunch.

52

Further south, in Texas, David Blinder received a similar call, and he responded with similar instructions. But when David put the phone down, he sat back to think closely about the implications of what Parker had told him.

Blinder knew that Winkelstein had shrouded his dealings under layers of subterfuge. But still, someone or some agency knew about this shipment, and it troubled him. This could be a weak spot in the entire plan. He had promised Bellamy and the Rolla group that he would provide the army to make their otherwise idealistic plans come to fruition, and he had a lot riding on procuring those large weapons that were being delivered, courtesy of the US Army and the Sovereign Citizens.

David Blinder had an intuition about Marie LeBrun. His source in the government had told him that she did special jobs for one of their high-level bureaucrats from time to time—jobs that were best conducted outside of legal government channels. That was part of the reason he had had her shadowed the week before: to let them know that he was onto them. In fact, all he had was a hunch, but it turned out to be a prescient one. He knew there was one person who could get the intelligence he needed on LeBrun. After thinking this through for a while, he put a call in to Samantha Stranger.

He had given Ms. Stranger a specially encrypted cell phone to be used exclusively for their contacts. He was routed through

Macau and several other East Asian cities, a miracle of contemporary technology that made it highly unlikely to be traced. In return for his generosity, Samantha was expected to answer right away or get back to him within thirty minutes on the same device, a copy of which he was now holding in his hand.

When there was no answer, Blinder did not bother leaving a message. She would know that she had received a call, and, since there was only one possible caller, she would know what to do. David Blinder turned his chair to look out the window behind his desk. He had great confidence in Samantha Stranger.

53

Sam felt the phone ring rather than hearing it because she had turned the sound off when they were doing their prep work. Still, she knew immediately it was from Blinder, and she also knew that he had chosen a most inopportune time to call. As soon as she felt the device vibrate, she checked her watch. She had thirty minutes.

Sam turned to Marie. They were both resting from their recent activity and were preparing to plan the next step. When Samantha told Marie about the call and the protocol, Marie frowned.

"Shit," she said.

Before she could follow up her assessment, the pair heard twigs breaking and the sound of muffled voices, maybe three hundred yards away. Their senses automatically went on high alert. The possibility that this could be a coincidence was not even considered by either of them. They were being tracked.

Sam and Marie grabbed their binoculars and scanned in opposite directions. "There!" whispered Sam. Marie turned in that direction but continued scanning the area on the way. "I see them," she whispered back.

"I count three men," Sam said.

"Check," Marie replied.

They took out their automatic pistols; the silencers were already attached.

They then executed a standard military drill: they each started crawling in a different direction toward the three men. The goal was to come at them from different angles but not on either side. If they did that, they risked placing each other in the line of fire. Placement was key: they needed to insert themselves at angles that would enable them to confront the men while closing off escape routes.

Communication switched to hand signals. When they were in position, they assessed the weapons the men were carrying. Two of them had standard-issue M-16 rifles. The third had a device attached to a tank on his back. The women's eyes widened slightly. A flame-thrower! These guys were serious. They both knew what they had to do. Marie hoped that these men were just dressed as US Army; the thought of killing American soldiers did not sit well with her. But neither did going down in flames.

She got the man with the flame-thrower in her sights and fired; within seconds, Sam got off two shots, one for each of the other men. They did not bother to search the bodies or check to see whether they were alive or dead. They crawled back to their bikes knowing that the likelihood that there were others was high.

The clock was ticking. While Sam wasn't exactly anxious about getting back to Blinder, her adrenaline was coursing through her body, as it naturally does in life-and-death situations. While she had to be deliberate in her decisions, the hormonal rush cleared her mind wonderfully.

She checked her watch. Twenty minutes had gone by since Blinder called. She turned toward Marie. "Keep watch," she said. "I have to return this call."

Marie didn't question her friend. She grabbed her weapon and started scanning the forest around them. Sam got close to the ground and punched the speed dial button on her phone. Blinder answered on the second ring.

"I would like you to research someone for me, Samantha," Blinder said in a soothing, seductive way. "A certain Marie LeBrun. I believe she worked for the CIA at one point. I think she is a sometime contractor for them. I would like any information you can find."

"Yes, sir," Sam said. "I'll get back with you as soon as I have the material."

She clicked off. Her body was still pumping adrenaline. She wasn't sure what was more demanding: killing three men trying to kill her or being tasked to investigate her partner by a man they were investigating. She told herself she had some time and got back up.

She motioned for Marie to remount their bikes. They both scanned the forest around them. Simultaneously, they figured that going back in the direction they came was the wisest choice, especially since all the vehicles were tagged for the Echelon satellite. They realized they might run into some resistance, but going south was probably an invitation for an ambush. Their mission was not fully accomplished, but a new wrinkle made itself felt: the need to stay alive.

54

Parker was growing impatient. He had given strict orders to find, interrogate, and eliminate those two agents, and he had not heard back from any of the half dozen men he had put on the job, the same six men whom Cooper had used to help with the shipment. He expected to hear back after he reported to Winkelstein and Blinder, but there was nothing. He sat in his car and drummed his fingers on the dash.

After what seemed like forever but was actually only about twenty minutes, his mobile phone beeped. It was the lieutenant he had put in charge of the surveillance team for the Army trucks moving south.

"Report!" he said, ignoring social pleasantries and reverting to his preferred military parlance.

"Three men down," a nervous voice said over the encrypted line. A pause. "No other contact."

Parker did not say anything right away. His mind was racing. They killed my men, he thought. Anger made his limbs hot. "What happened?" He spit the words out, a feature that was not lost on the lieutenant.

"We spotted them on bikes. They tried to lose us in the forest," the man replied, working hard to stay calm. "The men were looking for them with rifles and a flamethrower. The agents got the jump on them and mowed them down." The lieutenant's anxiety was not going down. But he wanted to make sure Parker had a clear picture of what happened.

"And now?" Parker said.

"The remaining men are still looking, but they are taking it very carefully. We also sent for backup."

Parker considered this. He recognized that there wasn't much to be done. The dead men were Sovereign Citizens in Army attire. He didn't bother to tell the lieutenant what he needed to do with the bodies. "Keep me posted," he said simply, and he hung up.

Parker thought for a minute. Then he put his car in drive and headed south. He had stationed himself some miles behind to be close enough to the action without being compromised, but he felt he needed to get closer. He might have to get his hands dirty. For an ex-Ranger, that was not an unwelcome prospect.

55

Sam and Marie got to their bikes and revved up the engines. They headed due north, hoping that they were moving away from more spotters. Of course, they could not be sure, but they both figured that taking the risk was better than sitting in the area where they had assassinated three men with weapons.

They kept to the forest for about three miles. At that point, it was close to the road, so they ducked the trees and foliage and got on solid asphalt; they gunned their engines north. They were simultaneously feeding information back to Max, who had been party to the action the whole time.

"I don't think they were Army regulars, Max," Marie said. "The Army hasn't used flamethrowers since, like, 1978." She was vague in her head but correct about the year. It was before she was born.

"That's correct," Max said. "Still, it was heavy equipment. And it is the kind of equipment that was no doubt stored at Fort Leonard Wood. There is clearly a traitor there."

"I think it's Cooper," Sam said. "He was the one who authorized the shipment. He has access to the complete underground vault where they store this stuff. And he was the one who escorted Winkelstein when he came to pay a visit a few days ago." She was trying to have a conversation and keep her eye on the road at the same time. This was a daunting task, since she was traveling a little over a hundred miles per hour.

"I did a little research on him," she continued. "Typical military: strong, silent type. Very conservative. Lives alone. A couple of drinking buddies; no close friends to speak of. Respected by his superiors. One of those NCOs who run the military no matter who is officially in charge."

"Okay," said Max. "We have to pull him in."

Being hunted by big men with outsize and illegal weapons sharpened one's sense of justice. "Would you like us to do it?" Marie asked.

"No," Max said. "We have some people in the Memphis field office who can be there in a couple hours. Let them handle it."

"What do you want us to do?" Marie asked.

"I want you to find Cherie Keenan," he said. He brought them up to date on his conversation with the police chief. "I want you to find her before the bad guys do."

That gave them a plan. They headed for Rolla, but they decided to bypass Fort Leonard Wood. They didn't know what lay in store for them there; nor did they want to get in the way of other operations. Even though it doubled the time of the trip, they agreed that it was the far wiser course.

herie Keenan and her children, of course, were nowhere near Rolla. They had passed through Iowa and were headed to Chicago. Cherie had been to the Windy City a few times; she liked it—for a Yankee city. It had a tough reputation, but she also felt it was a place where a woman and her three kids could get lost so long as they had enough cash. She was not incorrect about that.

She selected a Motel 6 on the far western edge of the suburbs of greater Chicago. She couldn't think of a more anonymous place. She paid for two adjoining rooms in cash and shepherded her kids into one of them, where they began their evening ritual as if they were still in their comfortable Rolla manse.

The children were noticeably quiet and compliant. She felt bad for them because she was sure there was no way they could possibly understand what their father had gotten himself into or how dangerous it was for all four of them. They had dinner at a local diner and acted as if fleeing their home in the middle of the day and driving all night to a strange big city was the normal course of events.

True to her charming Southern roots, Cherie Keenan had the ability to smile softly and carry on earnest chitchat no matter that her world and the worlds of her children were completely upended in a matter of days. Inside, she could feel the tears wanting to make themselves known. There will be time for that, she gently chided herself. Right now, survival was the most important thing.

After dinner and the final nightly rituals, Cherie kissed her children good night and closed the door to the room next to hers where they were staying. She checked the lock on the front door of that room half a dozen times, but she did it so smoothly that the children did not seem to notice. Or if they did they didn't comment on it. When she closed the door between the rooms, she deliberately did not allow it to click shut. A mild wind would open it, and she wanted it that way in case there was a sudden need to assist her children, to escape, or otherwise to defend them.

She got herself ready for bed and pulled back the covers. It was late—after eleven—but she felt a strong need to speak with someone. She knew calling Daniel was out of the question. She did not want to bother the police captain again; besides, she told him that she would call him tomorrow, which she fully intended to do. She thought of the friends she had in Rolla. So many of their husbands were involved with Daniel, and she just didn't know who to trust.

She began to cry softly and silently. She knew her first obligation was to her children; then to herself to care for them. But then she felt another need, something she had never felt in this particular way: she felt a need to help her country. Having grown up in the South, Cherie had heard talk all her life about the War Between the States and how sad it was that it ended in defeat. She used to feel the hope in the voices of her elders in her family that somehow, despite the century plus that had gone by and despite the progress of the United States in the modern world and despite the intervening wars that had claimed so many Northern, Southern, Western, and Eastern American lives, there was still this dim candle burning for an antique, mid-nineteenth-century ideal, for something that was no longer, for something she could not help believe at its base was just pathetic. It was like a child growing up and forever lamenting the loss of his childhood or his robust adolescent years. Clinging to the past never appealed to Cherie Keenan, and in the present she was a devoted citizen of the current United States of America. It was her home. She felt gooseflesh every time she heard or sang the national anthem or the other patriotic songs that make up the American songbook. For the life of her, she could not identify a single reason why anyone in their right mind would want to change the structure of government and indeed of civil society for over two hundred years. What was the matter with these people? What was the matter with her husband?

She thought it was too late to call anyone. But she decided before she turned off the light that she would do whatever she could for her country. She would call Chief McAlister early in the morning and ask him what she could to do assist the authorities. She would not crawl into a hole forever. This was a tactical retreat, not a rout. She would volunteer to be of whatever service she could. She knew this was the end of her relationship with Daniel. That part, while totally unexpected a couple of weeks before, was clear in her mind. It hurt like hell throughout the past week, but at this moment, in the shadowy room of a cheap hotel on the outskirts of Chicago, Cherie Keenan knew there was no way to resurrect that relationship, that marriage, or even that contact. She could not stand the thought of the man to whom she had been so devoted for so many years.

Armed with a type of resolve she seldom experienced in her life, she turned off the light and turned to face the slightly open door to the room where her children slept. She prayed that they could be proud of at least one of their parents; then she prayed for the courage to be that one before falling off to sleep.

arrin McAlister was not completely surprised when Cherie called him promptly at 8:00 a.m. the next day. It was consistent with what he knew about her. In addition, his social impressions had been powerfully validated by his conversation with Max the day before. He had been in the office since 7:00 a.m.

"Chief McAlister," Cherie began. "Did you check on the information I gave you yesterday?"

"Yes, ma'am, I did," McAlister said. He couldn't think of a single reason to dissemble. "I called Washington. They validated everything you said. They also filled me in on the larger picture. They asked me to do everything I could for your protection."

Cherie let out a sigh of relief. She hadn't been aware of how anxious she was. Those simple words felt better to her than anything she had heard over the past few weeks. Tears came to her eyes. "Thank you, Chief," she said.

McAlister continued. "But I can't protect you if I don't know where you are, Mrs. Keenan."

"Please call me Cherie," came the reply.

"Darrin," McAlister replied, nodding to an empty office.

There was silence on the phone. Cherie could not quite bring herself to let anyone know where she was just yet, no matter how much support she felt from the police chief; events were too much in a whirlwind. "Darrin," she finally said, "do you know where my husband is?"

"No, ma'am, we do not," Darrin said. His deputy had no luck finding him the day before, although every cop in the department was still looking.

Cherie thought about this for a moment. "Darrin, I am deeply appreciative of your believing me about this. I can't tell you how much that means to me. And I want to be of whatever assistance I can in this situation. I think Daniel got involved with some pretty disturbed but powerful people." A new thought occurred to her at just that moment. "And I wonder if my, um, departure might have put him in some jeopardy."

McAlister considered this for a moment. "It seems to me that is entirely possible, Cherie," he said. "But we won't know for sure until we find him, and we are still working on that." Then he decided to change tactics. "How can I help you now?" he asked.

Cherie thought for a moment. "I'm not sure. I am willing to help the authorities in any way I can, but I need to get my kids to a safe place, a place that would be hard for people to trace. So I can't take them somewhere Daniel would know about, such as my family. I'm not sure where to go."

Darrin considered this. Up till that moment, he hadn't given much thought to the fact that Cherie did not just disappear by herself, but she had three kids in tow. Not an easy feat. They must be some children, he thought.

"Cherie," Darrin said in a slightly softer, less businesslike tone. "It would help me if I knew the general area you were in. I might be able to help you."

Cherie took a long deep breath. There was something about Darrin McAlister that was earnest. She wanted to trust him. If she did not trust him completely, she trusted him more than any other human being she could think of at the moment. So she took another deep breath and made the leap. "I'm in the Chicago area," she said.

Chicago? McAlister thought. Why Chicago? Of course! That's exactly why she's there. Not a place anyone would expect. His respect for Mrs. Keenan notched up. He also felt this to be a stroke of luck. He was from northern Illinois and went to school in Chicago. He scanned his mind for contacts he knew and trusted in the Chicago area. Of course, he thought finally, Loyola University. He had gone to school there.

"Cherie," he said. "Let me make some calls. I'm from that neck of the woods, and I think I can find somewhere for you to put the children and then we'll go from there. Call me back in an hour."

"Thank you so much, Darrin," Cherie said. She felt she had made a good and lucky decision to trust Darrin McAlister. She thought about giving him her number, but decided against it. One step at a time, she told herself.

When he got off the phone, Darrin McAlister called Father Thomas Lemke, a Jesuit priest to whom he had been close at Loyola. Lemke was youngish when McAlister was a student there, and he probably was not yet fifty even now. They had kept in friendly if infrequent contact since Darrin's school days.

Father Lemke was very attentive when Darrin called. He listened closely as this former student and now chief of police gave him the broad outline of what had been happening over the past days.

"Jesus," Lemke said. "Darrin, how can I help you?"

"I need to find a place where Cherie can hide her children for a while. Maybe a few days, but maybe for longer. They are good kids. But Cherie's children need to be somewhere safe so she can assist the authorities. I've got a hunch she is one of the few leads in this whole mess. And she needs to be free to do that."

Lemke thought for a while. "I think I know a place. Let me check it out and I'll get back with you this morning."

"Thanks, Father," Darrin said. Even though he had known Tom Lemke as a friend and even a sometime colleague over the years, he could not quite bring himself to be overly familiar with him. Strong Catholic backgrounds aren't easy to surmount.

McAlister was relieved. He had implicit trust in Father Lemke, and if the good father said he could find a place, he would find a place. And it would meet all the requirements for safety and indeterminate length of time.

When McAlister put the phone down, his secretary walked into his office. "Chief," she said. "I've got the deputy on the line. Bad news."

McAlister swore to himself as he picked up the phone.

"Talk to me," he said.

"It's Daniel Keenan, sir," the deputy said. "We found him."

"Where?"

"Several places," the deputy said. "His body was dismembered. We found his head on his front porch and other body parts at the university and another at his private office where he conducted his consulting business."

"Jesus Christ," McAlister said through clenched teeth. He knew immediately that he could not bring Cherie Keenan back to Rolla. "Any leads?"

"We're working on that, but nothing just yet. It looks like the murder took place somewhere else and the parts were distributed to the various sites. The Special Case Squad is on the scene."

"Keep me posted," McAlister said.

58

Once Adam Wilson realized that Cherie had left town, he knew he had no choice but to eliminate Daniel Keenan. Cherie knew about the plan. Daniel was weak. Whatever qualms Wilson had about making a scene with Keenan's death at the beginning, he now knew that it was just too high a risk to keep him alive. He would deal with Mrs. Keenan in due course. Right now, he had to make sure everyone was ready to leave.

Besides, he reflected as he drove back to his hotel, this might serve as notice to anyone else who has second thoughts about their plan. Adam Wilson did not brook opposition to his schemes.

Given the fact that Keenan's death would garner attention, Wilson decided to do it with style, to make a statement. To warn the rest of his colleagues that there would be terrible consequences if the plans were not followed. It would also serve notice to law enforcement that they were not dealing with some cowardly crooks.

It wasn't hard to find members of the Sovereign Citizens to carry out the execution. It wasn't the first time the organization had to eliminate someone, and they had all the equipment, experience, and expertise they needed to do precisely that.

Wilson, of course, would be on his way out of town while the deed was being done. He was not stupid enough not to provide himself a rock-solid alibi for noninvolvement. Besides, he was certain no one could trace his destination.

He loved power.

The other members of his group were assembling at that very moment. In fact, he himself was headed to the gathering spot they had prepared in a mountain in Wyoming. Tomorrow was the day the mayhem was scheduled to begin. He chuckled to himself. He had gotten an early start. He was always precocious.

59

It took Tom Lemke only twenty minutes to follow up his hunch and secure the agreement of some good friends to house three children for an undetermined length of time. He called Darrin McAlister back within thirty minutes of the call Darrin placed to him.

"Darrin," he began. "I know a couple in Evanston who have a large house and are willing to mind the children for however long it takes. I didn't give them any details, but I know this couple. They've helped me before in some difficult situations. You can trust them." He paused just a moment. "I trust them," he said.

Darrin gave a sigh of relief. "Thank you, Father," he said. "This woman's name is Cherie Keenan, but I don't have her number. I have to wait for her to call me back. How do you think we should proceed?"

Tom Lemke thought for a moment. "We can be flexible. I'll let my friends know. They will be ready whenever needed. Just give me a heads-up when she calls and if she agrees to leave her children with them."

"Will do, Father. I can't tell you how grateful I am for this or how important this is to our investigation." The "we" he was referring to was himself, his department, and the federal government of the United States.

After he finished his conversation with Father Lemke, McAlister called Max in Washington, DC. He told him that Cherie had contacted him and that he had arranged a place for her to drop off her children for a length of time. He also told him that she was prepared to cooperate with the authorities and would do so when the children were settled.

"Okay," Max said. "Good work, Chief."

"One more thing," McAlister said. "We found Daniel Keenan's body this morning. It was dismembered and spread around all the places he lived and worked."

Max was silent for a moment. A chill ran down his spine. "Any leads, Chief?" he asked gently. Max knew how responsible men felt when someone was lost on their watch, and he figured Darrin McAlister to be a very responsible man. In this he was correct.

"Not yet," McAlister responded. "We're working on it."

"Keep me posted," Max said.

After he hung up, McAlister called to his secretary. "Kimberly, get me Lieutenant James on the line. When you get him on the phone, tell him I want updates every half hour."

Within a couple of minutes, he was speaking to Darryl James, his longtime lieutenant and senior deputy.

"What have you got, Darryl?" he said bluntly.

"Not much," Darryl said. "We did find his car parked downtown. There was blood on the front seats. We checked for witnesses. Some people said they saw Dr. Keenan downtown this morning. One man said he was holding his arm, as if it were injured. But nothing definite. We're checking out the businesses near where his car was parked. There's a bank, a couple hotels, and some restaurants. We may know more after we do some lab testing on the car."

"Good work, Darryl," McAlister said. "Keep me updated."

"Every half hour, Chief."

"Yup." Darrin knew he was geared up about this situation. A lot was happening on his watch, and he wanted to make sure he was on top of it as much as possible.

60

Cherie did not call Darrin back until the next day. She was torn. On the one hand, she was mightily relieved to feel that he believed her and was willing to help her. On the other hand, one of the things that was becoming much clearer to her as time went slowly on was that men were capable of such deception. She never would have believed her longtime husband would have gotten involved in such a crazy scheme, completely unbeknownst to her. So she was reluctant to trust any man too much.

But realistically she knew she had to do something; mistrust as a permanent fixture was neither a healthy nor a viable path. She was going back and forth in her mind as she and her children were having breakfast at a diner. She happened to glance at the television across the room, over the counter. To her surprise, she saw Darrin McAlister's face on the screen. She couldn't make out what they were saying, so she told her children to stay put, and she walked up to the counter to get a closer look.

What she saw made her jaw drop open. She stared immobile as pictures of her husband—archival images from various news stories past—flashed across the screen. Murdered! She was in such a state of shock that she wasn't catching exactly what they were saying. All she knew was that she had to get her children out of this place and quick.

She went back to the table and, as gently as she could, told the kids to finish breakfast. She started speaking constantly to keep their attention away from the television, as she kept a furtive eye on it herself. They had to go. As soon as the last bite of food was deposited in the mouth of the last child, she sprang up and paid the bill. When she was finished, she collected the children, who were accustomed even at their young ages to more leisurely mealtimes, and herded them out the door. They looked at each other with raised eyebrows as if something was wrong with their mother, the way siblings often do. But those glances were becoming routine.

Cherie shepherded her kids into the car and drove back to the motel. She put them in the room and told the oldest not to turn on the television.

She went to her room and called McAlister. He picked up on the first ring.

"Cherie? Is that you?" he said when there was silence on the line.

"Yes," Cherie said in a very soft voice. She was so filled with grief and anger and rage and shame she was barely able to breathe.

Darrin did not hesitate. "Cherie, I have found a man, a Catholic priest, who has some friends who can keep your children for a while—"

"I just heard about Daniel," Cheri blurted out, interrupting him. "Oh, my God, Darrin, what happened?"

Darrin winced. "We don't know all the details yet, Cherie," he replied less urgently. "We have some details about how he died, but it's too gruesome to talk about over the phone." Darrin hesitated just a moment. "I am so sorry for Daniel's death, but we have got to get you to a place where you can help us."

Cherie nodded as if Darrin could see her. "Okay," she said.

"I know a priest, a Father Tom Lemke. He's a Jesuit who works in the Chicago area. He has some friends who are willing to take the children for as long as you need them to. Then we've got to get you into protective custody somewhere." Not here, he thought.

"Okay," Cherie said meekly. She just didn't know what else to do.

"How do you want to proceed, Cherie?" Darrin asked. "I can give you Father Lemke's number or I can call him or I can ask him to contact you? Just tell me how you want this to go."

Cherie was too grief-stricken to think clearly. "Give me a moment, Darrin," she said. She took several long deep breaths in an effort to calm herself. "Okay," she said at length. "You call him and tell him I'll contact him. Then I'll call him and we'll go from there."

"Great," Darrin said flatly. He gave her Lemke's number.

After she hung up, Cherie stared at the wall of her motel room for some time. She was still in shock. As angry as she was with Daniel and even though it was she who slashed him with a knife, she never seriously contemplated the possibility that he might get himself killed. She recalled that Darrin used the word "gruesome" to describe Daniel's death. She mourned for a man she detested; she grieved for a man she lost two weeks ago. Not much of this made sense to Cherie, but she knew that she had to get her kids safe and then get in touch with the authorities. She wondered absently what protective custody meant. Jail? Witness protection? None of that seemed to matter.

She knew she needed some time. She hoped she would have some time alone, without the children, without anyone. She wanted her parents, who were both deceased. She wanted someone close. But just then, the only person to whom she felt a tie outside the little children in the next room was the dutiful chief of the Rolla Police Department.

The future did not look bright. But it looked serious and it looked important.

herie snapped out of her reverie and called Tom Lemke. As she waited for him to pick up, she idly wondered if she had ever had a conversation with a Catholic priest. She couldn't recall one.

Tom answered on the fourth ring. "Father Tom," he said.

"Father Tom, this is Cherie Keenan. I believe Chief Darrin McAlister of the Rolla Police Department spoke to you about me."

"Yes, Mrs. Keenan, he did," Lemke replied. "I am so sorry to hear about your husband."

"Thank you, Father," Cherie said.

Lemke recognized that Cherie did not want to go into that messy situation just now. That made sense to him. He suggested they meet at the north campus of Loyola University. He figured it was a landmark she could easily find, and it was close to Evanston where his friends lived. She agreed to meet him there in two hours.

When Cherie got off the phone, a lot of feelings were percolating inside her. She closed her eyes and forced herself to calm down, to take things one at a time, to think as clearly as she could about what she was doing. She took several deep breaths. She felt a slight lessening of tension in her body. She opened her eyes. Her senses seemed a little more acute; she could hear birds singing outside her motel room window. She took a final deep breath and got up to collect the children.

She sat her three children down to explain what was happening. Whenever Cheri undertook to speak to her children together, she assumed a teaching persona that she had developed years before when she taught elementary school. She liked to teach, and it was good preparation for dealing with her own children.

"Children," she began. "I know these past few days have been difficult for you, for all of us. Honestly, you have all been wonderful. You've done what I've told you to do with very little complaining. I am very proud of you." She paused a moment to stop a tear. "I could not have asked for better children.

"But now we have to do something different, something that is going to be hard on all of us. I need to return home to take care of some important business, and it involves things I have to do by myself. I cannot take you with me, as much as I would like to. What I have to do cannot be done with children around. I have found a nice couple who are willing to let you stay with them until I return."

Cherie looked at each of her children as she spoke. Daniel Jr., the oldest, was trying not to be scared and cry. Cynthia's face was trembling. And John, the youngest who was only two and a half, just listened. She hugged each of her children.

"So, I want you to continue to be the good children you are until I return. Do you understand?"

They all nodded. Even John who, after he saw his siblings nod, followed suit. And then he grinned and giggled.

Cherie chuckled. She loved these children. They were everything to her. Especially now that their father was dead. She faintly considered telling them this but knew this was not the time. They would find out soon enough.

Cherie packed the kids into the car and drove to Loyola. She got directions when she checked out of the Motel 6.

It took less time than she thought, and within thirty minutes, she was pulling the Lincoln onto Loyola Drive. Father Lemke had told her he would meet her at the end of that street, which dead-ended at Lake Michigan. To her surprise, she saw a trim, middle-aged man with a black clergy shirt and black slacks sitting on a rock. Must be him, she thought.

She pulled up to the end of the street. The priest stood up. She had told him what kind of car she was driving. She did not want this process to take any longer than necessary.

Cherie rolled down the window as he approached. "Cherie?" he said.

"Father Lemke?"

He nodded.

Cherie looked at the priest for a long moment. She thought maybe she should have been more careful; maybe should have arranged a code word or something. But he had come into her life via the good offices of Darrin McAlister, whom she had grown to trust. He also had a kind but serious look on his face, the kind that intimated, at least in Cherie's mind, that he had some idea of what was happening. And there was a matter of simple fatigue—she wasn't cut out to be a paranoid secret agent. She wanted help.

"Hop in," she said. The plan was for them to drive together to the Ausbangers in Evanston. Tom Lemke got into the passenger side. He looked over his shoulder at the three children huddled in the large rear seat. "Hi, guys," he said cheerfully.

Lemke gave Cherie directions. Then he dropped his voice so the children in the backseat could not hear. He explained that he had known the Ausbangers for many years. They were unable to have children of their own, and they had on several occasions housed children when Lemke had a need. They were discreet, didn't ask a lot of questions, and were unfailingly polite and caring.

None of this penetrated into Cherie's psyche much. She was doing what she was doing because it seemed like a logical next step in an outrageously illogical situation. She was trusting Lemke and the Ausbangers because Darrin trusted Lemke, and she trusted Darrin as much as she could trust anybody just now. But she felt as if she were in a play that someone else wrote and was directing.

She drove on in silence. Tom did not want to force a conversation, but he did want to give her a basic idea of how this would go, how to communicate, and other practical matters. Cherie listened closely, absorbing as much as she could.

When they got to the Ausbangers' home in Evanston, Cherie pulled the car into the driveway, turned off the engine, and sighed deeply. "Here we are," she said flatly.

Everyone got out and Tom led the troupe up to the front door, which opened immediately.

Tom and Denise Ausbanger both walked out onto the front porch. "Welcome to everybody," they said, almost in unison. Tom shook Lemke's hand. "Good to see you again, Father," he said. Denise gave Father Lemke a peck on the cheek.

Tom Lemke did the introductions, and everyone walked inside. Cherie was quiet, but her insides were beginning to roil. The thought of leaving her children was a turbulent one: she understood it was the best thing to do just now, but she was beginning to feel how these young people had been her anchor over these past days, and the thought of being without them suddenly frightened her. She knew she couldn't drag this out.

"Father Tom has told me a lot of good things about you," she said to Tom and Denise. "I can't thank you enough for taking care of my children for me." She paused for a moment. "I hope it won't be for long."

Tom Ausbanger spoke. "We are honored to do it, Cherie," he said softly. "It's the least we can do for Father Tom."

Cherie figured there was probably a story of interest behind those words, but she was in no mood to find out about it just then. All she wanted to do was leave. She stood up a little more abruptly than she intended and said, "I think it's best if I go now." She turned to Tom and Denise. "Thank you again," she said. Then she turned to Tom Lemke. "Thank you, Father. I am deeply appreciative of this." She could feel a tear in her eye, but she did not want to cry in front of the children. She took a deep breath and turned to her kids. She gave each one a warm embrace. She failed to keep her tears away; so did the children. John was getting a little agitated. He sensed that something bad was happening. "Mama!" he said, and he threw his arms around her neck.

Cherie finally untangled herself from the child's grip. "I will see you soon. I will call you every day," she said. And, after shaking hands with the adults in the room, she walked out of the house and got into the big empty Lincoln.

62

Abner did not have to wait long to learn about David Blinder's plans. Two weeks after he and David had dinner, his phone beeped, and an electronically disguised voice informed him that Mr. Blinder was on the other end of the phone. At first, Abner was suspicious, but the voice referenced the dinner in specific ways, and it explained how the encrypted voiceover was a security measure both for himself and for Abner.

Abner listened patiently. He had been doing some research on the Blinder brothers, and he learned that they were thorough, ruthless, and single-minded in pursuing their goals. And David was apparently the more controlling of the two. Abner figured he was on the line to take orders.

And he was. David Blinder wasted no time instructing him about the very specific things he wanted him to do. This included getting his key contacts to spread the word to select groups that the War Between the States was about to be resumed and to do everything in their power to aid and abet the forces of freedom from federal control. He directed that a chain of command be established that would enable the group to communicate with each other swiftly, and he informed him that hostilities would begin in the near future, not the distant one Abner's contingent had as their horizon.

Abner listened closely and jotted down some notes as David spoke. As if he could see him, however, David told him not to write down anything and simply to memorize what he was telling him. He instructed Abner to destroy whatever notes he had made already and to destroy them by fire as the two talked. Abner, who didn't smoke and who didn't carry matches or a lighter, was at something of a loss to do this.

But he stopped writing and focused on what was coming out of Blinder's almost garbled voiceover. As he listened, his excitement and his anxiety rose in tandem. He was exhilarated, but he felt unprepared. How could this possibly happen in a matter of weeks or months rather than years? he thought.

His thinking these things did not stop Blinder from educating him about how precisely events would unfold. In the back of Abner's mind, he realized that David Blinder was a man of uncommon intelligence, the type of person who, much as a composer of an opera might, perceives everything as a single vision, a panorama, a drama in which he could visualize every detail. Abner was awestruck.

He also did not feel entirely unprepared. Since the meeting of his group in St. Louis, morale among the Confederates, as they began referring to themselves, was high. They were eager to get on with the business of restarting the war and following through on their Declaration of Independence.

That was weeks ago, however, and Abner knew he needed some kind of organizational follow-up to build on the momentum of that fateful meeting. He focused on what Blinder had told him about an army. He had no idea what he was really referring to, but David Blinder obviously felt very strongly that he had an army capable of doing battle with the formidable forces of the United States government. Abner had no idea how Blinder could have raised an army without the knowledge of the federal government; nor did he imagine that a rag-tag, thrown-together group would be much of a threat to the highly trained and highly esteemed members of the US armed forces.

Of course, he did not have any specifics about the group, so he was grasping in the dark about this, but he remained skeptical.

Except for the fact that David and George Blinder rarely had a misstep on their way to fortune and control over the targets they selected. They were an uncanny pair whose string of successes was widely acknowledged and admired in financial and economic circles.

"Are you clear, Abner?" Blinder asked at length.

"Yes, I am clear, David," Abner replied. "I will do as you ask."

"Good," said Blinder. "I will give you further instructions as needed."

Abner nodded but didn't say anything. Blinder clicked off.

Abner needed some time to think. He would comply with Blinder's instruction for each of the members of his team, but he could take a little while to think about this in a broader perspective. He decided he needed to see Judith.

He caught up with her the next day at her condo in Birmingham, Alabama, where she was working as an emergency room physician on the night shift. She had left academic medicine a few years before because she couldn't stand the petty politics, the posturing, the holier-and-smarter-than-thou attitude that typified many academic institutions. She wanted to help people. So she turned to clinical practice, and emergency medicine was the most exhilarating practice venue she could find. It wore her out, but she went home every day feeling as if she had done some good in the world.

Judith was not home when Abner arrived, so he let himself in with the key she had given him right after she moved in. She told him then that it would make life easier, so long as she knew he was coming. And he always gave her advance warning.

The relationship was curious. In many ways it was passionate and loving, but it was also compartmentalized and episodic. When Abner and Judith were together, they talked a lot, sometimes for hours. Often they would complete each other's thoughts, the way some married couples do. They would make love with similar intensity and care. But when they parted, the intensity slipped into the background until next time. Each member of this pair knew it would be there again when needed. They both felt fortunate.

Judith was also the person with whom Abner could be most open about his plans for the resurrected Confederacy. He would not discuss it on the phone, however, not even with Judith; this was one of the reasons he needed to see her. He ordinarily did not hold back information from her, and she was astute enough to be a genuine asset in giving feedback and sharing her thoughts about almost any situation. But she knew nothing about Abner's contact with David Blinder, and Abner couldn't wait to tell her all the details.

While he was waiting for her, he put on some coffee and turned on the stereo softly. He knew Judith loved music, and it helped set the mood. He was standing by the kitchen counter trying to pin down the precise time he had last seen Judith. It had been over a month, he realized to his own surprise. As he was thinking these thoughts, he heard the key in the lock. Judith was home.

He walked over to greet her at the door, giving her a warm embrace and a sloppy kiss. "You know how long it's been since you've seen me?" he asked in that thick Georgian accent.

"Thirty-two days," Judith replied. "But who's counting?" She lingered in his arms for a while.

The couple walked over to the couch and sat close. "I have a lot to talk to you about, honey," Abner said. "A lot has happened."

Judith kicked off her shoes, folded her legs under her, and brushed her hair out of her face, getting comfortable. This was distracting to Abner, who found the simple sight of his lover and friend to be arousing and who delighted in her every little move. He smiled.

"So tell me," Judith said.

"A while back, I got a call from a man named David Blinder. You may have heard of him. He and his brother George were big operators back in the nineties. Hell, they were big operators in the seventies. Anyway, big money guys. Empire builders. The financial kind. He was at a service I did in Manhattan last year when I went back to my old congregation to visit." Abner got up to get coffee for himself and Judith. He kept talking. God, it feels good to talk to somebody about this, he thought.

"Anyway, it turns out that my new friend David Blinder is in cahoots with some other groups to foment rebellion among the states. He claims—and this is the part that is too good to be true—that he has an army capable of swinging a rebellion."

Judith had picked up her cup and was about to take a sip when she heard the word army. "An army?" she said.

"An army," Abner replied.

The couple sat in silence for a while, pondering what this meant.

Judith spoke first. "You mean that this man, Blinder, thinks or claims that he has an army capable of actually doing battle with the US military?"

"Yes," Abner affirmed.

"And you believe him?" she said.

Abner tilted his head sideways just a little. "I've done some homework on this guy, and he is a major operator. I'll need more proof, of course, but I am inclined to think that if he says he has an army, he's got something that's mighty close to being an army."

Judith was silent for a while. "What are you going to do, Abner?" she asked.

Abner sighed. "I got a call from Blinder yesterday. He gave me pretty specific instructions about what he wanted me to do. Basically, he wants me to organize my group in a communication network and have them identify as many sympathizers as they can before hostilities start."

"Hostilities?"

Abner nodded. "Blinder says that hostilities could start soon, within weeks or a couple months."

Judith stared across the room. She was trying to take this in. She knew that Abner's goal was to rend the Union and reestablish the Confederacy. She was not unsympathetic to that goal. But the thought of actual warfare and bloodshed was not so easy for her to bear. She was, after all, a physician, and she was devoted to healing and to preserving life. She knew it might come to this, but she thought it was way, way down the road.

She turned toward Abner, put her coffee cup down, and put her hand on his cheek. "Are you ready for this, sweetie?" she said.

Abner leaned his face into her hand and looked her in the eye. "I think this is going to happen if I'm ready or not, Judith."

A chill descended on the room.

63

Samantha and Marie pulled into the outskirts of Rolla, Missouri, just after four o'clock on Friday afternoon. They double-checked the contact information Max had given them. They were to meet up with Chief of Police Darrin McAlister. They were not to contact him by phone. They were simply to go to the police station and ask for him and then introduce themselves.

In the meantime, Echelon was tracking the Army trucks out of Fort Leonard Wood, and Max had a Special Forces Delta Team on alert. That gave the two women some breathing room as well as a sense that their mission had been productive.

When they got to police headquarters, Sam and Marie surveilled the building. They noted anyone who entered, snapping their pictures discreetly and forwarding them to Max for recognition. No one suspicious was noted. After checking with Max to make sure Darrin was in, they crossed the street and mounted the front steps.

"Chief McAlister, please," Marie said to the receptionist, a stout woman in her late fifties.

"Right this way," the woman said. She had obviously been briefed about their arrival. She took them to the door of McAlister's office and motioned for them to enter. Darrin McAlister stood up and walked around from behind his desk. He extended his hand to greet them.

"Welcome to Rolla," he said. Max had informed him that the two women would be showing up, so he wasn't surprised.

Marie and Sam nodded and sat down.

"Coffee?" asked McAlister.

"No, thank you, Chief," Marie said. "We are here to help you locate and protect Cherie Keenan." Samantha nodded.

Darrin appreciated the directness and businesslike attitude of the two women. "Here's what we know." He proceeded to tell them all the information Cherie had shared with him, including the assault on her husband. He also described the subsequent death of Daniel Keenan. He told them that it was his opinion that the manner of death was designed to send a message of some sort. He ended with the most recent information. "She dropped her kids off late this morning at a home in Evanston. This was arranged by a Catholic priest who is a friend of mine in the Chicago area." He paused. "She did not tell him where she was going. I am expecting her to call at any time."

"Chief," said Marie, "how confident are you that this office has not been bugged?"

"Up until yesterday, I didn't even think about it," McAlister said candidly. "Since then, we've had the office and the phones and Internet swept for bugs twice. Nothing showed up."

Marie glanced at Sam, who nodded slightly. They were pleased about this.

McAlister continued. "I've been in touch with Max, your contact, as you know. He has a helicopter on standby in the Chicago and northern Illinois area to pick up Cherie Keenan as soon as we locate her."

More nods from the two women. They were both warming to Darrin McAlister.

"How can we help you, Chief?" Samantha finally said.

McAlister sighed. "First of all, you can call me Darrin. This is the Midwest; we tend toward the friendly." He smiled a small smile.

"I understand that your priority is keeping Cherie Keenan safe and getting her in touch with the authorities in DC. I will do all I can to help make that happen." He paused for just a moment and looked out the window. "And then I'd like you to help me with Daniel Keenan's murder. I have a hunch that event is part of the larger picture."

"Okay," said Marie. "That's right. We are tasked to take Mrs. Keenan into protective custody and make sure she gets to a safe place. In the meantime, we will do what we can to assist your investigation." Marie glanced over at Samantha.

"I think you would be wise to start with Dr. Keenan's investments, Darrin," Samantha said. "According to our intel, he was to withdraw all money from all accounts before his departure. If you can determine if he did that, we can get an idea of the timetable of this group."

Darrin nodded. "I can do that," he said. He picked up the phone and turned away from the two women. He was obviously speaking to their IT person, directing her to collect information on Daniel Keenan's personal banking accounts.

Sam and Marie were impressed that a small town like Rolla had that capability.

"This may take a little while," Darrin said, putting the phone down and turning back to face the women directly.

"What has your investigation turned up about the murder?" Marie asked.

Darrin shook his head. "Unfortunately, not much. Daniel Keenan was last seen downtown. He was holding his arm, presumably because of the attack by Cherie. No one saw him enter any of the buildings. We are presently searching the hotels in the area. We think he may have met with some people from out of town."

Just then the phone rang, and Darrin turned to pick it up. He listened intently for a couple of minutes, then hung up. "It looks like Dr. Keenan only made it halfway through the dispersal process.

About half of his investments were liquidated, and the rest are still intact. Also, it looks like Cherie emptied a bank account the day she left. To the tune of about forty grand."

Samantha and Marie listened intently. This made sense to them. Cherie was running for her life. She may have snapped. Then Marie turned to Darrin. "Could we speak to the priest who helped her place her children?" she said.

Darrin nodded. "Sure. Let me call him first." He picked up the phone and dialed. He then left a voicemail message asking the priest to get back in touch with him as soon as possible. "He usually calls back quickly," he said to the two women.

The three were deep in silent thought when Darrin's phone rang again. Darrin picked it up, glancing at the caller ID tag.

"Father. Hello. I have a couple of women here from Washington who would like to talk to you about Cherie Keenan." He listened momentarily to the response. "Okay. Here they are." He passed the phone over to Marie.

"Father Tom," Marie began. "I was sent here to assist in the protection of Mrs. Keenan. We believe she has information critical to the federal investigation of a major criminal enterprise." Marie listened to Father Tom's response.

"Good," she said, continuing. "I am glad you are willing to help. Can you tell me about Mrs. Keenan's state of mind when you last saw her?" More listening.

"Thank you, Father. May we contact you again if we need more information?"

Marie handed the phone back to Darrin, who placed it back on the receiver. "He didn't have much information," she said. "He said it was obviously painful for her to leave her children with the family he chose, and she did not stay long. Father Tom thought she was crying when she left but trying to hide it from the children. He said she seemed determined."

Just then Darrin's cell phone rang. "Hi, Cherie," he said, the relief evident in his voice.

Darrin listened intently to the voice on the other end of the phone.

"Cherie, I hear you. We are glad you are willing to help, but we also want to protect you as much as possible. I am with two federal agents who were sent from Washington to help you." He listened intently for a few more moments.

"Yes, they are with me now."

He turned to the two women. "She wants to talk with you," he said. He handed Samantha the phone.

"Mrs. Keenan?" Sam said.

"Who are you?" asked Cherie.

"My name is Samantha Stranger. I am a contract worker for the CIA. I am a former agent. I work for a man named Max Grabel. He is the CIA official Darrin talked to when he contacted Washington."

There was silence on the phone. "How do I know I can trust you?" Cherie asked.

Samantha did not reply for a moment. "After what you've been through these past days, Mrs. Keenan, I don't know how you could trust anybody. But we are working with Darrin McAlister to help get you to a safe place so that you can help us."

Cherie closed her eyes. This whole situation seemed unreal. She was inclined to believe this woman she had never met, but she was fearful of trusting anyone, just as Samantha said. She took a deep breath. She trusted Darrin; that seemed okay. She trusted Father Tom; that seemed okay.

"Okay," she said. "How can we meet?"

"We have a helicopter standing by to pick you up—"

"Who will be on the helicopter?" Cherie interrupted.

"A two-man team who will rendezvous with us at a determined location."

"I would prefer someone I know. Perhaps you or Darrin."

Sam looked at Darrin and at Marie. "We'll be there, Mrs. Keenan. My partner and I and Chief McAlister." She was looking questioningly at Darrin, who nodded. "It will take us a couple hours to get there."

Cherie knew she had to take the next step. "I will give Darrin my phone number. Please have him call me when you get close."

"Thank you, Mrs. Keenan," Sam said. She handed the phone back to Darrin, who already had a pen in his hand.

Darrin jotted down the number and thanked Cherie one more time. Then he hung up. He exhaled slowly. "Okay," he said. "How do we proceed?"

Marie spoke up. "We have a private jet waiting on standby at the airstrip north of town." She glanced at Sam and Darrin. "Let's go," she said.

64

On the way to the airport, Marie explained to Darrin that Mrs. Keenan's telephone number would enable them to locate her precisely. Darrin did not seem surprised by this, but he didn't seem happy about it. He felt protective of Cherie Keenan, of her children, and of her privacy. But he knew the situation was unusual and critical. He gave Marie the number.

Samantha opened her computer and ran the number. Within a minute, she was looking at a GPS map of Cherie's exact location near Kenosha, Wisconsin, about an hour from Evanston. She zoomed in. It appeared that she was staying at a small roadside hotel. Sam got the street view and identified it as a Hampton Inn.

"Got her," she said. She looked at Marie and then at Darrin. "Thanks, Darrin. This will help a lot."

Darrin nodded.

By this time, they had arrived at the airstrip, where the Gulfstream was waiting, fully fueled and engines running. They hopped out of the car and walked the twenty feet to the plane. At the top of the stairs, Sam whispered Cherie's location to the copilot, who was greeting them. He nodded to her and then to the pilot.

As soon as they sat down and got belted in, the plane began to move down the runway. They were airborne within minutes.

No one spoke for a while. Darrin looked out the window, trying to get his bearings. It seemed that his normal life, the one he had

had for the past twenty years, the one he assumed he would have until he retired, was gone, replaced by something he was still trying to wrap his mind around. He was having great difficulty absorbing the implications of events that had been unfolding over the past several days. It wasn't that he didn't exactly trust the players, but he was acutely aware that his take on things could be way wrong. It was possible that Cherie Keenan killed her husband and left town with a bunch of money, made up a fantastic story, and was leading them on a wild-goose chase. It could be that the two women with whom he was heading north were on the opposite side of the one they claimed to be on. He didn't know Max Grabel from the Man in the Moon. He just didn't like not being sure of things.

Still, he had no real choice but to trust what instincts he had in this situation and do what he believed was the right thing. And that was why, for the first time in his life, he was sitting in a private Gulfstream jet barreling north to pick up a woman he only knew casually. He wasn't a praying man, but if he were he would pray that everyone in this little drama was who they said they were.

Samantha's thinking had taken a completely different turn. She was wondering how she was going to finesse information about Marie to David Blinder, who had asked for any and all info. She knew she and Marie had developed a cocoon around their relationship and that it was far from common knowledge, but she also knew David Blinder to be a ruthless and determined man who had enormous resources at his disposal. She would have to tell him something or deal with him somehow.

She fantasized telling him the truth: that Marie was her friend, lover, and partner; that they often worked together; that he would be better served with her on his side. But the truth didn't seem remotely applicable in this situation, especially given Blinder's lack of loyalty to the country that provided him so much. Revulsion rose from the pit of her stomach. I should kill the son of a bitch, she thought.

But that was an issue for another time. Just now she had to focus and coordinate with Max and Marie and Darrin to get Cherie Keenan somewhere safe. Max was suggesting a safe house in Chicago. In fact, he was on his way to that vicinity, just as they were. Sam couldn't think of a better alternative, so she decided to go along with the plan.

Marie's thoughts were different. She was thinking about the mole in Mueller's organization. She knew Robert Mueller to be an intelligent and devoted civil servant who surrounded himself with similarly trustworthy people. So who was the mole? Who was the son of a bitch who sold his country out? She was determined to find out, but just now she had no way to do that. She tried to put it out of her mind, but she knew that until that person was identified, all communication was suspect, no matter how careful the precautions. This did not sit well with Marie, and her stomach churned.

After about an hour, Darrin broke the reverential silence of the threesome.

"What is the plan once we locate her?" he said, looking first at Marie and then at Samantha.

Marie spoke first. "When we get close, you call her and arrange a place and a time. We drive there. You go up to meet her. She knows you; at least she knows what you look like. Then you tell her about us and signal us to join you. Then at least three of us and maybe all four get in a vehicle and proceed to a safe house, where Max and his team will be."

"Oh," said Darrin.

After another hour of mostly silent thinking, the plane landed at a small airstrip just west of Kenosha, where two black SUVs were waiting with the motors running. Three men in dark suits met the trio at the bottom of the retractable steps and escorted them to the vehicles. Their sunglasses contrasted with the setting sun.

Sam kept checking her GPS track on Cherie's phone. Cherie was either still at the Hampton Inn or she had left her phone there. Sam figured she probably had it with her.

It was about a twenty-minute ride.

or her part, Cherie couldn't be sure if she had made the right decision. Events seemed so out of her control, as they had for days now. It wasn't within her conception of herself that she would stab her husband with a knife; nor was it within her frame of reference that she would be a fugitive from justice.

That thought pulled her up short. That's precisely how she felt. Even though her only crime was to protect herself from her unexpectedly maniacal husband, she was the one on the run, on the lam. She was the one who had to run and hide her children and seek help like some pitiless runaway who completely lost a sense of direction in her life.

This made her angry. What had she done wrong? Okay, the slashing of Daniel was impulsive; it was bad. But he was preparing to take her by force. He was trying to subject her and their children to a crazy idea of pulling out of life and waging war on the United States of America. He betrayed his country and in the process betrayed his marriage and his family. Even though Cherie felt a twinge of grief and guilt for his death, she recognized that this man, largely unbeknownst to her, was the one who made the decisions that led to his demise. It was not her doing. She did not kill him. She hurt him, yes, but someone else was responsible for his death, possibly including himself.

These thoughts helped her quell some of the turmoil and uncertainty she was feeling about connecting with the government agents. She had no idea what she was about to do. Would they take her to a jail? Would they charge her with assault? Or even murder? It is possible, she thought, that somebody may think she killed Daniel. Spouses have been known to do that. She couldn't imagine she wasn't a suspect. She never forgot that Darrin described Daniel's death as "gruesome," but she never got the particulars about what that meant. She hoped she could ask him. She wondered if she had the courage.

She walked outside the small but pleasant hotel where she had rented a room for the night. The sun was setting, and the sky was a lovely shade of pink. She inhaled deeply the fragrance of southern Wisconsin. Oddly, it reminded her of home in the South. She loved flowers.

It was in the midst of these pleasant thoughts that she saw a black SUV pull up in front of the Hampton Inn. She chuckled at the thought that the government actually used those vehicles; they were much like the ones that appeared in TV crime dramas.

She did not move from her perch in front of the motel door. She saw two men get out of the vehicle and look in her direction. She was about to smile, when she heard the screech of another black SUV to her left. She looked up and saw two identical vehicles barreling toward the first.

Then she saw the first two men pull out AK-47s, a gun that moviegoers around the world could identify in an instant. She turned to the door a few feet away and pushed it open.

She heard gunfire and dropped to the ground. She couldn't tell if she was hit. She knew she needed to run. At first she crawled on all fours and then she got up on two feet and ran around to the back of the lobby, through the office, and out the window. The manager of the hotel was startled when she came through his office, but then he listened, not comprehending to the noise in front of the building.

He froze in place. Cherie lay panting on the grass behind the motel.

She listened for more gunfire from out in front. She wanted to see what was going on, but she was too scared to risk sticking her head around the corner.

She sank down with her back against the wall of the motel. She surveyed what was in front of her: big open space, not a lot of room to hide. She listened closely. She heard a woman's voice. She thought she recognized it. Then her cell phone rang.

She didn't recognize the number, so she couldn't decide whether to answer it or not. But ultimately she felt she had no choice. If she didn't answer, it would keep ringing and give away her location. She pushed the talk button. "Hello," she whispered.

"Cherie, are you all right?" Darrin's voice was intense.

"I think so," Cherie said meekly.

"Where are you, Cherie?"

No response.

"Cherie, we got those men who were trying to hurt you," Darrin said. "They're dead."

Cherie felt a mix of fear and relief and grief and sorrow. More death, more pain. She didn't even know those people.

"Cherie," Darrin repeated. Then he stopped talking. He had turned the corner of the building and spotted her. Soon he was standing over her behind the small hotel in a strange city. He looked down at Cherie, who was leaning in a seated position against the stucco wall of the motel.

He crouched down next to her. "Cherie," he said softly. "You are safe now."

Cherie did not say anything. She could not think. She could not speak. Tears began streaming down her cheeks. Darrin was barely able to stop his own. He put his arm around her and pulled her close. "It's okay," he kept repeating. "It's okay."

None of this felt okay to Cherie Keenan.

66

These events were not at all okay for Aaron McLaren, the man who had arranged the hit on Cherie Keenan and who had tracked her using ingenious computer methods. McLaren worked for David Blinder. He was in charge of Mr. Blinder's personal security. Part of his job was accessing the various databases used by federal departments, and it was he, not some old-fashioned mole, who was able to hack into government online and communication systems and obtain highly classified information, including real-time, day-to-day correspondence. It was McLaren who identified Marie LeBrun to Blinder and who conjured up Mario LaSalla, a perfect nobody who had just the right combination of limited intelligence, criminality, and hubris to do a thankless task for what was in Mr. Blinder's universe not much money.

McLaren had been following the events in Kenosha in real time. He was linked to the men he had tasked to take out Cherie Keenan. He knew they had a small window of time, but he felt certain that it would be sufficient to kill a single woman on her own in a strange city.

McLaren did not know for sure if his intrusions had been compromised or if it was just plain luck that led to the mission failure. In either case he started working on another option as soon as communication with his men ceased. He assumed they were dead.

He believed he did not have a choice. Reporting failure to David Blinder was equivalent in McLaren's mind to suicide, and while he might or might not share what happened on this particular day, he would much prefer to do it with the original mission completed. He did not want Blinder to have any questions about his competence.

The trouble was that it would take another couple of hours to get a team to where Mrs. Keenan was. He knew they were taking her to a safe house in the Chicago area: he knew where it was and he knew how it was laid out. What he did not know was how many handlers Mrs. Keenan had. By McLaren's count, there were at least five people and possibly more. His new team would have to be larger so it could assault the safe house and take out not just Keenan but whoever was protecting her as well. He started making calls.

Meanwhile, in Kenosha, Sam and Marie and Cherie and Darrin were sitting at a rest stop near the Illinois border. They were talking about what just happened. Everyone present shared the same uncomfortable feeling that the timely arrival of the government team was a matter of sheer luck. If they had been thirty seconds later, Cherie would have been killed.

"It wasn't exactly one hundred percent luck," Samantha said at length. "We were given a heads-up by Echelon that a large black SUV looking a lot like a government vehicle was heading toward the motel. Max had insisted that the satellite keep an eye on it as soon as he had the coordinates, which he got while we were still in the air."

Then Marie spoke. "It still means that our communication networks are compromised, Sam," she said. "We can't trust our own communications right now."

"And that means that the bad guys may know about the safe house," Darrin added. "I don't think it's safe to go there."

The two women nodded.

For her part, Cherie wasn't feeling especially safe. She had calmed down enough to recognize the close call she had, and she was grateful not to be alone with her own thoughts. But the situation became even more serious in her mind, much more serious than it had become even with her husband's death. She knew that she owed these people her life, and she was not about to back away from helping them now. But she also had a sense that their situation was precarious.

She spoke up. "Does anybody have any idea where the system was compromised?" she asked. "Was it the cell phone network? the computer network? the radio transmissions?" She looked at the three others.

"I think it's the computer network," Samantha replied evenly. "Our communications systems interface with our supposedly secure intranet to make them more efficient." She thought for a moment. "If I were hacking, I would hack there." She thought some more. "And it's consistent with the information the bad guys must have had."

"I agree," Marie said. "If they had known Cherie's location before we tracked her through the GPS system, they would have attempted to eliminate her sooner. So it's a safe bet they are reliant on the computer, not on the ordinary cell network. Besides, the cell network is just too massive to monitor unless you have a specific number."

Darrin shook his head. His technical expertise ended on the application side of things. He had no idea how computer networks actually worked. He was even a little fuzzy about what an "intranet" was.

"If I understand what you two are saying," he said, "the best way to communicate is through a cell phone, preferably a disposal one, such as the one Cherie has been using."

"Yes," Samantha replied. "Provided no one tracked it on a computer-based system, such as GPS."

"Gotcha," Darrin said.

The two-minute lull in the conversation was broken by Cherie. "Now what?" she asked.

"First thing is to get some of those disposable cell phones," Samantha said. "We can't use the one you had because it was compromised. That's why we left it at the scene."

"Then we contact Max and talk about the safe house situation," Marie added. "We cannot go there, but we may be able to fake it so that, if or when—and I mean when—another team shows up, we'll be ready for them."

That was something Darrin understood. "It would give me great pleasure to help you with that," he said.

As if on cue, the foursome got back into the vehicle and started driving south. Darrin took the wheel, as he was most familiar with the area. They headed toward Waukegan, where they were pretty sure they could find a place that sold disposable cell phones without drawing too much attention to themselves.

Samantha and Marie couldn't help but relive the close call they had: how they got an alert from Max, how they sped toward the motel just in time to see two men with AK-47s try to kill Cherie Keenan, whom they were sent there to protect. The men were obviously surprised by their arrival, but they were well trained. They started firing at the government vehicles as soon as they heard them approaching.

Fortunately, they were seriously outgunned by the weapons the women were carrying as well as by the team that had met them at the airport. The killers were killed without mercy and without a second thought. The backup team dealt with the bodies and the local authorities. The women and Darrin left as quickly as they could, which was immediately after securing the area and making sure there were no other snipers.

Local authorities arrived within minutes to investigate the scene, and federal agents arrived shortly thereafter. They swept for prints, photographed the bodies and the vehicle from every angle, and interviewed anyone within earshot. They took DNA samples and collected any forensic evidence they could find. Samantha and

Marie were pretty sure they wouldn't come up with much beyond the identification of the men involved. Whoever did this ran a very sophisticated operation.

Darrin pulled up to a Walgreens. "How many phones do we need?" he asked.

"At least three," Samantha said. "No," she corrected herself. "Make that four." She glanced at Cherie, who nodded.

As soon as they procured the phones, Darrin started driving again. He did not have a specific direction, but he knew he should probably drive south, toward Chicago.

Fortunately, Marie knew Max had an old-fashioned cell phone he used for just this kind of situation. She also knew the number by heart. She called him; he answered on the first ring.

"I am so relieved to hear your voice," Max said.

"Likewise," Marie replied. "It was touchy for a few minutes back there."

"Tell me exactly what happened," Max said.

Marie told him. She described how the men were dressed just like government agents, sunglasses and all. The vehicle was standard-issue US government as well. The only difference was that they carried AK-47s instead of the typical American weapons. They were obviously well trained. Probably ex-military.

Max listened intently. This conspiracy or whatever it was obviously had long tentacles. He was working on two plans at once: one to get Cherie and his team with her to a safe location, the other, to arrange an ambush to get whoever was going to show up at the Chicago safe house. He had no problem with either, but the fact that his agency had been breached gave him pause.

"Okay," Max said. "I can work with old-fashioned cell phones." He had long before arranged a private communication system with off-the-shelf phones of the type Darrin had just purchased. It was the safest form of communication in a dangerously interconnected world.

"I am arranging an alternate plan," Max said. "I want all of you to check in at the Public Hotel on North State in Chicago. There will be a reservation in the name of Rosalind Gruyere, one of Marie's aliases. They will give you a large suite on the top floor. This place is one of ours; we've used it in the past. It is well secured. We have shut down all computer access to it, and I am arranging all the plans on untraceable phones." Max paused for a moment. "But stay alert. I know our computer networks are compromised, but we can't be certain the penetration isn't even larger than that. I'll meet you there around eleven."

"Thanks, Max," Marie said. "I'll let the others know." She clicked off.

The foursome drove south is silence.

bner answered David Blinder's second call much more eagerly than the first. He was more comfortable the more he understood how Blinder worked. Abner had been in daily contact with his group, and they had been working tirelessly to make discreet contacts with Confederate sympathizers. What they discovered was even more energy for secession than Abner had imagined.

Gradually the outline of a plan made itself clear. And that plan was to seize power in the Southern states, one by one, once David gave the signal. Abner felt sure this was what Blinder wanted, and he was proud to be able to report on the progress he and his men had made.

David got straight to the point. "Abner, it's almost time," he said. "We will commence hostilities within a week."

Abner, though excited, was dumbfounded that events had moved so quickly. "We'll be ready, David," he replied. "My men have done their jobs admirably."

"I want all the details, Abner," David replied.

So Abner told him. He described how each man had identified a minimum of five other influential men in their respective states, vetted them carefully, and brought them into the scheme. Each man was enthusiastic. True Southerners had long tired of federal oversight, and they saw secession as a long-awaited development. They were eager to help.

Each state had a slightly different plan. Some were to ramrod legislation through the legislative body announcing secession; some chose to simply effect a coup d'etat, replacing the sitting governor with a sympathizer who would take over. All were prepared to do whatever it took to move their states out of the Union into what they perceived as freedom, the way the Founding Fathers originally envisioned America. They were filled with pride, enthusiasm, and a grim sense of determination.

David then shared with Abner how the military operations would be carried out. Some of these would take place on Southern soil; others in non-Confederate states. All would be precisely coordinated. It was imperative, David explained to Abner, that no action be taken until he gave the command. Abner could feel the eagerness in his new friend's voice, even the encrypted one.

After he hung up, Abner called Judith. He was beside himself.

"It's happening, honey," he said. "It will happen within a week."

Judith tried to be supportive. She loved Abner; she shared his love of the South and his Confederate inclinations. But the closer the time came, the more ambivalent she became inside her mind. While freedom appealed greatly to her, mayhem did not. She wanted to shield those feelings from Abner.

It turned out she did not need to do much. Abner was so excited, he barely gave her time to talk. He finally said he had a lot of other calls to make, that he loved her, and that he could call her back so they could arrange a time to celebrate what was to come.

Then he hung up. Judith stood in her apartment for a moment looking at the cordless phone in her hand. She started to shake. She was not sure she could be a part of this. No, it was worse than that. She was sure she could not be a part of it.

It had "disaster" written all over it.

In the early decades of the twentieth century, the United States military was a formidable force, but it was stretched far across the globe. Most of the fighting units were dispersed in other countries, and the installations within the US were, for the most part, training sites. Since there was generally no need for a military presence on the American land mass, this suited the times. However, it revealed a genuine vulnerability on the part of what was incontestably a mighty organization.

There were exceptions, of course. Fort Knox in Kentucky was staffed by a fully trained unit that guarded the nation's hoard of gold. That force routinely anticipated attacks and trained to repel them. Other units protected other key government installations. But for the most part, the emphasis on actual battle troops was abroad.

In addition, the military had another vulnerability. While they emphasized screening in their selection processes, it was possible for talented dissimulators to worm their way into the Army, even into the command structure. And the Sovereign Citizens, practiced at dissimulation, excelled in this. It was in this way that a relatively small force was able to entertain hopes of defeating a mighty but widely dispersed opposing force.

68

David Blinder sat back in his desk chair. He was at home in Texas, but he was working hard. He had been in contact with all of the resources he had identified to effect a crisis and the dissolution of the federal government. He looked up on his wall at the Gilbert Stuart portrait of Thomas Jefferson, the one that everyone thought was lost. David had spent considerable energy and resources to procure it, and he mused how similar his present activities were to that worthwhile pursuit.

David mused a bit about his motives. He considered that few people knew the stirrings of his heart, mostly because he acted as if he didn't have any. He was supremely private. He didn't think he had even shared the passion he felt with those closest to him, even his brother George. But David Blinder loved America, and he believed in his heart, along with his father, that the thirties spelled the beginning of the end of the American dream, the vision that the Founding Fathers had formulated: the United States as a place where freedom reigned as the highest value, where men were free to do as they pleased to get ahead as they saw fit, without the interference or regulation of an enormous bureaucracy. He shared this vision, and he wondered why so few others did relative to the population of the country.

But he had found those brave few, and he was ready to perform major surgery on the land mass that he loved. He would return it to its original configuration: a collection of free and independent states, just as the Declaration of Independence said.

These thoughts inevitably led him to think of his brother George. Even though David Blinder was heavily engaged in fomenting rebellion, the thought that kept nipping at the edges of his consciousness had to do with his older sibling. Since this project had gone live, George had gotten more and more distant. He did not inquire about the success of his efforts or even their status. David thought George was drinking more and knew that he had recently taken to puffing on cigars throughout the day rather than occasionally in the evening.

Ever since their last conversation about the project, when he realized that George was not so invested in the work as he was, David found himself in a dilemma. He and George had always been a team. No matter that it was David who did most of the leg work in their various enterprises, he had never withheld information from George, and he believed that George did not withhold information from him. They were for decades a team: a single unit, a unique, powerful organism. They had triumphed over great odds again and again. The bond the brothers had was powerful.

Now David was calling that notion of teamwork into question. If George was not with him, did that mean he was opposed to the plan? Would he consider sabotaging it somehow? David had a weakness for going straight to the worst-case scenario: it was a habit that had frequently been reinforced in practice, and it saved him a great deal of time and money over the years. That this happened at the expense of others' well-being or even their lives troubled him not an iota. David Blinder was an efficiency machine.

In his more lucid moments, David did not think George would do anything that would impede his plans; it was more likely that he just wouldn't be so helpful as David would like. But he needed to be sure, and in order to be sure he had to have a conversation with his older brother. He was not looking forward to it.

But duty was his standard, and he buzzed his butler, who arrived within a minute.

"Yes, sir?" Anthony said.

"Anthony, please find my brother George and ask him to join me in the library."

"Yes, sir," Anthony replied. And he left the room.

David stood up and stretched. He had spent the day coordinating with the Sovereign Citizens, identifying targets, and planning sequences or orders of battle and talking about how they would get their men and weapons into position. D-Day, as David came to think of it, was to happen between seven days and fourteen days from now. The precise timing was yet to be determined, but it would be set before a day more passed. David was beside himself with excitement.

He had also been in contact with Abner and his men and Adam Wilson and his group. Wilson's group had already been getting into place. That didn't matter to Blinder very much. He thought the plan of that group—taking themselves out of circulation altogether—was needlessly complicated and even a tad melodramatic, but it reflected the devotion of that highly religious cadre. He was a little concerned about the incident with Daniel Keenan, and he wondered absently if Aaron had taken care of the small matter of Dr. Keenan's wife.

Momentarily, George Blinder entered the library. "Hello, David," he said, and he ambled over to his favorite chair. Without thinking, he opened the humidor next to his chair and selected a cigar.

"George," David said. "We need to talk."

George looked at David as he lit his cigar. "'Bout what, David?" he said, his speech not nearly so crisp as it usually was, suggesting to David that his brother was less than one hundred percent sober.

David took a deep breath. "George, we have spoken for years about how intrusive, inefficient, unfair, and dictatorial the federal government has become. This was in part our father's legacy to us. You know I have been working with various elements of society to do something about this. Up until a few months ago, I thought you and I were on the same page, as we have always been through all of our many successful business ventures." He took another breath. "But since my activity has accelerated, you seem withdrawn, uninterested, and distant." He looked at his brother. "I have never experienced you like this. It's as if you disapprove."

It was George's turn to take a deep breath. He put his cigar onto the large crystal ashtray next to his chair. "You know, David," he began. "I have been a part of our success for many years, and I have worked to limit the interference of government in our business activities. I know how strongly our father felt about the federal government. But I have to say that in the back of my mind, I always thought that the notion of that going up a notch, to outright takeover or disbanding of the government, always seemed like a fantasy of ours. It is one I did not share. It was just something we tossed around during our free time." He looked at his brother darkly. "But I never thought it was something you took so seriously or would really act on."

There was silence for a few moments. David began to say something, but his brother raised his hand.

"These past months have been a trial for me, David," he said. "I love you; we have always worked together. Even though I admit that you did most of the heavy lifting in many if not most of our activities, I was always in the work." He shook his head, as if dismissing an unmentionable thought. "But now, well, I don't know. I think . . . I think this plan is foolhardy."

David looked at his brother in silence as the blood drained from his face. So it was true, he thought: George disapproves.

Neither George nor David said anything for a while. David was considering the best response to this shattering information. George was pondering his second cocktail of the early evening.

After some time, George got up and walked across the room to a bar and poured himself a scotch, no ice. He turned around and looked at his younger brother. "What are you going to do now, David?"

David looked at his brother. "To some extent, George, that depends on what you do. Are you going to obstruct my plans?"

George shrugged slightly. "I don't think I could do that if I wanted to, David. What I would like to do now is talk you into backing off this foolhardy plan." He took a sip of scotch.

David hesitated. This didn't even sound like his brother. Ordinarily, over many years, they were so close they often blurted out the same thoughts simultaneously. David was having a hard time functioning without that support. He felt as if he had lost a limb.

To his surprise, George continued. "I thought long and hard about saying this to you. You've always been the powerhouse, the one in our dealings who made things happen. I always saw myself as something like a fellow traveler, just somebody for you to kick ideas around with. But this . . ." He took another sip of scotch. "This idea, this 'project' you are involved in: it could ruin the Blinder family. It could destroy all we've built over the years."

David's head was swimming in conflicting thoughts. Why hadn't George brought this up before? Why was he so surprised? David never gave any indication to his brother that he was anything but deadly serious about the things the two of them talked about. David felt as if the floor were moving underneath his feet. He leaned back in his chair and looked up at the ceiling.

George ambled back over to his favorite chair. He relit his cigar, looking at his brother all the while.

David leveled his head and looked at his brother. "What are you going to do, George?" he said. There was no emotion in his voice.

"As I said," George replied, "I want to talk you out of this." He looked back at his brother. It was clear that he was making no progress. "But if I can't," he said, "I don't want to be a part of it."

What happened on David's face would have been a scowl, but not enough of his face shifted for that; it was more like an intensely neutral, penetrating gaze. "I have used family resources that implicate you every step of this project," he said acidly. "You do not have an option of not being 'a part of it.'"

George looked down at his drink. He had never quite experienced this side of his brother, but it did not surprise him. Others had. He had seen David angry before. He knew that, when David got angry, his voice took on a serious timbre unlike anything else George had ever heard. David did not get loud; he just got poisonous. One could feel the acid in the words that he spoke. He shook his head.

"Then I suppose there is not much I can do," he replied at length. "What would you have me do, David?" he asked.

David did not flinch. "Stay out of my way," he replied simply.

69

When McLaren's hastily assembled team got to the Chicago safe house where they fully expected to find Cherie Keenan and several other men, they were heavily armed. They had been told not to leave anyone alive: no witnesses.

They were dressed in Army combat uniforms and outfitted with non-Army weapons: AK-47s, hand grenades, rocket-propelled grenade launchers, and assorted handguns. There were six of them. McLaren was following with a real-time online linkup.

The house was on the south side of Chicago in a run-down neighborhood. This, plus the fact that it was dark, made it easier for them to approach the small bungalow in two armored SUVs. They positioned the vehicles about a half a block away in separate directions. The plan was to storm the building from two different angles, front and rear, kill everyone in it, and demolish the building completely.

Max's team of twelve members of the Special Activities Division of the CIA had set up a larger perimeter. They identified the vehicles immediately when they pulled up Cottage Grove. They were computer- and radio-silent. Hand signals and whispering were their primary modes of communication. They were in contact with Max, who was on-site and directing the operation via cheap, disposable cell phones.

The hope was to take the assault team members alive so they could be interrogated and linked to larger figures. To that end, Max's group was equipped with two separate kinds of ammunition: standard military firepower, including silenced M-16s, M-9 side arms, and a variety of gas and explosive grenades, as well as nonlethal Taser XREPs, shotgun Tasers designed to stun but not kill the target. These could be fired from a distance and had an instantaneous effect on the targeted subject, completely disabling the person. The professionalism of the initial team sent to kill Cherie Keenan was not lost on Max, and he made sure his SAD team had a full appreciation of just whom they were dealing with as well as a full complement of matériel to manage the situation.

Max would have preferred to have an AWACS plane or at least an observing drone assist in his operation, but he knew it was too dangerous to use any computer-dependent device. He would have to do this the old-fashioned way: hand-to-hand combat in an urban setting. He was stationed on the roof of an apartment building across the street from the safe house, and he had his binoculars trained on the incoming team. He had left a light and a fan on inside the safe house, hoping this was enough to create the illusion that there were people inside. He hoped he had the element of surprise on his side.

After he counted the men getting out of the SUVs, he motioned for his men to commence operations. The first team swung around in a pincer movement, surrounding the team that was approaching the house from the rear. With their silenced Taser rifles, they opened fire. They took out the driver, the only person remaining in the SUV, and then pumped Taser projectiles into the other two men.

The team leader signaled to his counterpart on the other team that the first assault group was down. The second SAD group swept down on the remaining assault team members. One of them got suspicious and turned and saw them coming. He opened fire, missing his target and collecting counterfire in return. The other two members of his team turned their weapons on their attackers but realized instantly that they were outgunned and outmanned. They were all neutralized with the same electrically charged ordnance.

Max followed his team, whom he had instructed to remain silent and to collect all electronic gear. They did so, and Max handed it over to his IT specialist, the best man he had, who was waiting in a van nearby. Another van came and collected the now bound assault team, all alive and all to be interrogated separately.

cLaren was listening closely via the secure Internet hookup he had established with his team. He had visual contact with them until they exited the SUVs. He did not hear the assault of the SAD team, but his men were trained to check in every two minutes. They ordinarily did this continuously, since the link was real-time. But when there was a pause, McLaren noticed. He did not say anything. He watched his Breitling Chronomat tick the seconds away. After ninety seconds, he was beginning to perspire. How could he not have gotten this right? He had all the data. At about a hundred and ten seconds, he heard an explosion. He listened more intently. "Check in," he whispered.

"Team one, checking in, proceeding as planned," came a reply. McLaren waited.

"Team two, checking in, proceeding as planned," came a second. Then: "We're busy here. Back to you soon."

McLaren was puzzled. The voices were encrypted and disguised, so he couldn't be sure if the words he heard were those of his men. But that was the protocol, so he was tempted to relax. He kept his eye on his computer and on his watch. He heard more gunfire, then another explosion.

George Halen, the IT specialist, had the assistance of two of the SAD guys to help him revive one of the men and demand the check-in protocol. In the minute or so that this took, he set up a protocol to track the communication link. The SAD team member's methods were not pretty, and at first the half-awake man resisted. However, his attention was procured, and he spit out the words. He knew he had a losing hand.

Halen understood he had only a few minutes before whoever was tuned in would realize that his mission had been compromised, so he worked as quickly as he could, searching the Internet connection for clues of the origin of the observer. He tried to send a reverse signal, but it got bogged down in a mass of data he didn't have time to figure out.

At the same time, McLaren's anxiety was returning. As soon as his watch hit one hundred and twenty seconds, his tension peaked. He thought it was possible that his team was somehow engaged in a firefight. But then he saw telltale signs of a tracer on his screen. He shut down the Internet connection and started breathing heavily. In his mind, he reviewed the steps he took to disguise the connection. He had used linkups from around the world; these things were nearly impossible to trace. Still, the fact that his mission failed was one thing; compromising his identity and his personal connection to the Blinder family was another. He gathered up his equipment, which primarily included a laptop, and left the late-night diner that he had selected for overseeing this operation. He got into his Maserati and sped away.

He had no idea where Cherie Keenan was.

"Shit!" said George Halen. He knew he was at a dead end. He would take all the equipment with him and go over it as carefully as he did everything, but he was not optimistic about finding what he was looking for, which was the origin of this mysterious but obviously highly skilled assassination network.

Part 4

★ ★ ★ ★ ★

bner was nothing but pleased. His men had expanded their network rapidly, and a plan was beginning to come into clearer focus.
A subplan, really, since the primary one was Blinder's assault on
the federal superstructure. Abner's role, and the role of his men,
was to prepare the way so that Southern government structures
were prepared and willing to declare themselves what they should
be: free and independent states. He got light-headed every time he
thought of it.

He believed that another meeting was in order. The enthusiasm
of his team was palpable, and he felt that energy could be usefully
directed. He decided to do this via a computer conference, so as to
avoid having people travel when they were in the midst of the work
they were sent out to do. This was easy to set up and encrypt and
did not take much time to arrange. He scheduled it for two days
hence.

He was in Georgia. His troubled marriage in St. Louis made
that agreeable city less attractive just now. In addition, he felt he
should do this work from his home state in the South. It helped him
feel clearer and more grounded. As painfully as he had abandoned
this state when he was young, he embraced it now. He felt safe, at
home. He thought often of his brave father, long since idealized in
his mind as a man of conviction, purpose, and strength, traits Abner
knew he himself had in abundance.

Abner thought of calling Judith prior to the meeting, but he was too excited. While contact with her generally calmed him down, on this day he did not want to relax. He did not want to relinquish the delicious feelings of anticipation and imminent success that coursed through his body. He wanted to be alone with himself. He was sure this was something the Christian saints felt when they faced adversaries in the ancient Roman Coliseum: filled with faith and hope and promise of success and reward.

His men logged on precisely at seven o'clock. Their small faces filled his large computer screen. In the corner, he could see his own image, with just the correct blend of equanimity and hopefulness. He asked each one to report what he had accomplished.

The news ran from good to unbelievably good. All of the men reported successfully recruiting key people who were willing, when the conditions were right, to put their financial and legislative weight behind secession. None of them thought that this would be a problem, so estranged had the state governance apparatuses become from Washington, DC.

The unbelievably good was the report that three of the eleven governors had privately agreed not only to secede by executive order but also to declare all federal facilities within their states—including all US Army facilities—property of the respective states; this in addition to declaring secession from the Union. Abner couldn't wait to make his report to Blinder.

The group spent some time strategizing about how to use that single-minded sense of purpose as leverage in the remaining states. Most of the men thought this was eminently doable, and they planned to meet with their respective governors privately as soon as that could be arranged.

Abner praised the men in his group. "You are all true patriots," he declared. "Thank you for the vital service you are providing to our country." He said this with such emotion, he could not prevent his eyes from glazing over just a bit. He allowed a single tear to fall down his cheek. Abner didn't care. Real men had feelings, and this was the pinnacle of his life's work. He could not have been prouder of what his men did and of what he did in this vital and blessed work.

After he logged off, Abner turned in his chair and considered what to do next. He knew contacting David Blinder was high on his list, but he wanted to savor his moment of success a little while longer before he contacted him. There was an undercurrent of subservience that he always felt with Blinder, an experience he was sure he shared with many people who did business with him. He did not think he resented that, or at least not much, but he wanted to spend just a little time nursing the high he was feeling before taking the next step.

He walked into the kitchen of the small apartment he had rented in downtown Atlanta and pulled out a bottle of his best Kentucky bourbon. He got a glass and put a couple of ice cubes in it before pouring himself three fingers of the amber liquid. He took his drink and walked out onto the small balcony overlooking the lights of Atlanta, the new capital of the South. Not a capital like Washington, DC, to which other states would be subservient, but more like the primus inter pares of Christianity's Church of Rome: first among equals. Atlanta deserved the distinction. No other city had been burned to the ground with such vengeance and hatred as Atlanta. No other American city suffered so much at the hands of Union forces. Killed by our own brothers, he thought bitterly. That's what the federal system wrought. No more! he declared silently to the city below him. I will avenge that injustice. Soon we will all be free of the yoke of oppression. Soon we will all be free.

He polished off his bourbon in one long gulp.

72

David Blinder was in fact delighted with the report from Bellamy. He was still struggling with the situation with his brother and was unsure what to do about it. That cast a long shadow over his planning and implementing, especially as the time grew short. But he couldn't help congratulating himself for finding Abner and using him to such good effect.

"You have done excellent work," he effused to Abner. "I am very proud of you."

Abner savored the compliment. But for someone who grew up essentially parentless, it seemed a little quaint if not patronizing. Still, he believed he had David Blinder's complete confidence.

"Abner," Blinder continued. "This is all going to happen soon, most likely within a week. I want you to wait for my call to put your resources in play. I will contact you directly."

"I'll be ready," Abner replied. And he had no doubt he would be.

"Good," said Blinder. And he hung up.

David turned his chair away from his desk to face the large window behind his desk in the library of his home in Texas. Everything seemed to be on schedule: all of his plans were gradually coming to fruition. He glanced over at the portrait of his father that hung over the mantel of the mahogany fireplace. You would be proud, Father, he said silently.

Then David swiveled back to the window. What was he going to do about his brother George? He mentally listed the options: kill him and make it look like an accident, or, better yet, make it look like some federales did it; have him essentially kidnapped and sequestered until hostilities ceased; or just trust that he wouldn't say or do anything to hinder the plans. But what was the word George used to describe the plan? Oh, yes: foolhardy. David shook his head. He knew the third option was just not possible. He would give it another day's thought. George was, after all, his brother.

In the meantime, he put the matter out of his mind and swiveled back to his desk. He had a coded sheet of paper that would no doubt look like gobbledygook to anyone who glanced at it, but it was his personal diagram for coordinating the assaults that would cripple the national government and compel the states to secede from the Union.

He thought about the Sovereign Citizens and how potent and how completely amoral they were as a group: disciplined, supremely secretive and paranoid, bent on destruction for vague, ill-defined ends; they just cried out for the kind of direction David Blinder provided. David could not believe his good fortune in penetrating their organization. He did something that the mighty federal government had never been able to do, and he was damn proud of that.

But the issue of George continued to plague him, despite his decision to postpone it a day. He realized that he was considering the death of his brother, a man to whom he had been intimately connected throughout his life, the only other human being who knew about David and his life in a detailed way. It struck David as odd that he could not identify a feeling when he thought of doing away with George. He saw it primarily as—what was the word?—an inconvenience just now.

But perhaps a necessary inconvenience. He could not risk George's spilling the beans either to someone outside the family or even to his spouse or someone else in the family. The Blinders were a notoriously tight-lipped group, even with each other. What David and George had throughout the years was special. David's wife knew nothing of his business interests, but George knew a lot about them. David's wife knew nothing of this most recent project, but George knew nearly all about it. Nobody in the Blinder family knew how cold-blooded David was, but George did.

David shook his head. It will be a damn shame to lose him, he thought.

73

For George's part, he realized within minutes of his brief conversation with his brother that he would get nowhere. As much as he admired David, he knew that, once his brother's trajectory was set, there was little that he or anyone or anything else could do to knock it off course. Throughout their career together, George saw this in the main as an asset. He and David could discuss something and within no time, it seemed, David would bring it about.

But George also knew how utterly unscrupulous David could be. He did not have any firsthand information that his brother killed anyone, but he knew for a fact that on six or seven occasions someone who was obstructing a Blinder plan ended up on the other side of the final horizon. He did not think David himself would do it—he was too fastidious for that kind of work—but he knew David had a wide network of connections; this included people who could do all sorts of dirty jobs. George knew that David was selective about what he told George about these matters: he never acknowledged that he hurt or killed anyone, and George never asked. George always felt it was his job to listen and to be supportive. He did not want to know if people were hurt or if laws were broken, and it was to no one's advantage for him to know those things. That was fine with him.

But this last project troubled George a great deal. He thought of his father's rants against the government and regulation and entitlements as more symptomatic of a hotheaded, hard-charging self-starter than the sober reflections of a wisdom figure. George loved his father, but he always thought he was a little off, a little too intense. Not unlike David, he mused. Politically, George was a closet moderate. He sang from the Republican songbook to his family and friends, but privately he thought the path of compromise worked well for the country. In an era of deepening radicalism, this sensible thinking was harder and harder to sell.

George did not doubt that his brother at least considered doing away with him. He didn't even think it was personal; it was just how David was. But George was not one to offer himself up to be martyred. He had an escape plan that he would implement at the first sign of danger. Now he was there. George figured that his last conversation with his brother was that first sign.

George's plan was not complicated, but he had developed it over time. He had suspected for some time that he might need to get away. He had sequestered enough money to sustain himself and had hidden it cleverly in a variety of shell company accounts on- and off-shore. He needed transportation. He was certain he could use none of the household vehicles, although there were many. Not exactly coincidentally, he had recently returned to riding his bicycle for exercise, along the lovely and mostly flat rural roads surrounding the Blinder property. He figured not even his brother would bother to have a bicycle tagged, especially one used by an older man for occasional exercise. The other part of the plan consisted of George's concocting an alternative identity, with an assumed name, a driver's license, and a passport. He had ample cash at his disposal. The only question was when to implement the departure. The more George thought about the timing, the more anxious he got. He figured that time was short; he could not escape the thought that it was time now. He elected to leave first thing in the morning.

Fortunately, George had a fairly clear idea how his brother worked. He knew that if he decided to do away with him, he would likely do it sooner rather than later, although he would certainly be constrained by carefully considering how it fit into his overall objectives. George knew a great deal about David's enterprises but not everything. He tried to plan on the basis of what he knew, but he understood there was an unavoidable margin of error because of David's natural secretiveness. George was blessed with the ability to listen patiently and listen well; he had an excellent memory. He had a stack of information that he thought was incriminating to his brother, and he selectively gathered it in a safe place to exonerate himself if any of this came to light. He also thought it might be useful if there came a time to negotiate.

But he also realized that a time for negotiation with David might never come. When he heard the timbre of David's voice, he believed he and David had passed a critical juncture. There would be no negotiation; there would be only David's decision, whatever it was.

George was saddened by all of this, but he saw no future for the relationship between himself and his brother. He saw clearly that David was passing a point where he would no longer be able to mask his involvement in a seditious plot that would mean the federal authorities would hound him until he was dead or behind bars. George shook his head. Pride goeth before the fall, he thought, and he knew from firsthand experience that David's pride knew no bounds.

For George's part, he was fully prepared to bid farewell to the pampered life he had lived as one of the richest men in the country and take up a less gilded if more anonymous retirement with fewer but safer perks.

So the morning after his brief and futile conversation with David, George awoke early in the morning. He kissed his wife on the forehead before he got out of bed and dressed as he always did. He went down to the breakfast room and listened intently to any noises in the Blinder compound. Nothing. He quietly opened the back door and slipped out. He had the bicycle that he would ride the three miles to town, where he would hop a bus to Dallas. Once there he would rent a car under his forged identity and drive south across the border to Mexico. From there he would proceed to a third country where he had established a new home. He had a backpack ready with everything he needed. He slipped out the back door.

As he pedaled down the road, George felt twinges of regret and twinges of freedom. He regretted that things had come to this point with his brother, but he felt free not only from the parlous plot in which his brother was engaged but also from the weightiness of being a publicly known and often feared person. He longed for quiet anonymity and for other people to treat him more or less like a normal person. He longed to pass his sunset years in a quieter, cozier, and less intense place.

When George got to the bus station, he went into the bathroom and changed his clothes. He did not do this because of the physical exertion of the ride but because he wasn't sure David didn't have all of his clothes outfitted with a GPS tracker of some sort. He brought with him some clothes he had purchased a few weeks earlier and kept hidden from everyone.

George didn't mind the bus ride. Even though he was born wealthy thanks to his hardworking father, George thought many of the accoutrements of wealth excessive. He really didn't see the need for a hundred-million-dollar Gulfstream jet when first class on most airlines was quite comfortable. But in America, people used their money for convenience, for show, or for any number of reasons, the significance of which mattered little to George. The jet was there because the brothers could afford it and because it offered a modicum of increased comfort and efficiency. And because it broadcast to the world that the Blinders were a cut above everyone else in the money game. Seems silly, George thought as he gazed out the window of the comfortable Greyhound bus that was traveling south.

It was at the bus station in Dallas that he first noticed a man watching him. Initially it was just a flash, a barely noticeable awareness that something was amiss. The man hadn't been on the bus; it was as if he were waiting for George at the Dallas station. As if he knew which bus he would be on. George sat on a bench in the middle of the station and watched the man who was surreptitiously trying to watch him. George did not look at him directly, but he kept his eyes cast in his general direction. The man glanced his way but kept his eyes on a newspaper he had in his hand. He was leaning against a pillar in the station reading a newspaper, something that people rarely do in the real world but often do in detective movies. All he needed was a cigarette dangling from his lips, George thought.

He realized that the odds of his being successful in this escape plan were at best fifty-fifty. If David sent this man, he must have had someone tracking me since I last spoke to him. Or maybe he's always had someone follow me and I just thought of it as a security measure. George took a deep breath.

Then the man with the newspaper started walking in his direction. George's pulse quickened. Is he going to kill me here? he thought. He glanced around. No one else seemed to notice anything amiss.

"Excuse me, Mr. Blinder?" the man said. And then he hesitated. "You are George Blinder, aren't you?"

"Yes, I am," replied George. He was too surprised to lie.

"Mr. Blinder, I have been a great admirer of you for a long time. I teach business at SMU, and the models you and your brother used to take over companies was just brilliant. It is an honor to meet you in person, sir."

George did not say anything for a moment. Then, "Why, thank you. And what did you say your name was?"

"Anderson, Keith Anderson," the man replied, extending his hand. Blinder shook it.

"It's nice meeting you, Mr. Anderson," he said.

"And you, sir. Good day." He walked off.

So much for anonymity in these parts, George thought. Time to get out of here.

He walked out of the station and hailed a taxi. "I need to rent a car," he said to the driver, who nodded and sped away.

amantha was thinking of how to finesse the situation with David Blinder's request for information about Marie when Blinder called her a second time within days, an unusual occurrence. "What do you have for me, Samantha?" his unctuous voice said.

"I'm still collecting data, Mr. Blinder," Samantha said. She was in a large suite of rooms in the Public Hotel in Chicago with Cherie Keenan, Marie LeBrun, and Darrin McAlister. Max had been there the night before but had left an hour ago to return to Washington. "I should have something solid later next week." She knew that Blinder preferred thoroughness to speed in most situations.

"There's something else I would like you to do as well," Blinder said. "I'd like you to run a check on my brother George. Find out any information you can. And this is a priority: I would like you to drop what you were doing for me and attend to this first. I want you to do this before you complete your work regarding Ms. LeBrun. Do you understand?"

"Yes, sir, I do," replied Samantha evenly, feeling both relief and wonderment about his agenda. "When would you like this information?"

"If you come up with anything unusual, I would like to hear about it as soon as possible," Blinder replied. "There is some urgency about this."

Samantha ventured a question. "Could you give me some idea of what I might be looking for?" she said.

A moment of silence on the other line. "Yes, I want to know if he has established any alternative identities, aliases, or things of that nature. I'd also like to know about hidden caches of money, secret bank accounts, and that sort of thing. Here is his Social Security number."

Samantha was still writing this information down when Blinder clicked off. She glanced over at Marie. "Sounds like trouble at the Blinder compound," she said. She could not wait to get this information to Max. She put the phone down to explain. "That was Blinder," she said. "He wants me to check on his brother George."

Marie's eyes widened. "Tell Max," she said. "He needs to know this right away."

"Agreed," she said, and she pulled out the disposable phone to make the call.

It turned out that Max was hardly surprised. He had been working to penetrate the Blinder security network for days, and he had assigned significant resources to the task. This included the Echelon satellite network, which tracked George's departure. Max had also activated a local operative by the name of Keith Anderson, who was to provide human intelligence on the ground.

"We are following George Blinder now. Sam, I want you to do what David Blinder asked you to do, but I want you to feed him inaccurate information. We will work that up to coincide with the intel you get on this. It has to look real and be borne out in case anyone checks. But give it a day. I presume even David Blinder knows this won't be easy."

"Got it," said Sam.

avid Blinder got two pieces of bad news within an hour. He was talking with Aaron McLaren, his chief of security, the man he had tasked with doing away with Cherie Keenan. McLaren was explaining how he had failed twice to kill a defenseless middle-aged woman with ex–Special Forces mercenaries. He did not respond to McLaren's tense explanations. Excuses, Blinder thought. I hate excuses.

As soon as he hung up, George's wife, Tilley, called him on the house phone. "Have you seen George?" she asked.

"No, Tilley, I haven't," David replied. In his mind, he scrolled through the options, and his brother's disappearance was not far from the top of the list.

"I haven't seen him all morning," Tilley continued. "David, I'm worried. It's not like George to wander off without letting me know where he is."

"I'm sure he'll turn up," David lied soothingly. "He's had a lot on his mind lately."

"You will let me know if you see him, won't you, David?" Tilley asked.

"Of course, Tilley," David replied. He hung up.

David Blinder took a deep breath. He looked at the antique clock on the wall that kept perfect time. It was eleven o'clock. He wondered how far George could have gotten. He also knew that he had to talk to McLaren again, even though his head of security demonstrated his rank incompetence in that other matter. David already had someone else in mind for the job. He scowled and considered his options.

He did not want to order a hit on George if McLaren had compromised his much-bragged-about anonymity in his penetration of the federal communication system. He wondered how extensive the damage would be. Would he have to postpone his plan if McLaren's access was shut down? Was it shut down? Was it in danger of being shut down? How far did the damage penetrate? Lots of questions.

Mostly because he was momentarily unsure what to do, he called Samantha back. There was something about talking with her that calmed him down. She was a beautiful, competent, strong woman who was completely businesslike and deferential in her dealings with him. It helped clear his mind just to talk to her.

Samantha answered on the first ring.

"Samantha," Blinder said. "The priority on gathering information about my brother just went up." He spoke in a calm, matter-of-fact voice. "I need that information as soon as possible." David could sense just a hint of desperation in his own voice, a sentiment he abhorred. He took a deep breath. "I will reimburse you accordingly," he said, believing, as he did, that money motivated more than anything.

"Yes, sir," Samantha replied. "I'll see what I can do today."

David's voice softened. "Thank you, Samantha," he said. "Thank you."

amantha and Marie had been in heated conversation since Blinder's first call. After they spoke with Max, they wondered if George Halen had made any progress with the captured equipment. George told Max that it might be possible to retrace the penetration paths that the hacker had used to compromise the federal system. He was trying to mine this enormous cacophony of data for specific information. George also told Max, however, that the odds were not in favor of that. He was working on it, but whoever constructed this maze knew what he was doing. Halen called him a genius.

The fact that George Blinder went missing right after the raids on Cherie Keenan failed was not lost on any of the federal agents or on Darrin McAlister. A picture began forming in their collective mind. All of a sudden, David Blinder became an even hotter item in the conspiracy theory.

Of course, Max and Halen had been working to penetrate Blinder's security for days. It was a daunting task. The Echelon satellite was tasked with deep surveillance of his house, meaning that it used heat-sensing technology to identify human or animal movement in the Blinder compound. It also kept a digital file of this for further examination. It was that piece of technology that traced George Blinder's departure.

They reviewed the file of the departure with a simultaneous feed to Samantha's laptop. It showed two people talking in the library in the evening. Then everyone in the compound retired to their respective bedrooms. David Blinder was the last to go to his. Then early the next morning, a solitary figure arose around 5:00 a.m., got on a bicycle, and pedaled into town. He was lost to the satellite after he was about a mile and a half from the Blinder house.

"My bet is that that's George," Max said.

"It's got to be," George Halen said. He adjusted the satellite to side-view the same visual field, which allowed them to track George Blinder for another half mile. It was far enough to identify the fact that he was headed straight to town.

"I'm checking transportation options for Wichita Falls, Texas," Samantha said. A few keystrokes later, she reported in: "About the only thing short of prearranged private transportation is a Greyhound bus station," she said. "And if he is on a bicycle, I'd say he's headed for the Greyhound station. Clever, in a way." She checked the schedule. A bus left at 6:15 a.m. for Dallas. Another left at 7:15 for Houston. There wasn't another until 11:00 a.m., and that went to Austin. "My guess is Dallas," Marie said, looking over Sam's shoulder. He could be there within a couple of hours, and then he could go anywhere. She glanced at her watch. "I imagine he's left for Dallas by now," she noted.

"Let's brainstorm this," Max said on the computer hookup. "Why would George Blinder leave so mysteriously? On a bicycle?"

Ideas poured out. He did something David didn't like; he was afraid of surveillance; he had a prearranged plan; he did not want to be tracked; David tried or would try to hurt or kill him; he was wanting to make a separate deal or negotiate separately with federal officials in case the "rebellion" didn't pan out as planned.

But no contact had been initiated from George Blinder. "How old is he, Sam?" Max asked. Samantha checked her computer. "He will be seventy-seven in two weeks," she replied.

Max thought. "We have a man on him, but he's keeping his distance," he said. It was clear a moment later that he was ready to make his next move. He picked up the phone. "Tell Anderson to locate George Blinder and make some kind of contact." He clicked off and sighed deeply.

There was quiet in the room. Then Darrin said, "It seems to me that if one of the big rats is jumping ship, things are about to escalate. Why don't we storm the Blinder compound and arrest these people?"

Max thought for a moment. "All the evidence we have isn't enough to get a warrant to do that, Darrin," Max replied. "What we have is a lot of speculation. But if we are correct—and I think we are—Blinder has done a great job of covering his tracks."

A sense of frustration and impasse settled over the conversation.

I
n his soul, David Blinder knew that the battle was about to begin. It might be a day or two or a week or two or even a month or two, but he doubted the latter. He felt the exhilaration that comes with combat on a grand scale. These kinds of emotional experiences stimulated him, sharpening his senses and clearing his mind. He was standing in front of the large picture window in his library surveying the lushly watered and fertile Texas soil that made up his large farm holdings surrounding the family compound. He knew there were soldiers stationed just outside his field of vision, soldiers whose sole purpose was to do his bidding. They were members of the Sovereign Citizens, but they had pledged their considerable firepower to protect him and his family. They were also waiting for his command to commence operations to bring down the federal government.

David felt a sense of euphoria sweep over him. He took a deep breath. It's about to begin. As he pondered his predicament throughout the day, he realized that, even with the breaches involved with McLaren's security and even with his brother's departure—maybe even because of these things—he needed to move up his timetable.

The SC forces were skillfully hidden among the civilian population. They looked like everyone else; they were trained not to draw attention to themselves. But in an hour's time, they could be armed and organized into military units, ready to implement the strategy that Blinder had devised to topple the federal superstructure. They had no uniforms—for the most part, they wore jeans, T-shirts, and heavy boots or running shoes—but they had distinctive markings known exclusively to each other. Outsiders, including federal military and law enforcement people, would have a hard time understanding that these ordinary-looking people were executing finely detailed and well-practiced movements designed to bring them down.

The SC squadrons were concentrated around key areas: One was the gold depository at Fort Knox, Kentucky. David was certain that capturing the nation's gold was a key piece of the federal government's losing all credibility. That was the first mission. Second, Daniel Cooper would lead his squadron of handpicked SC forces to take command of Fort Leonard Wood in Missouri, one of the largest ammunition depots in the country.

Third, Adam Wilson had promised that his group was capable of procuring or neutralizing the nuclear codes. This would not only remove a significant threat but would demonstrate to all the weakness and fallibility of the federal government. It would also rattle the federal chain of command.

Then there was Washington, DC. Blinder believed that he did not have to attack that citadel outright. All he had to do was isolate it and threaten it. With the nuclear codes compromised and heavy weapons aimed at the White House, Congress, and the Lincoln Memorial, sobriety would quickly befall the pampered bureaucrats of that erstwhile swamp. So at the appointed time, his troops would ring Washington, allowing no one to come in or leave. They would detonate an electromagnetic pulse machine to kill all electronic communication. They would take out a symbolic monument to let everyone know they meant business, and then they would simply hold them hostage while the states took care of their own rightful business.

While all this was happening, Abner's group as well as Wilson's would initiate secession. Abner's men were ready to have all the states of the old Confederacy announce secession, no matter what the bureaucrats in Washington did or said or wanted. Wilson would take care of other major centers, including California and the West Coast states and Texas and Oklahoma.

David Blinder looked at the portrait of his father. "The day is nearly here, Father," he said to the silent image. "Finally."

ax's head was swimming with information: data from the satellite feed, data from Halen, information coming in from boots on the ground. The arms shipment stolen from Fort Leonard Wood was traced through the Mark Twain National Forest via the GPS trackers until all movement came to a stop. By the time agents arrived to investigate, all they found were large empty trucks. No weapons, no people: not even fingerprints or other forensic evidence. The trucks had obviously off-loaded their cargo and scrubbed down the anonymous vehicles; the cargo vanished off the grid.

"Damn!" Max said.

Nor had Halen made much progress with the equipment they collected at the site of the attack on the safe house in Chicago. It was all state of the art, but that was a surprise to no one. The tracking mechanisms usually built into computer command sequences were self-eliminating, and Halen was at his wit's end trying to come up with some kind of useful information.

Even the men in custody weren't talking. They were obviously a hardened lot. Some of them had been identified as ex–Special Forces of the US military, but as yet they had not all been identified. They did not speak at all. They did not ask for attorneys or food or go on about their rights. They were mute. A tough bunch.

Max got on the phone to talk to Mueller at the FBI and bring him up to date. He called him on his personal cell phone. He described the penetration of the federal communication system as far as he was able to discern it, but he clearly gave Mueller the impression that it could be worse than they knew about. Mueller listened closely.

"I'll have to go to the President," Mueller finally said.

"Yes, you do, Bob," Max replied. "And soon. I think things are heating up. It might be a good idea to contact the military and give them a heads-up. They may even want to ramp up the alert status."

Mueller thought for a moment. "I'll discuss that with the President, and I will be in touch with them, Max. I'll get back to you about whatever decisions are made."

Max clicked off and called Cherie Keenan, whom he had not spoken to in what seemed like a long while.

"How're you doing, Cherie?" Max said softly.

Cherie didn't say anything for a while. Then she murmured, "Sometimes I just can't believe what's happening, Max. A week ago I was living a quiet little life in Missouri, and now all hell has broken loose." She tightened her grip on the phone. "I miss my kids," she said.

Max nodded. He had children. Even though he wasn't married now, he had been, and it had not been unsatisfactory. He had two kids whom he adored. "We'll get you back with them as soon as we can," he said.

Cherie took a deep breath. "I've also been trying to reconstruct any information I could about that group Daniel was hooked up with. I never thought about it at the time—it was just some more meetings that he had—but I've been trying to think if there was anything unusual." She frowned. "I haven't come up with much."

Max nodded. "This is a very well-planned operation, Cherie," he said. "You're not the only one coming up empty-handed."

arvey Winkelstein waited with uncharacteristic patience for boarding to begin on the Virgin Atlantic flight from New York to Paris. While he wasn't privy to the operational details of what was about to happen, he figured the safest place would be some other country, one far enough away to avoid trouble, especially the shedding of his blood, and to avoid being implicated in any way. He was feeling pretty smug, standing at a counter sipping his fat-free latte.

"Dr. Winkelstein?" a voice said from his left.

Harvey turned. "Yes?" he said.

"I am Agent Wallace from the FBI. I'm afraid you will have to come with me, sir." The man was polite but firm.

"What is this about?" asked Winkelstein. He did not move.

"We will explain it en route, sir," the agent replied.

"En route to where?" Winkelstein asked, still not moving. His face was forming into a defiant sneer.

The agent thought for a moment, then nodded to someone over Harvey's shoulder. A man Winkelstein had not noticed grabbed his arms and twisted them behind his back and put handcuffs on him. "Ouch!" said Harvey.

"It was our intention to avoid a public scene, sir," the agent said in a perfectly neutral voice. "But we have been instructed to take you into custody this way if you showed the slightest resistance. You will now come with us."

The man behind him pushed him forward. Harvey fell into step between the two agents. "I am afraid you are going to be very sorry you attempted this," Harvey said. He had allowed for the possibility that something like this might happen.

As they approached the end of the secure area, Harvey fully expected the SC troops to unburden him of these two federal agents. He saw two of them following him with their eyes. Jeans, sweatshirts, running shoes, characteristic insignia. No doubt their loose-fitting tops were hiding weapons. He smiled a small but sly smile.

But nothing happened. The agents continued to escort him through the security perimeter, across the hall, and outside into a waiting car. There were US Army troops positioned in large numbers along the roadway, all carrying automatic weapons. "What the . . . ?" Harvey said aloud.

Agent Wallace spoke but did not bother to look at Harvey Winkelstein. "Those friends of yours had no weapons, Dr. Winkelstein. We set up a separate perimeter in the event that there would be trouble. It seems that your men decided that a tactical retreat was the best course." He turned slowly to look at Harvey straight in the eye. "You are dispensable," he said without a trace of emotion in his voice.

Wallace texted Max that Harvey Winkelstein was in custody.

One for our side, Max thought. He called Darrin McAlister back in Chicago and told him. Darrin put him on speaker. "That was a lucky break, Darrin," he said.

Darrin nodded. "The more I learned about that low-life poseur, the more I wanted him in custody. It will be interesting to see what kind of information we get out of him."

Samantha chimed in. "I'm pretty sure we have a read on the money flow," she said. Her eyes were glued to the screen even though she was talking to the phone on the table. Max had no idea what she was talking about, but he had a lot of confidence in

Samantha Stranger. It was more important that she knew what she was talking about.

"What we need," Max said, "is the weapons flow. What happened to those weapons stolen from Fort Leonard Wood?" He knew Samantha didn't have the answer. He was half talking to himself.

Marie spoke up. "I think we can help you with that, Max," she said. She had been doing some checking of her own and had found completed transactions in the history of Winkelstein's dealings. She was developing a clearer idea of how he worked.

"He's such a snake," Marie said, "but he's a consistent snake. He's done some clever things to cover his tracks, but he tends to repeat the same patterns. I think I'm getting a lock on that."

Max listened intently to what Marie was describing. She walked him through how Winkelstein procured the weapons, transferred them to a third party, arranged delivery for the buyer, and transferred the weapons again. It was clever. There was no obvious connection between the procurement site and the delivery site. There was a complete lack of knowledge on the part of the third party, who collected only a small fee for storing the weapons for some period of time. It was Harvey Winkelstein himself who, of course, made hundreds of thousands of dollars on these transfers. He bought cheap and sold high. Age-old formula for the accumulation of capital.

"This still doesn't tell us where those weapons in Missouri went," Max said. He was getting nervous. True, collecting Harvey Winkelstein was a point for his side, but Harvey was a small if important frog in a much larger pond. He needed more information about the Blinders.

"Thanks for all your good work, everybody," Max said. "I need to make another call."

He picked up another cell phone. "Pick up David Blinder for questioning," he said.

It wasn't exactly the case that David Blinder was expecting an attempt to take him into custody. He thought someone in the government bureaucracy might try it, so he made arrangements to deal with it if it occurred. However, since McLaren had shut down his federal spy system to avoid being traced, he had no reliable way of knowing when or if an arrest or a detainment was coming. To bolster his safety, he kept his personal attorney at the guest house in his compound.

Samuel Waverly was a distinguished and accomplished attorney. Tall and silver-haired, with announcer-quality vocal skills, Mr. Waverly was a force to contend with in the courtroom, in the negotiating room, and in the delicate kinds of situations that were about to erupt at the Blinder compound.

When the butler alerted David Blinder that federal authorities were at the door, he speed-dialed Waverly and commanded him to accompany him to the reception parlor where he would meet with the agents. Waverly did not demure; he relished a good fight.

The agents were led into the spacious room and offered coffee or tea. They politely declined. They explained in straightforward terms that they had a warrant for Mr. Blinder's arrest and asked him politely to accompany them to the federal facility in Dallas for questioning.

"What is the charge?" Samuel Waverly asked.

"Conspiracy to commit murder, conspiracy to kidnap, and conspiracy to foment insurrection against the government of the United States," one of the agents said matter-of-factly.

Neither Waverly nor Blinder had any visible response. "That's quite a set of allegations," said Waverly after a while. "Let me see the warrant."

He sat down across from the agents and read it very, very slowly. Blinder sat expressionless, staring into space.

At length, Waverly spoke. "As you gentlemen are no doubt aware, an arrest warrant to be valid must be particular. In the court, this is referred to as 'particularity.' It means that the warrant must be specific enough to differentiate one person from another, especially if the person's name is a common one, as is Mr. Blinder's." He looked at the officers. "I am afraid we will be unable to comply with this warrant, as it does not meet the test of particularity." He handed the document back to the officers.

One of the agents had a slight smile on his face. "I am afraid you are incorrect, sir," he said. "This warrant clearly specifies David Blinder in Wichita Falls, Texas. That is very specific."

"Even a town like Wichita Falls may have several Blinders. As a matter of fact, I can attest that there are at least four David Blinders in this county. I am not incorrect. In addition, given the fact that my client has committed no crime, I find this entire effort ethically questionable."

The agents glanced at each other from their comfortable chairs. They did not expect this to be routine—it isn't every day one serves a warrant to one of the richest men in the country. "Mr. Blinder, you are under arrest. You have the right to remain silent . . ."

"No, he is not, sir," interjected Waverly. "Mr. Blinder could only be arrested if there were a valid warrant. As I have apprised you, this warrant is invalid because it is insufficiently specific. If you persist in this attempt to kidnap my client, I will be forced to advise him to call the local authorities."

The agents glanced at each other again, this time without a hint of a smile. Neither made a move to leave.

"I believe," continued Waverly, "that this meeting is over." He looked at Blinder. "David?" he said, nodding toward the door. David Blinder and Samuel Waverly got up and left without another word, leaving the agents alone in the parlor.

The butler returned momentarily. "May I get you gentlemen anything?" he asked.

"No," said the first agent. "We were just leaving."

David Blinder walked back to his office and closed the door. The fact that he had a warrant issued for his arrest was a game-changer, even though the two agents who tried to serve it were neutralized without much trouble. But he knew that another warrant and more agents would be showing up at his door, a possibility confirmed by Samuel Waverly.

He considered his options. One was to detain or eliminate the two agents before they could report back. That was a small time window, he thought: those men were probably already in contact with their superiors. He would have to let that part of the drama play itself out. But he believed he did not have much time. He tilted his head back and returned to the original idea. He picked up the phone.

"Take those two men," he said softly into the receiver, which he gently replaced on the cradle. This would buy him a little more time, as the FBI tried to figure out what happened to its agents.

But now David Blinder knew that it was time to act; what was close was now perforce immediate. He took in a long deep breath and looked up at his father's portrait. "The time is here, Father," he said. He shook his head and picked up the receiver again, hitting a speed dial number as he did so.

"Now," he said simply.

The Sovereign Citizens' real army, as opposed to the front organization they carefully sold to the public or to anyone else, especially government agents, who wanted to know, was prepared. They had already positioned their troops in areas where they could attack with maximum effect. They wanted and believed they had the element of surprise in their favor. They were a disciplined and well-trained lot.

Daniel Cooper got the call just after lunch. He texted his SC units who were also US Army regulars, and each man hurried to his predesignated spot. The command building in the center of the compound, including all communication networks, were surrounded within minutes.

The underground storage facility was also a designated target. Once they controlled all the munitions stored in that vast structure, no one, not even the US Army, could outgun them short of nuclear weapons. And those weapons, combined with the ones stolen just a week earlier, made the SC forces an even more formidable threat. They moved silently to take possession of it. Since they looked like and in fact were US Army troops, no one was the wiser. But now they took their orders solely from Sergeant Cooper.

The command building was a little more complicated. Four hundred men entered the building pell-mell. They stood around acting as if they were supposed to be there, careful to array themselves along the exterior walls. Once they got the signal from the team leader, they pulled out weapons and commanded everyone to get on the floor.

"We are taking control of this building," a young private shouted, waving his M-16 toward the now captive soldiers who were still trying to absorb what was happening. "On the floor." The other soldiers looked at each other and complied. They knew they were outmanned, outgunned, and out of the loop as to what was happening.

Nor did the SC units bother to inform them. They were practiced in the virtue of secrecy and had no intention of informing men who might be their enemies what they were up to. The US troops were rounded up, their weapons and mobile devices confiscated, and taken to the basement; the doors were bolted, and the commanding officer was placed under heavy guard.

Similarly, after a brief interlude, the SC troops at the munitions depot turned on their erstwhile compatriots and gathered them into a single chamber. More SC troops began arriving.

An announcement was made over the PA system for all troops to return to barracks. Being good soldiers, the men assigned to Fort Leonard Wood complied immediately.

When they got to the barracks they found a squadron of SC troops directing them to one room. The SC soldiers took any arms and electronic gear that the regulars were carrying. None of this seemed so unusual to the US troops.

Communication and traffic leading out of the entire fort was shut down, with the exception of encrypted communication between Sergeant Cooper and his superiors off-site. As far as the regular Army command structure was concerned, it was as if Fort Leonard Wood had fallen off the grid.

something similar but on a much larger scale was happening in and around Washington, DC. Thousands of SC troops formed a cordon around the entire city. Some troops, dressed as DC police officers, started directing traffic, preventing it from entering or leaving the District. All incoming and outgoing traffic in vehicle or on foot ceased.

At precisely 5:50 on that fateful afternoon, an electromagnetic pulse generated by a highly specialized piece of machinery shook the air throughout the Capital. All electronic devices, including cars, computers, bank machines, lighting, and everything else day-to-day life took for granted, stopped functioning for thirty seconds.

Moments later, a missile streaked across the blue late-afternoon sky. It hit the Lincoln Memorial dead center, pulverizing the limestone statue and the surrounding colonnade structure. Washingtonians, tourists, and government workers alike stood in numb disbelief.

SC troops poured into the city, surrounding the Capitol Building, the White House, and the Supreme Court. Smaller units were dispatched to the Departments of State, Justice, and Defense.

Across the Potomac, the Pentagon also came under siege. No one was let in or out. Communication lines were cut and electronic communication was jammed.

Drones appeared in the early evening sky. The city had fallen so quiet that the soft humming of the light aircraft could be clearly heard on the streets below. Uncomprehending citizens gazed up at the tiny aircraft, wondering who was controlling the dangerous machines.

Finally the silence was broken by a loudspeaker attached to a jeep. "Return to your homes or hotel rooms," the voice boomed. "Return to your homes or hotel rooms immediately!" It repeated this over and over and over again throughout the congested but frightened metropolis. The speaker on the jeep was dressed in battle fatigues, so the public did not know for which side he was speaking, if indeed there were two sides. People obeyed.

As evening fell more deeply on the Capital, the streets were deserted with the exception of heavily armed men. As night fell, the soldiers set up sandbag rings around the major public buildings they surrounded.

Fort Knox was similarly under siege. Another electromagnetic pulse shut down all communication while SC troops, whose weapons were shielded from the effects of EMP, stormed and overwhelmed the facility. The defenders were swept away in short order. Prisoners were rounded up and placed in a holding cell. Armored trucks rumbled down the Kentucky road to collect the USA's stash of gold.

At 7:45, all networks were ordered to make time available for a special Public Service Announcement to begin in fifteen minutes. Those who refused were threatened with being shut down. All complied.

At precisely 8:00 p.m., a tall, thin man with a somber expression on his face appeared on TV screens across the nation. He had a prepared script in front of him.

"I am here to announce to the American population that the government of the United States is no longer functional. It has been superseded by forces of the Sovereign Citizens, a large group of patriotic Americans who, together with our allies, decided they could not stand by and see their rights eroded, their incomes confiscated, and their freedom curtailed. This large group is supported by an even larger constituency of committed men and women who are willing to put their lives on the line for authentic American values. An interim council has been appointed to administer the government until such time as a new Constitution can be completed.

"Please go about your business. Understand that no one will be harmed unless they resort to violence against us. Such violence will be dealt with summarily and harshly.

"My fellow citizens, be aware that we are at a moment of great opportunity and great danger. We will do all in our considerable power to help ease the transition to a new governmental structure.

"Thank you and good night. God Bless America!"

Telephone exchanges across the South, indeed, across the country, lit up throughout the night. Abner's men, having already collected names and commitments from influential politicians, began calling in those commitments. Legislators were called into session late in the evening. Adrenaline kept everyone working throughout the night.

Those politicians who were not in the know were shocked to hear about detailed plans for secession. Many were not displeased, and, truth be told, the rumor mill had not been quiet for some weeks. However, the distance between rumor and reality is roughly similar to that between thought and action, and being confronted by the unfolding reality left many legislators wary and, for the most part, silent. Many squirmed uncomfortably in their seats.

Votes were not taken until the secessionists were certain of victory. Those who raised objections were fawned over, cajoled, and threatened in thinly veiled or not so thinly veiled ways. The tallies for the CSA side rose.

Across the continent, something similar was happening in California, where the argument was primarily economic. Members of Wilson's group had been talking for months with key legislators about the sad shape of the California state budget. That debt-laden state had been taking a hard if quiet look at the billions of dollars sent to the federal government every year. The fact that this money would solve every single local financial problem in the state was not lost on the legislators, an argument that had been repeated for months behind closed doors. Now that the conversation was out in the open, options appeared. Joining with the other Pacific states of Washington and Oregon vastly increased the geographic footprint and promised even greater wealth. There was a general sense of fatigue at the machinations of East Coasters, who often glanced patronizingly at their western cousins. The mood was agitated.

The governor, however, was equivocal: California was proud of its leadership position among the states that comprised the United States. He was unsure of his position in a new country. He wondered if the entire effort to break the US apart would ultimately succeed, despite the momentum and the apparent tactical success of the initial assaults. He intended to raise all these concerns except the one about his position in the State Assembly in Special Session.

When he walked into the Assembly Chamber to address both houses of the legislature, he knew that the argument was already decided. The shouting was entirely pro-California. He took a deep breath, knowing that he would have to deliver an extemporaneous talk.

He started with the widely known facts about the size of California's economy: between fifth and eighth in the world. From there he proceeded to wax eloquent about the American value of freedom and the tradition of liberation from oppression. It was not too difficult to cast the government in Washington, DC, as a foreign power. The governor was persuasive with a crowd of legislators that did not need much persuading. What they needed was confirmation and leadership, and those present felt keenly that both were provided by their sitting governor, a natural choice for the first chief executive of the about-to-be-liberated Commonwealth of California.

Texas and Oklahoma were likewise in contact. As they pondered the events in Washington and listened to firsthand reports about the heated debates among the Southern legislators considering secession, the sentiment for schism flourished. Texas had always had a measure of ambivalence about being a part of the USA, having been briefly its own country. Now that long-silent streak of nationalist pride asserted itself in grand style. Banquets were arranged; champagne began to flow. All provided at the expense of the Blinder family, proud Texans that they were.

86

Adam Wilson followed these events on a single tablet computer deep in Wyoming. He could barely contain his excitement. He was thinking that this was worth all the years of planning, all the trouble, all the lives lost. He was sure that he was on the right side of history and that he would be able to forge a Christian nation out of the states in the heartland of the United States. As soon as it was clear that secession was a fact and that the nation was splitting, he and his hand-picked group would offer their expertise, wealth, and guidance to bring about just such a place. He was in communication with his operatives on the ground.

He had also received the go-ahead from David Blinder's network. He knew that it would be only a matter of days before his group could return to their lives ready to pour every ounce of energy into creating the religious paradise he believed America was destined to become.

People die in times like these, he thought soberly. Adam Wilson did not regard himself as a killer; in fact, he had never killed anyone. But he knew that there were times when some individuals must be sacrificed to the cause. Such was what happened with Daniel Keenan, a fellow soldier who lost his nerve.

Wilson followed the sketchy reports that were coming in from CNN and other major news networks. Despite the announcement, specific details were hard to come by. All knew that something big was happening in Washington, but they were all woefully short on just how big.

Silence and confusion descended upon the United States of America.

87

Max was in his office in Langley when the lights went out and the humming noise of office machines fell silent. He heard the massive explosion across the Potomac. He could see smoke rising from the far end of the reflecting pool.

"Jesus Christ!" Max said. "It's happening."

Feelings of failure, impotence, and rage swept over him. But there was no one to share these with. He didn't want to tell anybody; what he wanted was to strike back with all the force he could muster. He ran out of his office into the command center of the sprawling building. People were running everywhere, trying to figure out what was happening.

"We are under attack!" Max yelled. Suddenly he no longer cared who within earshot was trustworthy and who was not. He did not fully understand how the subversives infiltrated government networks, but he had been thinking it could have been purely electronic.

By the time he got to the command center, the electronics were coming back online. The EMP outage lasted for about thirty seconds. He pulled out his cell phone and speed-dialed Mueller. No answer. He knew it would be futile to try the chain of command. Physical presence mattered most in this situation, and he had to make do with what he had.

The analysts, agents, and office workers who were available assembled in the large conference room that was the command center of the building. Max was shouting orders as fast as he could think of them.

"Shut down the facility!" he shouted to the armed security guards who were there. "Make sure nobody gets in or out. Be prepared for a major assault." In the back of his mind, Max was wondering why his building had not already been targeted. Bigger fish? Maybe, he thought.

Max ordered everyone else to be quiet and listen. He ran through an abbreviated version of what he had been investigating, the developments over the past week, and the serious threat multiple enemies of the United States were coordinating.

"This is no longer a lunatic fringe," he said with all the seriousness he could muster. "These are well-financed, highly trained professionals who are intent on pulling apart the country." Then he paused for a moment. He glared at everyone in the room.

"We have had internal security breaches," he said with acid dripping from his words. "Serious breaches. Some of these, maybe most of them, were, I believe, electronic. Our enemies have very sophisticated tools at their disposal, and they have been using them. We have been working on cracking it, but it's been tough. They may have withdrawn it or modified it because of our efforts, but we cannot be sure."

He continued to glare. "But my point here isn't about electronic surveillance or snooping. My point is this: if I believe any of you are engaged in treasonous behavior, I will shoot you myself."

Max knew that the eyebrows that went up slightly indicated that his shocking message had gotten through. He knew his career was over, no matter how this crisis came out. It's against two dozen regulations that he could think of to threaten employees with anything, much less death. He didn't care. He was fed up.

"Let's get to work," he said.

He divided the people up into task groups and assigned each one a mission: one to determine the extent of the damage; one to examine the political implications; and another to formulate a response—a rapid and powerful response. He also directed his agents to contact the field operatives in Texas to storm the Blinder compound.

Max paused for a moment to take stock; his cell phone rang. It was Mueller.

"The President has been taken to a safe location," Mueller said without introduction. "The alert status has been raised to DEF-CON 2. Preliminary tests show that, even though the President is still in control of the football, the coding system for the nuclear arsenal may be corrupted." He paused for a moment to collect himself.

"What do you think their next step will be, Max?" he finally said.

"I think it's going to be as political as it is military, Bob," he replied honestly. "They've been preparing this for years, and I think they will swing into action on the state level. They don't need to conquer the country; they just need to demonstrate its weakness." He paused for a bitter moment. "I think they believe they have done that."

Max could not hear Mueller nodding, but he knew he was. If he disagreed with what Max said, Bob Mueller would have said so. Max continued: "I'm coordinating a plan to neutralize their military forces, but they came in stronger than anyone predicted." He paused in thought for just a moment. "I'll get back with you."

The President, in fact, was not exactly in a safe location. He was in a lower-level security room beneath the White House, which was surrounded by hostile forces. He insisted that he would not leave.

He looked at the monitors arrayed in the front of the room: some sketchy news feeds about the attack; a lot of questions and possibilities, but little hard news. There was a lot about this situation that raised his ire, but the fact that they targeted the Lincoln Memorial for their first aggressive move infuriated him more than the hundreds of troops outside his front door.

"I want the men who did that," he said to members of his National Security Council, who were arrayed around the table. Heads nodded. Everyone knew there was more pressing business.

"The first thing we've got to do, Mr. President," said Joe Biden, "is clear out those troops upstairs."

Mr. Obama nodded. "What have we got?" he asked.

General Dempsey, the chairman of the Joint Chiefs, spoke up first: "We've got a division of soldiers at various facilities within thirty miles," he said. "It's going to take us a little time to get them coordinated."

"Isn't this what they've been training for?"

"Yes, sir, it is," Dempsey replied calmly. "But these people have surprise on their side." He glanced at the Intelligence Chief for just a moment. "We have a plan."

"How much time?" the President asked.

"Twelve hours," replied the General.

"Meanwhile," the President continued, "we need to get on the air and say something."

"We can do that from here, Mr. President," said his communications director.

"Okay. Let's do it."

Vice President Biden was stunned. The dream he had weeks ago felt like the premonition it was turning out to be. He turned to the President.

"What are you going to say?" he asked.

"I'm going to tell the simple truth, Joe," the President replied. "I'm going to tell people that fanatical groups of different stripes have decided on their own, without electoral approval or a democratic process, to grab power in the most powerful nation in the world, and that they did it in an immoral way for the most fanatical reasons." He looked soberly at his vice president. "And I am going to tell them that this will not stand. It can't stand. It would mean anarchy, and I will not allow that to happen on my watch." He paused again for just a moment, staring at the table before him. "Anything less would be bullshit," he said.

Joe Biden nodded, as did every head in the room. Mr. Obama knew that this was perfunctory. No one knew what to do. No one predicted action on this scale, even with the reports that he had heard a couple of weeks ago. Despite the fact that he directed his people to act on them, it was far too little, far too late. Now was the moment, and he was the guy. It was up to him to decide how the United States of America responded to the second civil war in its history.

Acknowledgements

As many writers have observed, producing a novel is a team effort. I am grateful to have had the assistance of talented and engaged professionals in the publication of this work.

I would like to thank Katherine Pickett, my editor, whose capable eye and willingness to comment proved invaluable. I would also like to thank Bonnie Spinola, who proofread the entire work. Cover design, interior layout, and production was done by Peggy Nehmen, whose persistence was matched only by her creativity.

I would like to thank my supportive and thoughtful friends, particularly Patrick Cacchione and Tom Cotter, who read the manuscript and gave invaluable feedback.

Finally, I would like to thank my family: my wife Patricia and our children Kate and Chris, whose candor and thoughtfulness were and forever will be welcome.

www.ingramcontent.com/pod-product-compliance
Lightning Source LLC
Chambersburg PA
CBHW070407260626
47161CB00001B/310